"[Palahniuk] is a writer of remarkable talent, willing to look unflinchingly at despairing lives and their often-warped quest for even momentary redemption. He's a painfully deft chronicler of the meaningless job, the poisonous relationship, and of all the myriad damaging and deadening effects of so-called normal life." —*The Boston Globe*

"Fiercely smart, and in Palahniuk's signature way of raging against the deadening sterility of modern life." —*The Philadelphia Inquirer*

"*Rant* flirts with government-mandated genocide, Greek tragedy, aberrant sexuality, substance abuse and audacious fusions of religion and violence, stitching together disparate elements to craft a surreal, poignant and darkly humorous quilt. . . . A piercing plea to push the galactic reset button." —*Fort Worth Star-Telegram*

"[A] brilliant and provocative take on where civilization just may be heading." —*The Hartford Courant*

"*Rant* is fast and true, savagely clearsighted and intelligent, a luxury to read. . . . The novel you might expect if Philip K. Dick met Denis Johnson and they took crystal meth together and spent a week telling one another everything they knew about epidemiology, economics, cars, coin-collecting, generational warfare, spiders and the physics of time." —*The Guardian* (London)

"A blunt portrait of its antihero's transformation from high-school rebel to nihilistic killer." —*Time Out New York*

"Zombies, government conspiracies, religious epiphanies, time travel, a postmodern Typhoid Mary, and a woman who mixes thumbtacks into her cookie dough—all are fair game in *Rant*. . . . Vintage Palahniuk, a grim thriller ride filled with his signature black humor, withering social commentary, and stomach-churning details." —*Bookmarks* Magazine

"A fitfully brilliant collection of remembrances from a young fictional nihilist." —*Entertainment Weekly*

"Religious themes pepper this dark tale of a naturopathic serial killer. Palahniuk won't disappoint fans who favor his obscene, psychological narrative style." —*Relevant* Magazine

"Cult author Chuck Palahniuk continues to push literary boundaries in strange—even forbidding—territories." —*Writer's Digest*

"Palahniuk pumps enough adrenaline into his gross-out fables to make even squeamish readers read on. For all the blood, guts, and bodily fluids that splatter his prose, he also knows that tenderness packs a punch." —Bloomberg.com

"*Rant*'s whiplash ride is wild enough to make you want to grab your own car keys and go party." —*Willamette Week*

Chuck Palahniuk

RANT

Chuck Palahniuk is the bestselling author of nine novels: *Fight Club*—which was made into a film by director David Fincher—*Survivor*, *Invisible Monsters*, *Choke*, *Lullaby*, *Diary*, *Haunted*, *Rant* and *Snuff*. He is also the author of the nonfiction profile of Portland, Oregon, *Fugitives and Refugees*, and the nonfiction collection *Stranger Than Fiction*. More than three million copies of his books have been sold. He lives in the Pacific Northwest.

www.chuckpalahniuk.com

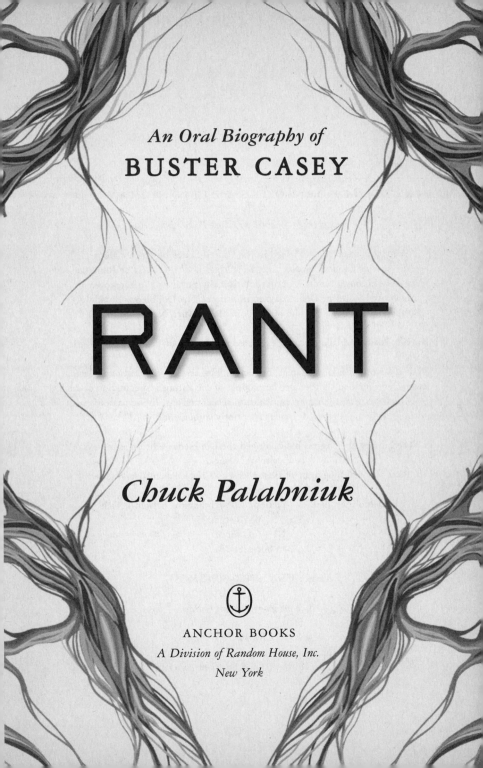

An Oral Biography of
BUSTER CASEY

RANT

Chuck Palahniuk

ANCHOR BOOKS
A Division of Random House, Inc.
New York

FIRST ANCHOR BOOKS EDITION, MAY 2008

Copyright © 2007 by Chuck Palahniuk

All rights reserved. Published in the United States by Anchor Books,
a division of Random House, Inc., New York, and in Canada by Random
House of Canada Limited, Toronto. Originally published in hardcover in
the United States by Doubleday, an imprint of The Doubleday Broadway
Publishing Group, a division of Random House, Inc., New York, in 2007.

Anchor Books and colophon are registered trademarks of Random House, Inc.

The Library of Congress has cataloged the Doubleday edition as follows:
Palahniuk, Chuck.
Rant : an oral biography of Buster Casey / Chuck Palahniuk.—1st ed.
p. cm.
1. Demolition derbies—Fiction. 2. Psychological fiction. I. Title.
PS3564.Y55R36 2007
813'.54—dc22
2006028918

Anchor ISBN: 978-0-307-27583-7

Book design by Michael Collica

www.anchorbooks.com

Printed in the United States of America
10 9 8 7 6 5

For my father, Fred Leander Palahniuk.
Look up from the sidewalk. Please.

Do you ever wish

you'd never been born?

Author's Note: This book is written in the style of an oral history, a form which requires interviewing a wide variety of witnesses and compiling their testimony. Anytime multiple sources are questioned about a shared experience, it's inevitable for them occasionally to contradict each other. For additional biographies written in this style, please see *Capote* by George Plimpton, *Edie* by Jean Stein, and *Lexicon Devil* by Brendan Mullen.

1 – An Introduction

Wallace Boyer (☼ *Car Salesman*): Like most people, I didn't meet and talk to Rant Casey until after he was dead. That's how it works for most celebrities: After they croak, their circle of close friends just explodes. A dead celebrity can't walk down the street without meeting a million best buddies he never met in real life.

Dying was the best career move Jeff Dahmer and John Wayne Gacy ever made. After Gaetan Dugas was dead, the number of sex partners saying they'd fucked him, it went through the roof.

The way Rant Casey used to say it: Folks build a reputation by attacking you while you're alive—or praising you after you ain't.

For me, I was sitting on an airplane, and some hillbilly sits down next to me. His skin, it's the same as any car wreck you can't not stare at—dented with tooth marks, pitted and puckered, the skin on the back of his hands looks one god-awful mess.

The flight attendant, she asks this hillbilly what's it he wants to drink. The stewardess asks him to, please, reach my drink to me: scotch with rocks. But when I see those monster fingers wrapped around the plastic cup, his chewed-up knuckles, I could never touch my lips to the rim.

With the epidemic, a person can't be too careful. At the airport, right beyond the metal detector we had to walk through, a fever monitor like they first used to control the spread of SARS. Most people, the government says, have no idea they're infected. Somebody can feel fine, but if that monitor beeps that your temperature's too high, you'll disappear into quarantine. Maybe for the rest of your life. No trial, nothing.

To be safe, I only fold down my tray table and take the cup. I watch the scotch turn pale and watery. The ice melt and disappear.

Anybody makes a livelihood selling cars will tell you: Repetition is the mother of all skills. You build the gross at your dealership by building rapport.

Anywhere you find yourself, you can build your skills. A good trick to remember a name is you look the person in the eyes long enough to register their color: green or brown or blue. You call that a Pattern Interrupt: It stops you forgetting the way you always would.

This cowboy stranger, his eyes look bright green. Antifreeze green.

That whole connecting flight between Peco Junction and the city, we shared an armrest, me at the window, him on the aisle. Don't shoot the messenger, but dried shit keeps flaking off his cowboy boots. Those long sideburns maybe scored him pussy in high school, but they're gray from his temple to his jawbone now. Not to mention those hands.

To practice building rapport, I ask him what he paid for his ticket. If you can't determine the customer needs, identify the hot buttons, of some stranger rubbing arms with you on an airplane, you'll never talk anybody into taking "mental ownership" of a Nissan, much less a Cadillac.

For landing somebody in a car, another trick is: Every car on your lot, you program the number-one radio-station button to gospel music. The number-two button, set to rock and roll. The number-three, to jazz. If your prospect looks like a demander-commander type, the minute you unlock the car you set the radio to come on with the news or a politics talk station. A sandal wearer, you hit the National Public Radio button. When they turn the key, the radio tells them what they want to hear. Every car on the lot, I have the number-five button set to that techno-raver garbage in case some kid who does Party Crashing comes around.

The green color of the hillbilly's eyes, the shit on his boots, salesmen call those "mental pegs." Questions that have one answer, those are "closed questions." Questions to get a customer talking, those are "open questions."

For example: "How much did your plane ticket set you back?" That's a closed question.

And, sipping from his own cup of whiskey, the man swallows. Staring straight ahead, he says, "Fifty dollars."

A good example of an open question would be: "How do you live with those scary chewed-up hands?"

I ask him: For one way?

"Round-trip," he says, and his pitted and puckered hand tips whiskey into his face. "Called a 'bereavement fare,' " the hillbilly says.

Me looking at him, me half twisted in my seat to face him, my breathing slowed to match the rise and fall of his cowboy shirt, the technique's called: Active Listening. The stranger clears his throat, and I wait a little and clear my throat, copying him; that's what a good salesman means by "pacing" a customer.

My feet, crossed at the ankle, right foot over the left, same as his, I say: Impossible. Not even standby tickets go that cheap. I ask: How'd he get such a deal?

Drinking his whiskey, neat, he says, "First, what you have to do is escape from inside a locked insane asylum." Then, he says, you have to hitchhike cross-country, wearing nothing but plastic booties and a paper getup that won't stay shut in back. You need to arrive about a heartbeat too late to keep a repeat child-molester from raping your wife. And your mother. Spawned out of that rape, you have to raise up a son who collects a wagonful of folks' old, thrown-out teeth. After high school, your wacko kid got's to run off. Join some cult that lives only by night. Wreck his car, a half a hundred times, and hook up with some kind-of, sort-of, not-really prostitute.

Along the way, your kid got's to spark a plague that'll kill thousands of people, enough folks so that it leads to martial law and threatens to topple world leaders. And, lastly, your boy got's to die in a big, flaming, fiery inferno, watched by everybody in the world with a television set.

He says, "Simple as that."

The man says, "Then, when you go to collect his body for his funeral," and tips whiskey into his mouth, "the airline gives you a special bargain price on your ticket."

Fifty bucks, round-trip. He looks at my scotch sitting on the tray table in front of me. Warm. Any ice, gone. And he says, "You going to drink that?"

I tell him: Go ahead.

This is how fast your life can turn around.

How the future you have tomorrow won't be the same future you had yesterday.

My dilemma is: Do I ask for his autograph? Slowing my breath, pacing my chest to his, I ask: Is he related to that guy . . . Rant Casey? "Werewolf Casey"—the worst Patient Zero in the history of disease? The "superspreader" who's infected half the country? America's "Kissing Killer"? Rant "Mad Dog" Casey?

"Buster," the man says, his monster hand reaching to take my scotch. He says, "My boy's given name was Buster Landru Casey. Not Rant. Not Buddy. *Buster*."

Already, my eyes are soaking up every puckered scar on his fingers. Every wrinkle and gray hair. My nose, recording his smell of whiskey and cow shit. My elbow, recording the rub of his flannel shirtsleeve. Already, I'll be bragging about this stranger for the rest of my life. Holding tight to every moment of him, squirreling away his every word and gesture, I say: You're . . .

"Chester," he says. "Name's Chester Casey."

Sitting right next to me. Chester Casey, the father of Rant Casey: America's walking, talking Biological Weapon of Mass Destruction.

Andy Warhol was wrong. In the future, people won't be famous for fifteen minutes. No, in the future, everyone will sit next to someone famous for at least fifteen minutes. Typhoid Mary or Ted Bundy or Sharon Tate. History is nothing except monsters or victims. Or witnesses.

So what do I say? I say: I'm sorry. I say, "Tough break about your kid dying."

Out of sympathy, I shake my head . . .

And a few inhales later, Chet Casey shakes his head, and in that gesture I'm not sure who's really pacing who. Which of us sat which way first. If maybe this shitkicker is studying me. Copying me. Finding my hot buttons and building rapport. Maybe selling me something, this living legend Chet Casey, he winks. Never breathing more than fifteen inhales any minute. He tosses back the scotch. "Any way you look at it," he says, and elbows me in the ribs, "it's still a damn sweet deal on an airplane ticket."

2—Guardian Angels

From the Field Notes of Green Taylor Simms (℃ *Historian*): The hound dog is to Middleton what the cow is to the streets of Calcutta or New Delhi. In the middle of every dirt road sleeps some kind of mongrel coonhound, panting in the sun, its dripping tongue hanging out. A kind of fur-covered speed bump with no collar or tags. Powdered with a fine dust of clay blown off the plowed fields.

To arrive at Middleton requires four solid days of driving, which is the longest period of time I have ever experienced inside an automobile without colliding with another vehicle. I found that to be the most depressing aspect of my pilgrimages.

Neddy Nelson (℃ *Party Crasher*): Can you explain how in 1968 the amateur paleontologist William Meister in Antelope Spring, Utah, split a block of shale while searching for trilobite fossils, but instead discovered the fossilized five-hundred-million-year-old footprint of a human shoe? And how did another fossilized shoe print, found in Nevada in 1922, occur in rock from the Triassic era?

Echo Lawrence (ℂ *Party Crasher*): Driving to Middleton, rolling across all that fucking country in the middle of the night, Shot Dunyun punched buttons, scanning the radio for traffic reports. To hear any action we'd be missing out on. Morning or evening drive-time bulletins from oceans away. Gridlock and traffic backups where it's still yesterday. Fatal pile-ups and jackknives on expressways where it's already tomorrow.

It's fucking weird, hearing somebody's died tomorrow. Like you could still call that commuter man, right now, in Moscow, and say: "Stay home!"

From DRVR Radio Graphic Traffic: Expect a gapers' delay if you're eastbound on the Meadows Bypass through the Richmond area. Slow down and stretch your neck for a good long look at a two-car fatal accident in the left-most lane. The front vehicle is a sea-green 1974 Plymouth Road Runner with a four-barrel carb-equipped 440-cubic-inch, cast-iron-block V8. Original ice-white interior. The coupe's driver was a scorching twenty-four-year old female, blonde-slash-green with a textbook fracture-slash-dislocation of her spine at the atlantooccipital joint and complete transection of the spinal cord. Fancy words for whiplash so bad it snaps your neck.

The rear car was a bitchin' two-door hardtop New Yorker Brougham St. Regis, cream color, with the optional deluxe chrome package and fixed rear quarter-windows. A sweet ride. As you rubberneck past, please note the driver was a twenty-six-year-old male with a nothing-special transverse fracture of the sternum, bilateral rib fractures, and his lungs impaled by the fractured ribs, all due to impact with his steering wheel. Plus, the boys in the meat wagon tell me, severe internal exsanguination.

So—buckle up and slow down. Reporting for Graphic Traffic, this is Tina Something . . .

Echo Lawrence: We broke curfew and the government quarantine, and we drove across these stretches of nothing. Me, riding shotgun. Shot Dunyun, driving. Neddy Nelson was in the backseat, reading some book and telling us how Jack the Ripper never died—he traveled back in time to slaughter his mom, to make himself immortal—and now he's the U.S. President or the Pope. Maybe some crackpot theory proving how UFOs are really human tourists visiting us from the distant future.

Shot Dunyun (ℂ *Party Crasher*): I guess we drove to Middleton to see all the places Rant had talked about and meet what he called "his people." His parents, Irene and Chester. The best friend, Bodie Carlyle, he went to school with. All the dipshit farm families, the Perrys and Tommys and Elliots, he used to go on and on talking about. Most of Party Crashing was just us driving in cars, talking.

Such a cast of yokels. Our goal was to flesh out the stories Rant had told. How weird is that? Me and Echo Lawrence, with Neddy in the backseat of that Cadillac Eldorado of his. The car that Rant had bought for Neddy.

Yeah, and we went to put flowers and stuff on Rant's grave.

Echo Lawrence: Punching the radio, Shot says, "You know we're missing a good Soccer Mom Night . . ."

"Not tonight," says Neddy. "Check your calendar. Tonight was a Student Driver Night."

Shot Dunyun: Up ahead, a sliver of light outlines the horizon. The sliver swells to a bulge of white light, a half-circle, then a full circle. A full moon. Tonight we're missing a great Honeymoon Night.

Echo Lawrence: We told each other stories instead of playing music. The stories Rant had told, about his growing up. The stories about Rant, we had to piece them together out of details we each had to dig up from the basement of the basement of the basement of our brains. Everyone pitching in some memory of Rant, we drove along, pooling our stories.

Shot Dunyun: The local Middleton sheriff stopped us, and we told him the truth: We were making a pilgrimage to see where Rant Casey had been born.

A night like this with everybody in town asleep, the little Rant Casey would be ham-radioing. Wearing his headphones. As a kid, a night like this, Rant used to turn the dial, looking for traffic reports from Los Angeles and New York. Listening to traffic jams and tie-ups in London. Slowdowns in Atlanta. Three-car pile-ups in Paris, reported in French. Learning Spanish in terms of *neumático desinflado* and *punto muerto*. Flat tires and gridlock in Madrid. *Imbottigliamento*, for gridlock in Rome. *Het roosterslot*, gridlock in Amsterdam. *Saturation*, gridlock in Paris. The whole invisible world of the traffic sphere.

Echo Lawrence: Come on. Driving around any hillbilly burg between midnight and sunrise, you take your chances. The police don't have much to do but blare their siren at you. The Middleton sheriff held our driver's licenses in the beam of his flashlight while he lectured us about the city. How Rant Casey had been killed by moving to the city. City people were all murderers. Meaning us.

This sheriff was boosting some kind of Texas Ranger affect, plugged into and looping some John Wayne brain chemistry. Boost a drill sergeant through a hanging judge, then boost that through a Doberman pinscher, and you'd get this sheriff. His shoulders stayed pinned back, square. His thumbs hooked behind his belt buckle. And he rocked forward and back on the heels of his cowboy boots.

Shot asked, "Has anybody been by to murder Rant's mom yet?"

This sheriff wore a brown shirt with a brass star pinned to one chest pocket, a pen and a folded pair of sunglasses tucked in the pocket, and the shirt tucked into blue jeans. Engraved on the star, it said "Officer Bacon Carlyle."

Come on. Talk about the worst question Shot could ask.

Neddy Nelson: You tell me, how in 1844 did the physicist Sir David Brewster discover a metal nail fully embedded in a block of Devonian sandstone more than three hundred million years old?

From the Field Notes of Green Taylor Simms: You might see Middleton from the air, flying between New York and Los Angeles, and you'll always wonder at how people can exist in such a place. Envision ratty sofas abandoned on porches. Cars parked in front yards. Houses half off their foundations, balanced on cinderblocks, with chickens and dogs sleeping underneath. If it looks like a natural disaster has occurred, that's only because you didn't see it beforehand.

Neddy Nelson: How do you explain the fact that an Illinois housewife, Mrs. S. W. Culp, broke open a lump of coal and found a gold necklace embedded inside it?

From the Field Notes of Green Taylor Simms: Despite the dreary scenery, it's all very sexual, these towns. It's only the individual who attains an early beauty and sexuality who becomes trapped here. The young men and women who acquire perfect breasts and muscles before they know how best to use that power, they end up pregnant and mired so close to home. This cycle concentrates the best genetics in places you'd never imagine. Like Middleton. Little nests of wildly attractive idiots who give birth and survive into a long, ugly adulthood. Venuses and Apollos. Small-town gods and goddesses. If Middleton has produced one remarkable product in the tedious, dull, dusty history of this community, that extraordinary product was Rant Casey.

Echo Lawrence: "The big reason why folks leave a small town," Rant used to say, "is so they can moon over the idea of going back. And the reason they stay put is so they can moon about getting out."

Rant meant that no one is happy, anywhere.

From the Field Notes of Green Taylor Simms: The central metaphor for power in Middleton, and especially within the Casey family, was the staging of their Christian holiday meals. For these events—Easter breakfasts, Thanksgiving and Christmas dinners—the family members were divided between two distinct classes. The adults dined with antique china that had come into the family generations before, plates with hand-painted borders, garlands of flowers and gold. The children sat at a table in the kitchen, but not actually one table, more a cluster of folding card tables butted together.

Echo Lawrence: In the kitchen, everything was paper, the napkins and tablecloth and plates, so it could all be wadded up and shit-canned. When the Casey adults sat down to break bread, they always said the same blessing: "Thank You, God, for these blessings of family, food, and good fortune which we see before us."

From the Field Notes of Green Taylor Simms: Aging family members still stalled at the children's table prayed for salmonella. For fish bones stuck in windpipes. The younger generations held hands and bowed their heads to pray for massive strokes and heart attacks.

Echo Lawrence: Rant used to say, "Life's greatest comfort is being able to look over your shoulder and see people worse off, waiting in line behind you."

Shot Dunyun: Before Party Crashing nights, when our team would go out for dinner, Green Taylor Simms would watch and sneer while Rant ate every food with the same fork. Rant wasn't a dumbshit, he just never got past using a plastic spoon.

Behind Rant's back, Green used to call him "Huckleberry Fagg."

From the Field Notes of Green Taylor Simms: Mr. Dunyun refers to Rant as "The Tooth Fairy."

Echo Lawrence: Get this. Around midnight in Middleton, Shot Dunyun and I parked at the turn-off to their farmhouse, next to a mailbox with "Casey" painted on it. In the middle of a lot of crops, the house was white with a long porch along the front, a steep roof, and one dormer window looking over the porch: Rant's attic bedroom with the cowboy wallpaper.

Bushes and flowers grow close to the foundation, and

mowed grass spreads out to a chain-link fence. We could see a barn painted brown, almost hidden behind the house. Everything else is wheat, to the flat circle of the horizon going around every side of Neddy's Cadillac. Shot fiddled with the radio, hunting for traffic updates.

From DRVR Radio Graphic Traffic: Just a heads-up. Watch out for the two-car fender bender along the right shoulder, westbound at Milepost 67, on the City Center Thruway. Both vehicles appear to be wedding parties, complete with the tin cans tied to their rear bumpers. Traffic is slow, as drivers rubberneck to watch the brides and grooms scream and throw wedding cake at each other. Be on the lookout for bridesmaids and white rice in the roadway . . .

Echo Lawrence: Shot fell asleep, snoring against the inside of the driver's door. I kept waiting for a sign Irene Casey was still alive and no mysterious stranger had strangled or stabbed her to death yet.

Neddy Nelson: Tell me how in 1913 did the anthropologist H. Reck discover a modern human skull buried in Early Pleistocene soil of the Olduvai Gorge? Explain how modern human skulls have also been unearthed from Early Pleistocene and Middle Pliocene strata in Buenos Aires, Argentina, and Ragazzoni, Italy, respectively?

Shot Dunyun: We walked around their cruddy cemetery, a mess of lawn-mowered weeds, but we couldn't find Rant's grave. How weird is that? We found the best friend's name in a phone book, Bodie Carlyle, then found his trailer at the end of a dirt road. Tumbleweeds piled window-deep against it, and a pit bull chained and barking in the dirt yard. This was hours before sunrise. We didn't even knock on the trailer door.

Echo Lawrence: Forget it. I never did see Irene Casey. We didn't even knock on her door. For all we knew, she was already dead inside that farmhouse.

Wallace Boyer (◯ *Car Salesman*): Sell cars long enough and you'll see: Nobody's all that original. Any lone weirdo comes from a big nest of weirdos. What's weird is, you go to some pigsty village in Slovakia, and suddenly even Andy Warhol makes perfect sense.

Echo Lawrence: Give me a break. At dawn, that redneck sheriff pulls up next to our car and bullhorns that we're in violation of the federal Emergency Health Powers Act and the I-SEE-U curfew. We didn't want to leave Mrs. Casey unprotected, but the Big Chief Sheriff points his gun at us and says, "How about you-all come into town for some questioning . . ."

From the Field Notes of Green Taylor Simms: In Middleton, sleeping dogs have the permanent right-of-way.

3—Dogs

Bodie Carlyle (☼ *Childhood Friend*): Wintertime, Middleton dogs run in a pack. Regular farm dogs hereabouts, they'll
tear off and disappear, except you can hear them howling and
barking at night. Other dogs, people car-dump them at the
side of the road. Abandoned. City folks figure any dog can
fend for itself, turn wild, but most mutts will starve until
they're hungry enough to eat the shit left by some other
varmint. The shit's crawling with fly eggs. Most of those let-
go dogs die of worms.

Other dogs, they pack together to stay warm. The dogs
that survive. The pack runs down rabbits and mule deer.
Come winter, the farm dogs hear the packs howling over a
fresh kill down in the trees along the river at night, and the
farm dogs take off.

A pet dog hears that howl, and, no matter how much you
call, even the nicest dog forgets his name. Except for their
howling, all winter, they're as gone as dead. Snow starts to
fall and your pet dog, your best friend, is nothing but the
wolf-man sound of far-off howling in the dark. Sound carries
forever when the air turns cold.

Wintertime, a kid's worst nightmare was walking home

after dark and hearing a dog pack, all that howling and snapping, coming closer and louder in the dark. Something with a
zillion teeth and claws. Folks come across a mule deer caught
by a pack, and the skull might be the biggest chunk left. The
rest of any hide or skeleton you'd find in bites, tugged apart
by teeth and scattered all over. With a rabbit, you might find
one little foot in a mess of fur, spread everywhere. Blood
everywhere. The rabbit's foot, with a little wet, soft fur, just
like folks carry for luck.

The Caseys' dog, it ran with the packs every winter up
until it disappeared. Used to jump on the sofa, look out the
windows at night, ears up to listen, when the packs were
roaming. Hunting. Those packs, more rumor than anything
real you ever saw. Half legend. The only monster we have
hereabouts. More than half. The idea those dogs, maybe even
your own dogs, would go crazy and hunt you. Your own dogs
might track you home after school. Trail you through the
brush alongside the road. Stalk you. Your own dog would run
you down and yank you apart, bite by bite. No matter how
much you might call out "Fido" or tell him "Stay," tell him,
"Sit!," the dog you housetrained from a pup, spanked with a
newspaper, that dog will snap his teeth together on your
windpipe and rip out your throat. Fido would howl over your
dying and drink the blood still pumping hot out of your own
loving heart.

Sheriff Bacon Carlyle (☼ *Childhood Enemy*): Don't ask me
to feel sorry for him. Even in grade school, Rant Casey was
begging to get killed some terrible way. Snakes or rabies. The
Caseys, their dog, they named it "Fetch." Some sort of half-
hound, half-beagle, half-Rottweiler, half–bull terrier, half-
everything mongrel. That's the name Chester Casey gived the
dog: Fetch.

Edna Perry (☼ *Childhood Neighbor*): If you'd care to know, the three of them Caseys called each other by different names. Irene Casey called her husband "Chet." He called her "Reen," short for "Irene," and only to her face. Nobody else called Irene Casey that. Rant called Chester "Dad." Irene called her son "Buddy," but his father called him "Buster." Never "Rant." Only Bodie Carlyle called him Rant.

History is, Rant called Bodie "Toad." No lie.

Everyone gave a different name to everyone else. Buster was Rant was Buddy. Chester was Chet was Dad. Irene was Mom was Reen. How folks lay claim to a loved one is they give you a name of their own. They figure to label you as their property.

Sheriff Bacon Carlyle: Same as dumping a dog, the worst thing a man can do is turn himself loose.

Echo Lawrence (☾ *Party Crasher*): Listen up. Rant would tell people: "You're a different human being to everybody you meet."

Sometimes Rant said, "You only ever is in the eyes of other folks."

If you were going to carve a quote on his grave, his favorite saying was: "The future you have tomorrow won't be the same future you had yesterday."

Shot Dunyun (☾ *Party Crasher*): That's bullshit. Rant's favorite saying was: "Some people are just born human. The rest of us, we take a lifetime to get there."

Bodie Carlyle: I remember Rant used-to saying, "We won't never be as young as we is tonight."

Irene Casey (☼ *Rant's Mother*): Used to be, Buddy walked with his Grandma Esther to church on Sundays. Good weather, Chet and I would drive Buddy to Esther's place and drop him off. Little Buddy made it a habit, seeing how she didn't have nobody to walk in with. She only lived a glance down the road from Middleton Christian. An old lady in her little church hat, and a little boy wearing a clip-on bow tie, holding hands and walking along a dirt road, they made a picture to touch your heart.

One Sunday, we're through the opening hymn, through the first Gospel reading, and halfway into the sermon, but Buddy and Esther still ain't arrived at the church. We're passing the basket for the collection offering, and the church door busts open. A pounding comes up the steps outside, pounds across the church porch boards, and the big door swings open so hard the inside knob punches a hole in the vestibule wall. With all the heads turning, craning to look, little Buddy stumbles inside, panting. Leaning forward with a hand braced on each knee, the door still open behind him and sunlight bright around him, Buddy's panting, his hair hanging over his eyes, trying to get his breath. No bow tie. His white shirt tails hanging out.

The Reverend Curtis Dean Fields says, "Would you kindly close the door."

And Buddy gasps and says, "She's bit."

He catches enough breath to say, "Grandma Esther. She's sick, bad."

Being cold weather, I figure a dog pack, could be a dog bit her. Wild dogs.

Sheriff Bacon Carlyle: Don't hate me for saying, but no Casey never paid to fix that hole Rant punched with the doorknob in the church wall. Even accepting he done it *by accident*.

Irene Casey: Buddy says a spider done bit Esther. From the look of it, a black widow spider. Buddy and his grandma was walking, halfway done, and she stopped, stood still, dropped his hand. Esther shouts, "Lord!" and uses both hands to rip the hat off her head, the pins pulling out ribbons of her gray hair. A sound, Buddy says, same as tearing newspaper in half. Her black church hat, round and black, about the size of a bath-powder box. One swing of her hand pitches that hat at the dirt ground. Both Esther's church shoes stomp that black satin in the dust. Her black shoes, gray with the dust. Dust stomped up in a cloud around her black coat. Her purse swings in her other hand, and she waves Buddy back, saying, "Don't you touch it."

Still pinned to the hat, tore out at the roots, thick hanks of Esther's gray hair.

With one church shoe, Esther toe-kicks the hat over, and the two of them squat down to look.

Mixed up in the dust and gravel, the mashed-up veil, and the crumpled satin, just barely bending one leg, flexing one leg, is a spider. A dusty black spider with a red hourglass on its belly.

From the Field Notes of Green Taylor Simms (ℂ *Historian*): Cousin to the shoe-button spider of South Africa, of the genus *Latrodectus* of the comb-footed spider family, the black widow nests in isolated places such as unused clothing or outdoor latrines. Until indoor plumbing became prevalent, bites from the black widow were most commonly inflicted on the buttocks or genitals of the victim. More recently, the spider is more likely to bite when trapped between clothing and the victim's skin—for example, when a spider nests in a seldom-worn shoe or glove.

Irene Casey: Granny Esther touches the top of her hair, two fingertips feeling between the strands of her hair, stepping the curls one way, then the other, until she touches a spot that makes her mouth drop open and her eyes clamp shut. When she opens them, Buddy says, his grandma's eyes, they're blinking with tears.

She clicks open her purse and fishes out a tissue. When Esther presses the tissue on top of her head, Buddy says, when they looked at the tissue, they seen a red spot of fresh blood. It's then Esther told him, "Fast as you can, run get your pa." Esther Shelby lowered herself to one knee; then sitting, then laying in the dust on the shoulder of the road, she says, "Boy, be fast!"

Echo Lawrence: Rant says his granny told him, "Run fast, but if you ain't fast enough, remember I still love you . . ."

Cammy Elliot (◯ *Childhood Friend***):** Kill me if I'm lying, because I ain't, but Middleton dogs turned wilder when the wind blowed too hard. A real gust of wind and all the trash cans go over. Dogs love that.

The first lesson a gal learns in sixth grade is what a septic tank can't digest. Any female trash, you have to wrap it in newspaper and bury it, special deep, in the garbage. The honeywagon comes to pump out your tank and he finds more than just natural waste, it's an extra cost.

'Course, when the wind blows over a garbage can, depending on the household, you have dirty Kotex flapping everywhere. Those gusty days, it's everybody's Aunt Flo has come to visit. Pads and napkins walking off, a regular army drove by the wind. Wrapped and losing their newspaper, they're showing dark blood coated with sand and cockle burrs. Pincushioned with cheatgrass seed. Every trash can that blows over, that army of throwed-away blood gets bigger, marching in the one direction of the wind. Until they come to a fence. Or a cactus.

Shot Dunyun: Close by, Rant could hear the dog packs barking and snapping. He didn't want to leave his grandma, but she told him to get going.

Cammy Elliot: No lie. A regular three-strand barbed-wire fence will look Christmas-decorated with those white puffs. Walk too close and you'd see the condoms snagged there, same as so many dead party balloons. Flapping green or gray or light blue, every rubber with some white mess still hanging heavy in the end.

Flapping at you in the wind, snagged on those pricks of sharp wire, you got panty liners and big strap-on, heavy-day pads. Smooth and ribbed rubbers. Brands of condoms and sanitary napkins you never saw on the shelf at the Trackside Grocery.

Old blood and chunks so black it could be road tar. Blood brown as coffee. Watery pink blood. Sperm died down to almost-clear water.

Blood is blood to most folks, mostly menfolks, but you'd be hard-pressed to match any two tampons pinned on a mile of barbed-wire fence.

Here and there, you'd find pubic hairs. Blond, brown, gray hairs. A good wind kicks up and all the folks of Middleton, we're hanging out, same as birds on a telephone line. Like some 4-H display at the county fair.

Sheriff Bacon Carlyle: If you ask me, the worst part was keeping your dogs inside the house. Folks didn't even need to see the spunk and blood snagged out on the barbed wire to know the wind had dumped somebody's trash. The dogs would turn crazy, whining and digging at the bottom of doors, scratching the paint and wearing out the rugs, to get at that smell so faint only a dog nose would pick it up.

It's different than needing to go outside and do their business. Dogs smell those rubbers and pussy plugs swinging in the hot wind, and dogs start to slobber.

God forbid you open that door. Most folks got right on the phone, blaming each other for the mess and calling someone else to come pick up.

Cammy Elliot: Country around here, it's so flat folks can see from anywhere to anywhere just by looking. Regular folks hold to too much dignity to go hiking out in the face of a Sex Tornado. Nobody wants the community watching them harvest the shame like so many ripe tomatoes.

It's either all the folks pick up their own, or nobody will.

Always, a big showdown. A decency stalemate.

Mary Cane Harvey (◯ *Teacher*): If I wasn't still teaching, Lord, the tales I could tell you about Buster Casey. An exceptional young man.

Sheriff Bacon Carlyle: Don't forget how some folks, including the FBI, was saying his Grandma Esther was Rant's Victim Number One.

Mary Cane Harvey: Buster never got higher than a C in any language-arts course, but there was a sense that Buster would build you the entire world out of just sticks and pebbles and the few words he'd learned. I'd compare it to Tramp Art that men make in prisons, or sailors used to make on voyages that took months. For example, scale models of the Vatican built out of wooden matchsticks, or the Acropolis assembled from sugar cubes glued together. These are artworks based on limited materials and tools, but requiring enormous amounts of time and focus. Monuments to patience.

Bodie Carlyle: To show you how popular Rant got by senior year, one night our dogs took to howling and digging at the door. The wind was blowing, and you didn't need sunshine to see it was the usual Sex Tornado.

Rant came knocking at our kitchen door. While my mom was on the phone laying blame, Rant waves me to come outside. Throwed over one shoulder, he's lugging an empty burlap bag.

Seeing the gunny sack, my mom shakes her head no at me. But I kick the dogs away from the door and trail Rant into the dark outside, the wind snapping our hair, snapping our shirt collars up on one side.

At the fence line, a wad of white stuffing is flapping in the wind, wild and alive as a rabbit in a trap. Condoms flapping like gray tongues tipped with spit. Rant plucks a rubber free and holds it under his nose, the foamy spunk too close to his top lip, and he sniffs. He says, "The Reverend Curtis Dean Fields." He smiles and says, "I'd know that stank anywhere."

Rant drops the trash into his bag. He plucks a pussy plug, this one with just an itty-bitty dot of red in the middle of that white pillow. The red looking black in the moonlight, Rant sniffs it and frowns.

He sniffs again, with his eyes closed this time, and says, "It's LouAnn Perry, all right, but she must be back taking those fluoride pills . . ."

Rant offers me the red dot, but I shake my head.

Before anybody decent has showed up to help, Rant's picked the length of our back fence, guessing every dick and pussy.

Mary Cane Harvey: There's so little to stimulate young people in Middleton. Social life is centered around the church or school events. The grange hall hosts a get-together every weekend, sometimes a cakewalk come springtime, and a craft fair going into the holiday season. Or the Cub Scouts will organize a haunted house as a fund-raiser around Halloween.

Bodie Carlyle: Rant Casey had a dog's sense of smell. A human bloodhound, he could track anything. From staying out late at night, he could smell even better. By being the most popular boy in school, he knowed the name behind every smell. And by twelfth grade, all these talents, they finally started working together to his advantage.

"Look at this," Rant says, and shows me a white pillow with a tight red flower in the center. Little as a violet. Without even sniffing it, he says, "Miss Harvey from English class."

The howl of invisible dogs on the wind, the sound slipping around us.

It's Miss Harvey, he can tell, on account of the red shape. "Makes a 'pussy print,' " Rant says, one finger drawing around the outside of the red stain. "A hundred times more personal than your fingerprint." The stain, he says, looks exactly like a kiss of her down-below parts.

You didn't have to ask how Rant knew the shape of Miss Harvey's parts. Same as animal tracks in the snow or sand, he could hand-draw you the kiss of a wide-ranging variety of local pussy. Native-born or just passing through. Just seeing how far a rubber was rolled down, Rant could reckon what dick it come off.

A ways off, in the kitchen window of my house, you could see my mom's outline standing at the sink, one elbow raised up and poked out sideways, her hand holding the outline of the telephone pressed to the side of her hair. Maybe watching us. Probably watching us.

Rant plucked another wad of white, splashed with a dark stain. He sniffed it and looked back toward my house.

I asked him, "Who is that?" and nodded at the old blood.

This new pussy print, a flower bigger than Miss Harvey's, a sunflower compared to her little violet.

And Rant opened his bag, saying, "Forget it."

No, really, I said, and reached for it. "Let me smell."

Rant dropped the sunflower-big stain into his burlap bag. He walked a step away from me, walking down the fence line, saying, "I'm pretty sure it's your mom's."

My mom, watching. Her ear still looking for blame over the phone.

Walking out with Rant Casey, time had a habit of getting stopped. That moment, another when time got stuck. That moment forever and always doomed to keep happening in my head. Those stars, the same old hand-me-down stars as folks still wish on now. Tonight's moon, the same exact moon as back then.

Sheriff Bacon Carlyle: Between the time it took Rant Casey running to church, and the time we took getting back to old

Esther, the dog packs had already found her. Irene's mama. They left her something awful to come pick up.

Bodie Carlyle: If Rant Casey ever fucked my mom, I didn't never have the balls to ask.

4—Fake Stars

Echo Lawrence (☾ *Party Crasher*): Before Rant had started kindergarten, but after he'd started sleeping in a regular bed, every day his mother put him down when the little hand of the kitchen clock was on the two, until the little hand was on the three. Yawning or not, Rant had to stay on that bed, up in his attic room, with his pillow propped against the wall. In bed, he hugged a stuffed rabbit he called "Bear."

Picture the moment when your mom or dad first saw you as something other than a pretty, tiny version of them. You as them, but improved. Better educated. Innocent. Then picture when you stopped being their dream.

If the sun was bright, and Rant could hear dogs barking outside, he'd say, "Bear wants to go play . . ."

When he wasn't tired, Rant would say, "But Bear isn't sleepy . . ."

Ruby Elliot (☼ *Childhood Neighbor*): Girls who gone to school with Irene Shelby, we know how close Buster Casey come to not getting born. Irene being no older than thirteen when Chester took up with her, fourteen when the baby come due. To be honest, Irene was none too happy, her being the only gal stretch-marked and breast-feeding in ninth grade.

Edna Perry (◎ *Childhood Neighbor*): You best swear I didn't tell you this, but before Buster come, Irene used go on how she wanted to paint pictures and carve statues. She didn't never figure what kind. Went as far as Dr. Schmidt, trying to not have that baby. Went to Reverend Fields at Middleton Christian, asking permission to give it up. It didn't help none: Her own ma, Esther Shelby, told her that baby would be born a flesh-and-blood curse of the Devil.

Echo Lawrence: Irene, she'd press her lips on Rant's little forehead. Sitting on the edge of his bed, she'd shake her finger at the stuffed rabbit and say, "We still need a nap." She'd say, "Let's count our stars until we're sleepy." Rant's mother would make him count one . . . two . . . all the stickers pasted to the ceiling paint. Four, five, six, and she'd walk out of the room, backward, and close the door.

Ruby Elliot: No lie, but Esther had her own child, Irene, about that same age. Chet Casey was the only voice that helped little Rant come into the world. Chet and Irene got hitched, but she had to quit school. Nowadays, folks see the path Buster Casey took, the plague he started, and it's hard to not figure Irene made the wrong choice.

Echo Lawrence: For that hour alone, looking straight up at the ceiling, his eyes not focused, Rant's finger, it explored the warm, deep world inside his head. Every two o'clock, Rant would lay there and pick his nose. Fishing out gummy strands of goo, he'd roll these between two fingers until the goo turned black. The black goo ball sticking to one finger, then his thumb, never falling, no matter how hard he shook his hand. Every gummy black little ball he'd reach up and paste on the wall above his pillow, the white paint peppered with black lumps. Stuccoed with black goo balls mashed flat, printed with loops and whirls, a thousand copies of Rant's little fingerprint. Souvenirs from the travels inside his head. Always the same portrait of the index finger of Rant's right hand. This spotted rainbow, this arching mural of black dots spreading wider as his little-kid arm grew longer The dried goo up close to his pillow, it was just black specks, dusty keepsakes from when he was really small. A hundred naps later, the dots were big as raisins, spread as high and wide as Rant could reach, flopped on his back, his head propped on the pillow.

The ceiling of his childhood bedroom Irene Casey had pasted with bright star shapes that glowed green when you turned out the light.

The head of Rant's bed was a negative night sky. There, sticky black dots outlined other constellations. Until that day, Rant didn't see the difference.

Edna Perry: If you can keep a secret, the first life that maniac Rant Casey wrecked was Irene's. The first bright future he ever ended was his mama's.

Echo Lawrence: That two o'clock when Rant stopped being an angel, his mother was tucking him in for his nap. Leaning over his pillow, she kissed her little Buddy sweet dreams. His round face sunk into his pillow. Rant's long eyelashes fanned down against his pink cheeks.

If you look at old pictures, Irene Casey is so pretty. Not just young, but pretty the way you look when your face goes smooth, the skin around your eyes and lips relaxed, the pretty you only look when you love the person taking the picture.

Rant's mother is the pretty young mom, the nudge of soft lips on his face beside his ear. She's the breath, the whisper of "Sleep tight" with the smell of cigarettes. The candy smell of her shampoo. The flower smell of her skin cream.

Her breath saying, "You're Mommy's little treasure."

Saying, "You're our little angel."

Most mothers talk the same way, in the moment they're still one person with their child.

"You're Mommy's perfect little man . . ."

That moment, before the cow eyeballs and the rattlesnake bites and high-school erections, here's the last moment Rant and his mom will ever be that close. That much in love.

That moment—the end of what we wish would last forever.

Dr. David Schmidt (◐ *Middleton Physician*): In my opinion, both the Caseys made unlikely parents. It's been my experience that plenty of young people look at their newborns as a practical joke. Maybe a punishment. A baby just is; it ain't made of chrome for you to tool around in. A baby ain't going to land you a job behind a desk with air-conditioning.

Chet Casey, he looked at that baby like his worst enemy and best friend, combined.

Echo Lawrence: That naptime, Rant's mother leans over the bed. With one hand, she finger-combs the hair off his little forehead, his bright-green eyes looking up at her, his eyes too big for his face. His eyes counting her stars.

She stands to go back to the kitchen or the garden or the television, and Rant's pretty young mother, she stops. Still half leaned over his bed, she looks at the wall above his pillow, her eyes squinting and twitching to see something on the plaster. Her lips peel open a little. Her gray eyes blinking and blinking, looking hard at the wall, her pretty, pointed chin sags against her neck. And with one hand she reaches forward, one finger poked out a little, the fingernail ready to pick at something on the white paint. The smooth skin puckered into a ditch between her eyebrows.

Rant twists on his bed, arching his back to look.

His mother says, "What's this . . . ?"

And her fingernail taps something, a black lump, a wad, a bump of something almost soft, a mashed raisin that flakes off and falls next to Rant's head on the pillow. A little black fingerprint next to his face.

Rant's mother, her eyes roll to follow the sweep of black dots across the wall, the swarm of gummy smudges that spiral down to her angel's head on the pillow.

As Rant used to say: "Some folks are just born human. The rest of us . . ."

In one way, we're all the same. After a heartbeat of looking, we all see dried snot. We know the sticky feel of it underneath chairs and tables.

Reverend Curtis Dean Fields (○ *Minister, Middleton Christian Fellowship*): Little Rant, wasn't no sin he wouldn't commit. No, little Buddy growed up sinner enough for their whole entire family.

Echo Lawrence: Here's one of those moments that last the rest of your life. A scene Rant saw flash before he died. Time slowed down, stopping, stopped, frozen. The only island you'll find in the vast, vague ocean of your childhood.

In the years of that moment, Rant's mother, her face buckled and clenched into wrinkles. Her face turned to muscles instead of skin. Her lips peeled back, thin, to show the full length of each tooth, beyond that her pink gums. Her eyelids twitched and trembled, her hands curled up, withered into claws. In the forever of that moment, the pretty young woman leaning over Rant's bed, she looked her new hag's face down at him and said, "You . . ."

She swallowed, her throat jumping inside her stringy neck. Shaking her ancient claws at the spotted wall, she said, "You are . . ."

On his back, Rant twisted to see his pride, his collection.

We all have this moment, when your folks first see you as someone not growing up to be them.

Irene's fake, pasted-on stars versus Rant's mural of real snot.

His pride as her shame.

Logan Elliot (○ *Childhood Friend*): It's no lie. That Casey kid done nothing above ordinary except pull up roots and burn bridges.

Shot Dunyun (☾ *Party Crasher*): Times like that, you look like a failed experiment your parents will have to face for the rest of their lives. A booby prize. And your mom and dad, they look like a God too retarded to fashion anything better than you.

You grow up to become living proof of your parent's limitations. Their less-than-masterpiece.

Echo Lawrence: His mother looked down at little Rant from the full height of standing straight, and she said, in a deep voice Rant had never heard, a voice that would echo inside him for the rest of his life, she said:

"You disgusting little monster."

That afternoon, Rant quit being to his mother what his "Bear" was to him. That was the real moment he was born. The start of Rant as a real person.

For the first nap of his new life, that afternoon, Rant fell asleep.

From the Field Notes of Green Taylor Simms (ℂ *Historian*): That next Thanksgiving dinner, after the black widow spiders had stung old Granny Esther to death, Irene Casey abandoned her seat in the kitchen. However, Rant's Great-grandmother Hattie stood next in succession for a place at the adult table. The line of succession was as clear as the names and dates written inside the family Bible.

Shot Dunyun: How creepy is this? By the end of that Thanksgiving, old Granny Hattie's twitching and scratching. The fox-fur piece she wears to every occasion—two or three red-fox pelts with the fucking heads and feet stuffed, pinned so they run around her neck—the shitty thing is jumping with fleas.

It's beyond creepy. People that old, it only takes a gust of wind to kill them. A broken hip. A bee sting. Just one mouthful of tuna bake gone bad. Like black widow spiders, flea bites, you're talking another natural part of the glorious redneck lifestyle. It could've been chipmunks or marmots or deer mice, rabbits, sheep, or rock squirrels, but something in their natural world's left its fleas behind. First, Granny Hattie complained about a sore throat and a headache. A stomach ache. Hattie is gasping for breath. An hour in the hospital, and she's dead of pneumonia.

From the Field Notes of Green Taylor Simms: The last rat-borne epidemic of bacterium *Yersinia pestis* occurred in Los Angeles in the years 1924 and 1925. It was traced to the widespread practice of destroying prairie-dog colonies by introducing animals infected with the plague. By the 1930s, 98 percent of the native marmot population was destroyed, but the remaining 2 percent remain asymptomatic carriers of bubonic plague.

Echo Lawrence: He used to wake up with a yelp. In his nightmares, Rant said his grandmother's little flirtation veil, the black lace would start to shift. The hat seemed to come alive, tearing itself to shreds, and the black threads crawled down her cheeks, biting, and his Grandma Esther, screaming. In those dreams, Rant could hear dogs bark but not see them.

Sheriff Bacon Carlyle (○ *Childhood Enemy*): Them dreams was his feeling guilt, plain and simple. Over Rant's killing those old women. Over spreading his infection.

Shot Dunyun: Those little fluff balls that look so cute in nature films, every year an average of twenty people cross paths with a plague-infected ground squirrel or chipmunk. Their lymph nodes balloon, their fingertips and toes turn black, and they die. The people, I mean. Not the fluff balls.

Echo Lawrence: Go ahead, ask Irene Casey about Rant's bedroom wall. She ended up hanging wallpaper. To her, dried snot was worse than asbestos.

Even as an adult, in his own apartment, the wall above Rant's bed wasn't anything you'd ever want to touch.

Irene Casey (○ *Rant's Mother*): Near as I recall, we did put up wallpaper in Buddy's bedroom, when he was going on three or four years old. A pattern of cowboys roping horses, and some cactus, on a background of chocolate brown, something that wouldn't show dirt. Awful dark, but practical for a boy's room.

The rest, about a wall covered with dried boogers—that never went on. Buddy was a beautiful child. A regular little angel. We did paste stars on his ceiling, those stickers that glowed in the dark, little cowboys under the stars. That part is true, but the rest . . . I wouldn't never call my baby a monster or no curse from the Devil.

And Buddy wouldn't never tell folks that story.

5–Invisible Art

Bodie Carlyle (☼ *Childhood Friend*): Weeks out ahead of
Easter Sunday, you could smell the vinegar on Mrs. Casey's
hands, worse than pickling season. Mrs. Casey would keep a
pot of water boiling. First to hard-cook her eggs. Then
another pot of water to boil with vinegar, add chopped junk
for color, and dye her eggs.

The Caseys, their house was in the country, but they buyed
their chickens already dead. The worst thing you could say
about somebody hereabouts is they buyed their eggs, but
Mrs. Casey buyed hers. Only the white ones. Leghorn eggs.
Mostly on account of Easter.

Coming in through the Caseys' kitchen screen door—
spreee . . . *whap*—you'd find Mrs. Casey with both elbows
up on the table. Her reading glasses slid down to the tip of
her nose. Her head tilted back. In the middle of the table, a
white candle, fat as in church, burning with the smell of
vanilla. Around the candle flame, a clear pool of melted
wax. Mrs. Casey, she'd dip an embroidery needle into that
wax, and she'd hold a white egg in her other hand. Holding the egg at the top and bottom, with a finger and

thumb, so she can turn it, she'd write with melted wax on the shell.

You couldn't help yourself, you had to stop and watch.

From the Field Notes of Green Taylor Simms (ℂ *Historian*): The young hang mirrors in their homes. The elderly hang paintings. And, if I may make an ungenerous observation, residents of rural communities display crafts—those dubious products of spare time, limited motor skill, and inexpensive yarn.

Bodie Carlyle: Invisible as spy writing, only Mrs. Casey could tell where the white wax disappeared on the white egg.

The stove would be crowded, with boiling out of every pot a different smell. Onions. Beets. Spinach greens. The stink of red cabbage. Black coffee. Plus the vinegar smell. In each pot, a different color: yellow, red, green, blue, or brown. Everything boiled down to the color of the cooking water. No lunch ready.

Her eyes crossed, looking straight down her nose, so concentrating on the wax that her mouth hanged open, red lipstick every day of the year, without looking up, she'd say, "If you two are chewing tar, spit it out." She'd say, "You'll find graham crackers over the stove."

Me and Rant.

If you stood there long enough, maybe she'd say how the wax was to keep dye off the egg. At her elbow would be hardcooked eggs that still looked white, but in truth were half decorated with the parts where dye couldn't go. Just watching her, it could slip your mind how you had an ant hill waiting outside. Or a dead raccoon. Even a box of wood matches.

Even being hungry for lunch, you'd get nosing into Mrs. Casey's egg work.

From the Field Notes of Green Taylor Simms: It's compelling that so many cultures practice a meticulous yet transitory art form as a spiritual ritual, prayer, or meditation.

Bodie Carlyle: Her elbows on the table, one hand dipping her embroidery needle in the wax, her other hand holding the eggs, not looking at Rant and me, one day Mrs. Casey says, "Pull up an egg or get out." She says, "You're making me nervous."

Mrs. Casey gave us each a needle and a cold hard-cooked egg and told us not to shake the table any. "Get an idea in your head," she said. And she showed how to dip the tip of a needle into the candle and bring one clear drop of wax back to the shell of a store-bought leghorn egg. "Draw your idea with the needle," she said. Drop by drop. White on white. Invisible. A secret.

Rant says, "You tell me. I can't figure what to draw."

And his mom says, "Something'll come."

From the Field Notes of Green Taylor Simms: Whether it's Piranski eggs or the sand mandalas of Tibetan Buddhists, their common theme is to somehow achieve an intense focus and complete absorption of the artist's attention. Despite the fragile nature of the artwork, the process becomes a means of stepping outside of the temporal.

Bodie Carlyle: Rant, me, and Mrs. Casey around that kitchen table, all leaned together around that candle with the little flame drowned in sun from the window over the sink, drawing stuff only we could tell, none of us figured to be hungry. None of us, anything more than the wax and egg in our hands. Even with the pots of greens and onions boiling, the kitchen air nothing but steam and food smell, none of

us so much as jumped when the screen door went—spree-
whap—and Mr. Casey stood standing there.

"What's for lunch?" he says.

"Thought you were eating at the diner," says Mrs. Casey,
still looking cross-eyed on her egg.

Rant stopped, just holding his egg, not dipping back
drops of wax from the candle. Rant's hands and breathing,
froze solid.

Me, I was drawing a wax day on my egg, a sun with rays, a
tree, my house, a wax cloud in the sky, but only I could tell.

Mr. Casey, he says, "Irene." He says, "Don't do this to the
boy."

And Mrs. Casey says, "You told me you were eating at the
diner."

Leaned over the stove, sticking his nose in the steam above
each pot, sniffing, Mr. Casey says, "Don't ruin him."

Still staring cross-eyed at her egg, the invisible secret of
her idea, Mrs. Casey says, "Do what?"

Rant not drawing anything.

And Mr. Casey says, "Don't ruin the boy for getting married." And he reached for the bowl of eggs beside her elbow
on the table. The eggs, plain white but really halfway decorated with all morning of her secret writing. Invisible art.

"Not those," Mrs. Casey says, her eyes snapped up, looking
over the tops of her eyeglasses.

But already two eggs gone, disappeared inside Mr. Casey's
hand.

And yelling loud, outdoors loud, Mrs. Casey says, "Not
those!"

Mr. Casey turns to the window and—tap-tap-taps—the
eggs against the sink edge to peel them.

Me, I drew a wax bird in the sky, flying over my house, invisible. I put itty-bitty drops of wax in the tree to make apples.

Lunchtime that day was the first I ever felt time get stuck. With Rant and his mom frozen solid, the smell of egg sulfur and vinegar dye and vegetables boiled to stains, a week, a summer, a hundred birthdays come and went. We sat with the sun stopped a century, smack dab in the window above the kitchen sink.

Even the clocks held their breath.

Mr. Casey ate the eggs, looking out the kitchen window, his shadow making the candle flame bright enough to see on the table. The hard-cooked smell of sulfur from the peelings he dropped down the drain. He gobbled the two eggs and the screen door went—spree-*whap*—behind him.

After that, the sun moved to touch one edge of the window frame. Time came unstuck. All the clock hands started back to tick.

Sheriff Bacon Carlyle (◯ *Childhood Enemy*): Don't make Chet Casey the villain for the crimes his boy done. My take is you're not born loving nobody. Love is a skill you learn. Like house-training a dog. Maybe a talent you do or do not build up. Like a muscle. And if you can't learn yourself to love blood family, then you'll never truly love. Not nobody.

Bodie Carlyle: The first egg Mrs. Casey spooned into the dye, that's the first time all afternoon we saw each other's secret picture.

Wood-spooning my egg into the pot of boiled red cabbage, the stink of vinegar and farts, she dipped the egg out colored blue. Sky blue. Blue except where the wax showed a tree with apples, a house, a cloud, and a sun in the blue sky. My house, where I wanted to get home to before Mr. Casey come back.

Spooning her own egg into the pot of boiled-down beets, Mrs. Casey dipped it out all red. Blood red. Red except for, all around, the fancy work of wax lines, complicated as spiderwebs or lace curtains. But not curtains—words, handwriting. Fancy as poetry you'd find in a valentine card. Too fancy to read.

Spooning up Rant's egg, his mom says, "What color?"

Green, Rant says.

"Green it is," she says.

She stirs the egg around in the pot of soggy, slimy spinach greens. Dipping the egg out of the pot, the wax lines make it look striped, side to side. Sectioned up to make squares.

Rant touches a finger to the egg. Touches it a second time. He lifts it from the spoon his mom holds. Pinching it by just one end, Rant dips the egg a little ways into the pot of boiled onions. The yellow dye.

Lifting the egg out, Rant holds it, striped half green and half yellow. The white lines of wax cutting the sides like the lines on a world globe at school.

"That's a beautiful pineapple," Mrs. Casey says.

"Ain't a pineapple," says Rant.

The half-green, part-yellow egg, striped into little squares by the white lines of wax. Between two fingers, at the top and bottom, Rant holds up the green-yellow egg, saying, "It's a MK2 fragmentation grenade."

Packed with granulated TNT, he says. Throwable up to a hundred feet. With a burst radius of thirty-three feet, a cast-iron body for shrapnel. A kill radius of seven feet.

Rant sets the hand grenade on a kitchen towel, where the other eggs, my blue one and his mom's red one, are drying out. And Rant, he says, "Let's make lots more."

Echo Lawrence (ℂ *Party Crasher*): According to Rant, the garden was his mom's territory; the lawn, his dad's. Irene told time by the flowers in bloom. First crocus, then tulips, forget-me-nots, marigolds, snapdragons, roses, day lilies, black-eyed Susans, and sunflowers. The spinach, then the radishes, the lettuce, and the early carrots. To Chester Casey, one week equaled time to mow the grass. One hour meant time to move a lawn sprinkler. We all live by different clocks and calendars.

One Easter, Rant said his mom hid the eggs among the tulips and rosebushes. She gave him a basket and told him, "Happy hunting, Buddy."

Rant still has the scar on his hand where the spider bit him.

Bodie Carlyle: Easter morning, Rant's reaching under a plant or a rosebush and he pulls back his hand. Rant's eyes go— kah-*sproing*—big and bugged-out—looking at the spider perched on the back of his hand skin. He slaps it away, but underneath, the spot's already gone red and puffed up. The veins crabbed up, dark red, branching away from the throbbing, hot tooth marks.

Rant goes back to the kitchen, crying, holding out his bit hand, the fingers already swoll up big and stiff as a catcher's mitt.

Mr. Casey takes one look at his boy, one hand swolled and red, the other hand swinging a pink Easter basket of colored eggs, tears rolling down Rant's cheeks, and Mr. Casey tells him, "Pipe down."

Shot Dunyun (ℂ *Party Crasher*): The church scene where his Granny Esther keeled over, dead, that's still fresh in Rant's mind. The way her dentures bit into her tongue.

Bodie Carlyle: Mrs. Casey, she's in the bathroom, putting on her finishing touches before church.

Mr. Casey swats Rant on the seat of his best Sunday pants and says not to come back inside until he's found all the eggs.

Rant still holds out one fat hand, sobbing it's a black widow spider, sobbing how he's going to die. Sobbing how bad it hurts.

His dad turns him around by the shoulders and shoves him back, saying, "Soon as you bring back all those eggs, we'll get you some medical attention." Latching the screen door to keep Rant outside, Mr. Casey says, "If you don't take too long, maybe you won't lose that hand."

Sheriff Bacon Carlyle: Rant always went on about leaving home, getting out and hand-picking himself a new family, but to my way of seeing that's never going to happen. If you don't accept your folks for all their worst ways, no stranger can ever measure up. All Rant learned himself is how to leave folks behind.

Bodie Carlyle: Dressed-up Rant in his bow tie and white shirt, his black patent-leather shoes and belt, his plain, regular Easter egg hunt, it's now turned into a Race Against Death. His little hands are knocking flowers to one side, busting stems. His feet tramping down petunias. Crushing carrot tops. With every heartbeat, Rant can feel the poison in his hand pumped closer to his brain. The sting of the bite, fading to numb, first his hand losing feeling, then the most part of his arm.

His mom come outside to find him panting in the dirt, facedown in the compost pile that's left of her garden, dirt stuck to the web of tears spread out around each green eye.

Echo Lawrence: So they left him there. They got in their car and drove off to Easter morning services.

Again, that moment, the end of what we wish would last forever.

Bodie Carlyle: Rant never found more than those three eggs. They come home and that's all he had to show for a whole day of hunting. Three eggs and the spider bite, his hand already shrinked back to kid-size.

That spider, it's that black widow spider that got Rant hooked on poison.

Even after Mrs. Casey waded into her garden, all the plants mashed and dug up, she couldn't find a single one of the Easter eggs she'd hid. The rest of that summer, her garden was ruined. Another week, and Mr. Casey's yard would be, too.

Echo Lawrence: Get this. Rant told me he'd found all the eggs, then stashed them in a box, hidden in some barn or shack. Every week, he'd sneak out two or three eggs and stick them in the deepest part of the grass, just before his dad would mow the lawn. By then, the eggs had turned fugly black, the worst kind of rotten.

Every time his dad ran over one with the power mower, you'd have exploded stink—everywhere. On the mower blade, on the grass, all over his father's boots and pant legs. Rant's hand-painted hand grenades, turned into land mines. The lawn and the garden were both disaster areas. Rant said inside the chain-link fence was a jungle. Black stink sprayed on each side of the house. Everything gone so wild you couldn't see the porch. Driving up, you'd think no one lived there.

Bodie Carlyle: He dyed eggs gray with a red stripe, made to match CS gas ABC-M7A2 riot grenades. Light green with a white top half, to be AN-M8 smoke grenades. Mrs. Casey, she bottled the leftover boil water. Jars of bright red and yellow, blue and green, they were all she had left of her garden. So the sun couldn't fade them, she put the jars in the back of a cabinet above the fridge.

The rest of the year, Rant used to sneak out drops of those colors. Summer into Christmas, he'd dig his dad's dirty shorts out of the laundry pile, and Rant would eye-dropper spots of yellow into the crotch of every pair.

After every sit-down piss, Mr. Casey would dangle his dick, trying to get out the last stray drop. Blotting with a square of toilet paper. But every week, more yellow spots in his shorts. It almost killed his pa when Rant switched to using drops from the red food color.

Echo Lawrence: As an adult, Rant's favorite way to skip work was to put a drop of red food coloring into each eye and tell his boss he had conjunctivitis. You know, pinkeye. For a week's sick leave, he'd use yellow to imply hepatitis. Rant's real master stroke was to arrive at his job and let someone else see his eyes, red or yellow, and make the boss force him to go home.

Rant would arrive at my place with his bright-yellow eyes, and we'd cruise the field for a tag team.

Bodie Carlyle: Mr. Casey spent big bucks trying to cure a bladder infection he never did have. He swallowed so much antibiotics he couldn't take a solid shit most of that year.

Echo Lawrence: Before he died, Rant gave me a white hard-boiled egg. He said he'd written something on the shell with white wax, but it's impossible to read, white wax on a white shell. If anything happened to him, Rant said only then could I dye the egg and read the message.

By now, that egg is so old I'm afraid to touch it. If the shell cracks, with the smell that'll come out, I'll be evicted.

Bodie Carlyle: After Rant took off to the city, after he died, the FBI come and grilled me. You should've seen how their eyes lighted up when I told them about the Easter hand grenades.

Irene Casey (○ *Rant's Mother*): The winter after Chet quit mowing the yard, all winter, dog packs used to come roll on their backs. To work the stink into their fur. The same dogs that tore up Grandma Esther. Makes no sense, how dogs can hanker after something so awful. A stink bad as pain, dogs seem to wear it with pride.

6—The Tooth Fairy

Bodie Carlyle (○ *Childhood Friend*): Don't laugh, but one landmark summer, a stick of licorice cost you five dollars in gold. A regular plastic squirt gun set you back fifty bucks.

The spring of the Tooth Fairy upset the whole, entire Middleton standard of living.

First happened is Rant come to my house a Saturday, with his Scout kerchief tied round his neck, and him telling my mom we needed the entire day to collect old paint cans for a recycling merit badge.

Before thenabouts, Rant and me was just-neckerchief Scouts. If all your folks could buy you was the yellow kerchief for round your neck, you was the bottom rung of Cub Scouting. Other boys, well-off boys, had the midnight-blue uniform shirt. Rich boys had the uniform shirt and pants. Milt Tommy boasted the regulation Scout knife and scabbard, the Scout belt with the brass buckle, and the compass that you could hook to hang off the belt. Wore his shoulder sash sewed all over with merit badges to every meeting.

Brenda Jordan (○ *Childhood Friend*): Promise not to tell, but a time we were dating, Rant Casey told me about a stranger. The time his Grandma Esther lay dying, a stranger drove up the road from nowheres. Said he'd look after Esther, and he told Rant where to find the gold. Just a tall old man, Rant says.

That old man told he was Rant's real, true daddy, come visiting from the city. That stranger told how Chester Casey was nobody.

Bodie Carlyle: Didn't matter how hard you earned it, a Scout merit badge with all that fancy 'broidery still cost five dollars. Rant and me weren't getting none of those badges.

That summer, we pushed a wheelbarrow, going to farms to knock on doors. Asking: Can we take away any rusted cans of old, dried paint folks might have stacked round the place? Cub Scouting scrap-metal project, Rant tells them, and folks smile, only too happy to be rid of old cans. All Saturday, until Rant and me collect us a pile in his folks' barn.

Rant screwdrivers the metal lid off one can, and the insides is solid pink paint left over from a bedroom ain't been that color since forever. Forgot colors of handed-down rooms of farmhouses all over. No surprises. Just dead paint. Until Rant pries open a can and the insides is packed with newspapers, some balled up, some papers is wrapped tight round something hard. Rolled open, inside the newspaper balls is old bottles. Black-blue glass from old-time-ago bottles. Little face-cream and medicine jars.

The newspaper feels soft as pool-table felt, not white paper but yellow, full of crimes to end all crimes, wars and plagues preached to be the end of the world. Every year of newspaper announcing another new end of the world.

Hartley Reed (◯ *Proprietor of the Trackside Grocery*): One kid, the Jordan girl, she brung in a handful of gold coins.

Most of them Liberty Head dollars going back to 1897. Found out, later on, she'd took a rock and hammered apart her grandma's dentures. Traded those loose teeth for this "Tooth Fairy money," the kids called it. Brung the coins to me, and took home a dollhouse come special-order from the Walker's catalogue.

Bodie Carlyle: Inside them paint cans is stuffed coin money. Gold and silver coin money, packed tight to stay quiet. Some stamped with eagles fighting snakes, and some coins with pretty girls or old men, the girls showed standing, hardly dressed, but the old men showing just their wrinkled face.

"Gold bugs," Rant says, folks not trusting governments or the bank. Nor neighbors, nor family. Nor wives. Lonely alone misers, Rant says, stockpiling gold and silver and heart-attacking with their life's secret unshared.

Rant says you can't call it robberying if the owners is dead and if the right and lawful heirs wasn't loved enough to get told about the money being hid. Pirate treasures. Those paint cans lined up on shed shelves, rusting in barns and the trunks of abandoned cars.

Turns out Rant knowed the money was around, not in every paint can but enough, knowed it for a long time, but didn't bother to fetch any cans until he'd figured how to reason us having such riches. Two just-neckerchief Scouts, without scratch to buy the merit badges coming to us, now spending gold and silver money with dates on it going back a hundred and more years.

Hartley Reed: Supply and demand. Nobody pointed a gun to make those kids spend their money. Funds was their money, to buy whatever they wanted. Just natural, when demand increases so do prices. When you get every kid in town bidding up cherry Fizzies, the cost is bound to inflate.

Bodie Carlyle: The inflation is how Rant figured to launder our pirate treasure. Starting with our most best friends in fifth grade, we asked around: Who had a tooth loose? Any kid with a coming-out tooth—cha-*ching*—we gived him a silver or a gold coin and tell him to say the Tooth Fairy brung it. Fifth grade, most kids figure the Tooth Fairy's a lie, but our folks ain't told us as much.

Every weekend, we're collecting paint cans, pushing that wheelbarrow down longer roads to get to more far-off farms, isolated spreads where the real left-behind money's gone to pile up.

And every week, we're giving kids more gold and silver to tell their folks is from the Fairy for a baby tooth.

Most folks knowed here's a lie, but moms and dads not wanting to admit their own lying about the Tooth Fairy and Santy Claus and all. Us lying to our folks, them lying to us, nobody wanted to admit to being the liar.

None of the other fifth-graders ratted on Rant or me, since they want to keep the money and figure more's coming.

Everybody caught trapped in the same Tooth Fairy lie.

You can get plenty of folks telling the same lie if they got a stake in it. You get everybody telling the same lie and it ain't a lie, not no more.

Livia Rochelle (☼ *Teacher*): A year I was teaching fifth grade, the Elliot girl brought me a gold coin and asked how much it was worth in trade for Tootsie Rolls. We looked up the coin in the library, and it was a two-and-one-half dollar Liberty Head, dated 1858. The obverse side showed a woman's profile, crowned across her forehead with the word "Liberty," and thirteen stars going around her.

According to the book we checked, that gold piece was valued at fifteen thousand dollars.

My fear was that she'd stolen the coin, so I asked how she'd come to have it. That Elliot girl, she told me the Tooth Fairy left it in exchange for a tooth she'd lost, and she pointed a finger to show me a gap in the side of her smile. A molar toward the front was gone, just a baby tooth.

Bodie Carlyle: Bicuspids brung five dollars, gold. A molar, ten. Silas Hendersen claimed to lose twelve incisors, nine canines, and sixteen wisdom tooths in the passing of that summer vacation. Was older kids selling their teeth to fifth-graders for a half-cut of the Fairy money. Kids 'tempting to pass off horse tooths, dog tooths, big cow tooths chewed down to the stub and roots. Got so Rant Casey turned tooth expert. Knowed a silver filling from mercury amalgam. A real broke tooth from a pried-off crown. Piled up in Rant's bedroom, he had soup cans of folks' teeth, then cigar boxes, shoe boxes, then shopping bags. The Middleton Tooth Museum.

Making all the fifth grade rich, it didn't look as suspect, Rant and me being rich. But for every gold or silver coin we passed on to a kid, we held back two for each of us. Rant holding back double what I did, not spending his.

After plenty of money come into play around town, what Rant and me spended only looked reasonable. Regular, compared to the new standard of living.

Team captains took money on the side, so even the loser-est ball player could pitch an inning. Teachers at Middleton Elementary would take a couple hundred under the table in exchange for a report card of straight A's. Was babysitters bribed a hundred dollars in sterling silver so kids could stay up, watching movies past midnight.

Livia Rochelle: Mr. Reed at the Trackside Grocery was only too happy to sell them candy. Another reflection of the time, the grocery took out the "Gifts for M'Lady" section and extended the toy and hobby selection all the way down to frozen foods. For a year, it seemed as if half the store was candy bars and air rifles and dolls. You had to drive clear to Pitman Mills for a new filter for your furnace, but the Trackside stocked seventeen different colors and sizes of bottle rockets.

Bodie Carlyle: We learned folks will sell anything to anybody if the money's enough. Inflated the whole entire Middleton economy. Flush with Tooth Fairy cash, kids didn't clamor to mow lawns. Returnable pop bottles and beer bottles piled up alongside the shoulder of roads.

Hereabouts, folks called it the "trickle-up" theory of prosperity. All the kids rich. All the adults smiling and wheedling and playing nice to get that money.

Looking back, we sparked a boom and rebirth of little downtown Middleton. Kids bought new bikes, and the Trackside finally paved its parking lot. Kids going back to school that fall, they wore lizard-skin cowboy boots. Rodeo belt buckles studded with turquoise. Wristwatches so heavy they made a kid lope to one side when he walked.

The second boom come at Christmas, with Santy Claus stuffing gold and silver in the stockings of fifth-graders, didn't matter good or bad.

Livia Rochelle: In my classroom, I tried to impress on the students that reality is a consensus. Objects, from diamonds to bubble gum, only have value because we all agree they do. Laws like speed limits are only laws because most people agree to respect them. I tried to argue that their gold was worth infinitely more than the junk they wanted to trade for, but it was like watching Native Americans sell their tribal lands for beads and trinkets.

The children of Middleton really were driving our economy. Within the week, that little Elliot girl was sneaking Tootsie Rolls in class. By junior high school, she had a face like raw hamburger meat.

Echo Lawrence (ℂ *Party Crasher*): The spooky part is, except for Rant, most people in Middleton had no idea how far someone had gone to acquire that gold.

Mary Cane Harvey (◯ *Teacher*): The children told me about one woman selling shaved ice in a paper cone with cherry syrup, two cones for a gold dollar. You'd watch kids take two bites and drop the rest in the playground grass.

Money you don't work to earn, you spend very quickly.

Brenda Jordan: The Tooth Fairy come different to every family. At the Elliots', they wrapped a lost tooth in tissue and slept with it under a pillow. In the morning, inside that tissue was the money. The Perrys, they dropped the tooth in a glass half full of water and set it on the kitchen windowsill. In the morning, instead of the tooth was money. The Hendersens done the ritual same as the Elliots, but they used a lace doily they called "the tooth hankie." The Perrys always used the same glass, a fancy cut-glass jigger they called the "tooth glass." My family, we put the tooth in water but we left it sitting, overnight, on the bedside table. Near a window left open a crack for the Fairy to fly inside.

The sole and only time I almost told on Rant Casey was one night I changed my tooth in the glass for an 1897 Morgan silver dollar. But in the morning, it was just a regular quarter-dollar, dated modern. I knowed my folks had switched and took the real money, but I had to act happy.

Cammy Elliot (☾ *Childhood Friend*): Adults lying about the Tooth Fairy. Kids lying. Everybody knowing that everybody was lying. Then adults selling helium balloons for a hundred bucks to kids who didn't know any better. Adults stealing from kids, then merchants stealing from folks. Greed on top of greed.

Cross my heart, the summer of the Tooth Fairy destroyed all credibility anybody had in Middleton. Since then, nobody's word stands up. To everybody, everybody else is a liar. But folks still smile and act nice.

Shot Dunyun (☾ *Party Crasher*): That next Thanksgiving, Rant's Granny Bel is in line for a seat at the adult table. Then his Uncle Clem. Then Uncle Walt and Aunt Patty. Rant says his mom stood there and counted on her fingers—four, five, six relatives would have to die before she'd eat like a grown-up.

Before the end of that Thanksgiving dinner, Rant's Granny Bel was already sweating with fever. Bel's running a fever of 105 degrees, but complaining of the cold. Her other symptoms include dizziness, fatigue, and muscle aches. Rant says Granny Bel can't catch her breath because, it turns out, her lungs are filling with fluid. Her kidneys have failed. Halfway to the hospital, Rant says his Granny Bel's stopped breathing.

Echo Lawrence: It turns out, lucky Grandma Bel's been infected by a killer virus. It's called the "hantavirus," and you get it from something Rant called the "white-footed mouse."

The mouse shits, and the shit dries into dust. You breathe the shit dust, and the virus kills you inside of six weeks.

She's an old lady wearing red lipstick, with powder on her nose.

Rant says the county tested the talc in Bel's compact, and of course it was half mouse shit. The dried, ground-up dust of wild-mouse turds. The powder puff was loaded with shit dust. Mystery solved. Kind of solved.

Shot Dunyun: Don't get the idea Rant Casey was some kind of naturopathic serial killer—spiders, fleas, mice, and bees— but you could make that argument.

Bodie Carlyle: Just a little part of my gold bought me that midnight-blue Cub Scout shirt and pants, bought the Scout knife, the belt, and the compass. Since Milt Tommy was a sixth-grader and didn't get no treasure, I paid him a hundred bucks in gold for his sash with every merit badge already sewed to it. Every badge from First Aid to Good Citizenship.

Folks really will sell you anything for the right price.

And I learned a cash-bought merit badge ain't worth shit.

7—Haunted House

Bodie Carlyle (◎ *Childhood Friend*): The only gold money Rant spent was, one day he pushed a wheelbarrow down the road, all the way to the Perry Meat Packing plant.

Reverend Curtis Dean Fields (◎ *Minister, Middleton Christian Fellowship*): Inside the grange hall, the annual haunted house consisted of old oilcloth tarps, smelling from train diesel, hung up to make a pitch-dark tunnel you'd walk inside. How folks hung the tarps, it made the tunnel turn right and left, turning back on itself to confuse you and make the walk last long as possible. Kids waited at the start, and Rant took them through one at a time. Kid stuff inside. At the far end was a party with a costume contest, cake, and candy. One year, a piñata.

Inside, the tunnel was pitch-dark except when lights flashed to show something scary. The far end was most dark, and Rant would blindfold you. He'd put your hand in a big mixing bowl full of cooked elbow macaroni stirred with cold butter, and he'd tell you, "This is brains." You'd feel a bowl of grapes coated with corn oil, or peeled hard-cooked eggs, and Rant would say, "These is pulled-out eyeballs." Pretty tame stuff these days. Hard for a kid's imagination, standing in the dark, feeling a bowl of warm gelatin water while Rant Casey says, "This is fresh blood . . ." Anymore, it's pretty hard for imagination to make that seem horrible.

Luella Tommy (☼ *Childhood Neighbor*): At the party end of the haunted tunnel, kids is gobbling cake and playing Ducky Ducky. Playing Pass the Orange. Kids ask can they have napkins to wipe off their hands, after touching the pretend brains and lungs and scary junk. Other kids just wipe their hands on their costumes or on each other.

The little Elliot girl comes out the tunnel, red up to both elbows. Real red. Crying. Dressed as a little angel with tissue-paper wings stretched on coat-hanger wire and a wire halo dusted with gold glitter, the Elliot girl wipes her eyes with one hand and smears red across her face. The Elliot girl, just sobbing, she says, "Rant Casey put a real live heart in my bare hand . . ."

And I told her, "No, honey. It was make-believe." I spit on a napkin to wipe her face and said, "That heart was just a plain old peeled tomato . . ." My first fear is she's scared. I'm kneeled down, wiping her face with a paper napkin, and the paper's coming apart. Then I see how sticky the red is, gumming her skirt together in folds. Sticky and blotched with dark spots. Clots. Not just red food color. And there's a smell. On top the diesel stink of those old tarps, that creosote smell same as railroad ties on a hot day, I can smell a sweet kind of marigold, kind of potty smell of meat gone bad.

Glenda Hendersen (☼ *Childhood Neighbor*): For God's sake. All the kids, just their fingers, one hand or both, some their arms and their costumes, little pirates and fairies and hobos, but they're all smeared with blood. Red blood so old it's gone black. Touching the cake, they got blood on the vanilla icing. Blood on the ladle for the fruit punch, and the orange for Pass the Orange. Fingerprints of blood all over the soda crackers for playing Whistling Crackers.

On the concrete floor of the grange hall, leading out of the tarp tunnel, come an army of little footprints, the tread marks of sneakers and sandals, all printed in sticky blood. Lowell Richards, from the high school, he borrows a flashlight and goes to take a look.

Sheriff Bacon Carlyle (☼ *Childhood Enemy*): Worse than the worse-ever police crime-scene photo.

Luella Tommy: Folks rumored maybe Irene Casey brung home and froze her afterbirth when Buddy was born. My first impression was, could be, Buddy made it a scene in the haunted house: the Hanged Man, the Ghost, the Vision of Hell, and Irene Casey's Placenta . . .

Thank God I was wrong—but not by far off.

Polk Perry (☼ *Childhood Neighbor*): Wouldn't have sold Rant Casey those eyeballs if I'd knowed what that runt had planned. What went on, that's a surefire sign the Casey boy would grow up to be a killer.

Lowell Richards (☼ *Teacher*): In the dark, Rant Casey holds the Hendersen boy's hand, dipping that hand into bowls. In the circle of my flashlight, bowls of blood thick as pudding. Bowls of slaughterhouse lungs. Pig and steer lungs, gray and heaped up. Bowls of squirmy gray brains, all busted and mashed together. Bowels and kidneys slopped on the floor.

There's one salad bowl rolling with different-size eyeballs. Cow, pig, and horse eyeballs all staring up, smudged with bloody fingerprints. All this mess starting to warm, starting to stink. Kidneys and bladders and cookie sheets heaped with intestines.

Polk Perry: History is, it's just a nightmare. Cut-off tongues laying everywhere.

Lowell Richards: With me watching, Rant Casey held the Hendersen boy's hand open, palm-up, and set something shining and dark in the fingers, saying, "This is a heart . . ."
A huge dead cow's heart.
And the Hendersen boy's giggling, blindfolded, and squeezing the heart. Blood oozing out the cut-off tubes.

Bodie Carlyle: It's spooky to consider, us turning teeth into gold and gold into eyeballs. Things in life is either flesh or money, like they can't be both at the same time. That would be like somebody being both alive and dead. You can't. You got to choose.

Sheriff Bacon Carlyle: Him being a Casey, 'course he made it look by accident. Told folks he thought that's how the haunted house was set up, always. Said he didn't know pillars of the community as trusted and honored and respected as Scout den leaders, grown-ups, would lie to little kids. Just like a Casey to play dumb. Rant said how since forever kids looked forward to touching brains and lungs. Said it was nothing scary to touch old macaroni. Rant made the old, respectable way we did things, using grapes and food color, sound like the shameful crime.

Lowell Richards: Rant Casey wasn't evil. He was more like, he was trying to find something real in the world. Kids grow up connected to nothing these days, plugged in and living lives boosted to them from other people. Hand-me-down adventures. I think Rant wanted everybody to experience just one real adventure. As a community, something to bond folks.

Everybody in town seeing the same old movie or boosting the same peak, that doesn't bring folks together. But after kids came home, their costumes matted with blood, blood under their little fingernails for a week, and their hair stinking, that had folks talking. Can't say they were happy, but folks were talking and together.

Something really did happen that only belonged to Middleton.

Shot Dunyun (ℂ *Party Crasher*): It wasn't only the boosted experiences that bothered Rant. It was dipshit kids done up as soldiers and princesses and witches. Eating cake flavored with artificial vanilla. Celebrating a harvest that didn't occur anymore. Fruit punch that came from a factory. A ritual to placate ghosts, or whatever bullshit Halloween does, practiced by people who had no awareness of that. What bothered Rant was the fake, bullshit nature of everything.

From the Field Notes of Green Taylor Simms (ℂ *Historian*): In Africa, people don't believe in the Tooth Fairy. Instead, they have the Tooth Mouse. In Spain: Ratoncito Pérez. In France: La Bonne Petite Souris. A tiny, magical rodent that steals teeth and replaces them with spare change. In some cultures, the lost tooth must be hidden in a snake or rat burrow to prevent a witch from finding and using the tooth. In other cultures, children throw the tooth into a roaring fire, then, later, dig for coins in the cold ashes.

By first believing in Santa Claus, then the Easter Bunny,

then the Tooth Fairy, Rant Casey was recognizing that those myths are more than pretty stories and traditions to delight children. Or to modify behavior. Each of those three traditions asks a child to believe in the impossible in exchange for a reward. These are stepped-up tests to build a child's faith and imagination. The first test is to believe in a magical person, with toys as the reward. The second test is to trust in a magical animal, with candy as the reward. The last test is the most difficult, with the most abstract reward: To believe, trust in a flying fairy that will leave money.

From a man to an animal to a fairy.

From toys to candy to money. Thus, interestingly enough, transferring the magic of faith and trust from sparkling fairy-dom to clumsy, tarnished coins. From gossamer wings to nickels . . . dimes . . . and quarters.

In this way, a child is stepped up to greater feats of imagination and faith as he or she matures. Beginning with Santa in infancy, and ending with the Tooth Fairy as the child acquires adult teeth. Or, plainly put, beginning with all the possibility of childhood, and ending with an absolute trust in the national currency.

Shot Dunyun: Talk about frustrating. All that pretense and reality in flux: Gold worth penny candy. Sugar worth gold. Macaroni passing as brains, and adults swearing the Tooth Fairy was real. Even the way a bizarre cultural delusion like Santa Claus can drive half of annual retail sales. Some mythological fat asswipe drives our national economy. It's beyond frustrating.

That night, even as a little boy, Rant Casey just wanted one thing to be real. Even if that real thing was stinking blood and guts.

From the Field Notes of Green Taylor Simms: Each holiday tradition acts as an exercise in cognitive development, a greater challenge for the child. Despite the fact most parents don't recognize this function, they still practice the exercise.

Rant also saw how resolving the illusions is crucial to how the child uses any new skills.

A child who is never coached with Santa Claus may never develop an ability to imagine. To him, nothing exists except the literal and tangible.

A child who is disillusioned abruptly, by his peers or siblings, being ridiculed for his faith and imagination, may choose never to believe in anything—tangible or intangible—again. To never trust or wonder.

But a child who relinquishes the illusions of Santa Claus, the Easter Bunny, and the Tooth Fairy, that child may come away with the most important skill set. That child may recognize the strength of his own imagination and faith. He will embrace the ability to create his own reality. That child becomes his own authority. He determines the nature of his world. His own vision. And by doing so, by the power of his example, he determines the reality of the other two types: those who can't imagine, and those who can't trust.

Reverend Curtis Dean Fields: No matter how well you seal it, wax or varnish, a wood floor can hold an odor. Clear cedar, tongue-in-groove boards like the grange has, the end part of summer you can still smell what happened. Hot weather. Took only one child to vomit her cake—Dorris Tommy, I believe—and the stink set off so many others you couldn't never tell who was number two.

Danny Perry (○ *Childhood Friend*): Weren't nothing but blood and barf, like a sticky carpet covered the whole floor.

Blood and barf. History is, that's how come folks started calling Buster Casey his nickname—"Rant." On account of every kid doubled over and making nearabouts the same sound. Kids yelled "Rant!" and up comes vanilla cake and frosting. Yelling "Rant!" and spouting out purple fruit punch.

Middleton folks, if they're sick or drunk, they'll still say, "I feel I'm going to Rant," if they're close to throwing up.

Bodie Carlyle: Before Rant moved to the city, he gived me twenty-four gallon milk jugs full to the neck with folks' lost teeth. From little baby teeth going back to grandfolks' mouths, dug out of trunks and keepsake boxes. By my account, the suitcases he hauled to the city, they held nothing but gold money.

Rant, he called those milk jugs "The Middleton Tooth Museum."

8—Pacing

Wallace Boyer (○ *Car Salesman*): Your truly effective car salesman, he hands you his business card, first thing. That salesman says hello, tells you his name, and gives you his card, because human behavior studies show that 99 percent of customers use the business card as their excuse to exit the dealership. Most car buyers, if they hate you, even hate your cars, they still feel bad for wasting your time. If they can ask for your card, the customer feels better about bailing out. You want to trap most shoppers, you hand them your card the minute you meet them: They can't escape.

In the first forty-three seconds you meet a stranger, experts in human behavior say that, just by looking at them, you decide their income, their age, their brains, and if you're going to respect them. So a smart salesman wears a decent suit. He doesn't scratch his scalp and then smell his fingernails.

A landmark study, out of Cal State LA in 1967 and proved a bunch of times since then, it says 55 percent of human communication is based on our body language, how we stand or lean or look each other in the eye. Another 38 percent of our communication comes through our tone of voice, the speed we talk, and how loud. The surprise is, only 7 percent of our message comes through our words.

So a smart salesman, his big talent is knowing how to listen.

We call it "pacing" a customer: You match your breathing rate to his breathing. He taps his foot or drums his fingers, you do, too, and match his speed. If he scratches his ear or stretches his neck, you wait twenty seconds and do the same. Listen for his words and watch where his eyes roll as he talks. The majority of customers, they learn through vision, and most times their eyes are looking up—to the left if they're remembering information, but they'll look to their right if they're lying. The next group learns by hearing, and they'll look side to side. The smallest group learns by moving or touching, and they'll look down as they talk.

The visual people will say, "Look," or "I see what you mean." They'll say, "I can't picture that," or "See you later." That's Echo Lawrence: always eyeing you.

Your audio customers will say, "Listen," or "That sounds good," or "Talk to you soon." For example, that Shot Dunyun guy: Makes almost no eye contact, but if you talk fast, sound excited, he'll get all worked up.

Your touch-based customers will tell you, "I can handle that." They'll say, "Got it," or "Catch you later." That's the young kid, Neddy Nelson: Stands too close to you, and he's always tapping you, touching you with his fingers, to make sure you'll listen.

In really effective pacing, a salesman adopts the learning style of the customer—visual or hearing or touch—to the point of looking up or sideways or down at the ground while you talk. Your goal is to establish common ground. Not everybody enjoys baseball or even fishing, but every person is obsessed with himself.

You are your own favorite hobby. You're an expert on you.

All a good salesman does is make eye contact, mimic your body language, nod or laugh or grunt to prove he's spellbound—those noises or gestures, they're called "verbal attends." A salesman only has to prove that he's just as obsessed with you as you are with yourself. After that, the two of you share a common passion: you.

There's lots more comes after that: embedded commands, objection bridging, hot buttons, tie-down and add-on questions, control questions . . . you name it.

Any good salesman will tell you: Before a customer cares how much you know, that customer wants to know how much you care.

And your truly effective salesman, he knows how to fake that he really, truly does give a shit.

9–Fishing

Bodie Carlyle (◎ *Childhood Friend*): Living, alive animal fur is what my fingers would finally come across. Rant just egging me to push my arm deeper into the ground. My fingers slippery with grease. Most of me sun red, stretched out on the sand, my hand's crawling down, colder than cool, into the dark of a varmint hole. Skunk, maybe. A coyote or gopher den.

Rant's eyes on my eyes, he says, "Feel anything?"

My hand blind, touching a tangle of sagebrush roots, smooth rocks, then—hmmm—fur. The soft hairs moving off, out of my reach down the tunnel.

Rant saying, "Go after it."

A gust of wind takes off with our crumpled sheet of tinfoil still greasy from Mrs. Casey's leftover meatloaf. The ground beef and oregano we each worked our digging hand through, the meatloaf wedged deep under our fingernails and slippery between our fingers. And my hand, lost somewheres underground, stretched beyond where I figured it would get, I reach to feel that fur and the rattle of a fast heartbeat underneath. That heartbeat almost as fast as mine.

LouAnn Perry (◯ *Childhood Friend*): History is, the girls Rant liked, he used to kiss. Boys, he took them out animal-fishing. Both ways it was a test of your faith.

Bodie Carlyle: Summers, most folks would go fishing, over along the river in hot weather; Rant would head the other way.

It wasn't nothing to find Rant walked straight all morning out in the desert, laid down flat on one side, his arm disappeared up to the elbow in some dirty hole. Didn't matter what critter—scorpion, snake, or prairie dog—Rant would be reaching blind into the dark underground, hoping for the worst.

That black widow spider on Easter Sunday, since it didn't kill him, Rant figured to hunt down what might. "I been vaccinated against measles and diphtheria," Rant used to say. "A rattlesnake's just my vaccination against boredom."

A cottonmouth bite he called "my vaccination against doing chores."

Pit vipers, just about half the time they forget to inject their venom. According to books, Rant says, rattlesnakes, cottonmouths, they truly are more scared of you. A human being, giving off so much heat, that's what a pit vipers sees. Something so big and hot shows up, and it's all a snake can get done to unfold those swing-down fangs and—kah-*pow*—sink them in your arm.

Nothing more pissed off Rant than getting a dry bite. Pain but no poison. A vaccination without the medicine. Those double holes marching up his arms, ringed around his shins, no red welts. Dry bites.

Instead of river fishing, Rant walked out beyond the back porch, beyond the barrel for burning trash, past the machine shed, out into the fields leased out for alfalfa, the Rain Bird sprinklers—tick-tick-ticking—shots of water into the hot sunshine. After the alfalfa came the horizon of Russian-olive trees, shaggy with their long silver leaves. Over that horizon come the sugar beets. After the beets, another horizon. Beyond that, a barbed-wire fence piled solid with tumble-weeds trying to get inside. Kotex and rubbers snared and flapping, full of Middleton spunk and blood.

Beyond that, another horizon. Three horizons outside the Caseys' back door, you found yourself in the desert. Rant called his walking out to get animal bit, he called it: "gone fishing."

Irene Casey (○ *Rant's Mother*): The fire ants should've been a red flag. Buddy never come in the house without his hands and feet being all over a red rash of ant bites. Pain you'd expect to make most kids cry, Buddy wore it no worse off than a heat rash.

Bodie Carlyle: His folks didn't hear the half of it. Rant could roll up his sleeve at school and count off the bites: red ant, hobo spider, scorpion.

"More of my vaccinations," Rant used to say.

All through ninth grade, Rant would ask to be excused from playing Friday dodgeball against the twelfth-graders on account of a fresh rattlesnake bite. While the rest of us got creamed to hell, Rant would pull off one sweat sock and show the coach a fat, red foot. The two poke holes leaking clear ooze you'd take for venom.

Between him and me, this was his vaccination against playing dodgeball.

To Rant, pain was one horizon. Poison, the next horizon. Disease was nothing but the horizon after all them.

From the Field Notes of Green Taylor Simms (☾ *Historian*): The black widow spider only kills about 5 percent of those it bites. An hour after the bite, the neurotoxin a-latrotoxin spreads throughout the victim's lymphatic system. Your abdomen contracts into a solid washboard of rigid muscle tissue. You might vomit or sweat profusely.

Another common symptom is priapism. It's nature's cure for erectile dysfunction. Rant never told his parents, but that Easter was the first time he'd ever experienced an erection. Sex and insect venom were completely collapsed in his childhood psyche.

Echo Lawrence (☾ *Party Crasher*): That's the secret behind Rant's craving for snakes. Even in the city, he needed to find a black widow or a brown recluse before he was worth anything in the sack. Getting a "booster shot," he used to call it.

Don't try this at home, but the result is a dick that stays hard for hours. On demand, and big as a gearshift. A little calcium gluconate and everything goes back to normal.

Sheriff Bacon Carlyle (☼ *Childhood Enemy*): The only why Rant Casey got himself bit was to catch a buzz. Poison being just another drug to abuse. Another high. Speaking as an officer of the law, I can tell you an addicted addict ain't like regular folks. By the end of this story, you'll be pretty near shocked what Rant done to get and stay strung out.

Bodie Carlyle: Don't ask me. I never did figure out the attraction. While other kids was sniffing gasoline or model-airplane glue, most summer days, Rant would be belly-down in the sand next to a sagebrush. Most kids around here, they'd be escaping from reality, while Rant was trying to get ready for it.

Those dirty holes, under those rocks he'd tip up a crack, those places where he couldn't see, that was the future we was so scared about. After he'd stuck his hands into the dark, and not died from it, after then Rant wasn't so scared. He'd roll up one pant leg and point his foot out straight. He'd sit in the desert and poke this bare foot down in a coyote burrow, slow, the way folks test bathwater with their big toe. In case it's too hot or cold. Watching him, Rant would plant both hands braced in the sand, his eyes shut tight, holding one big breath inside his chest.

In the bottom of that hole, a skunk, a raccoon, a mother coyote with pups, or a rattlesnake. The feel of soft fur or smooth scales, warm or cool to the touch, then—kah-*pow*—the mouth grab of teeth, and Rant's whole leg would shake. And Rant never pulled back, not the way most folks would, doing more damage as the teeth hung tight. No, Rant let the mouth let loose. Maybe snatch tight a second time. Sink deep. Let go. Get bored. Then a sniff of warm breath against his toes. Underground, the feel of a wet tongue licking up his blood.

Out of that hole Rant would pull his foot, the skin tore up and mangled, but licked clean of dirt. His clean skin bleeding—drip-drip-drip—pure blood. His eyeballs nothing but big black pupil dialed all the way open, Rant would be pulling off his other shoe and sock, rolling up the second pant leg, and shoving another bare part of himself into the dark to see what might happen.

The whole length of summer, Rant's toes and finger would be frayed skin, fringed with dripping blood. One bite of venom, one little squirt of poison at a time, Rant was training for something big. Getting vaccinated against fear. No matter the future, any terrible job or marriage or military service, it had to be an improvement over a coyote chomping on your foot.

Echo Lawrence: Get this. The first night I met Rant Casey, we were eating Italian, and he says, "You never been snake-bit?"

He's wearing a coat, so I have no idea about how *mutilated* his arms look.

As if this is my shortcoming, he keeps goading me, saying, "I can't believe a person could live so long and never been sprayed by a skunk . . ."

As if mine has been a life of utter caution and deprivation.

Rant shakes his head, looking and sighing at his plate of spaghetti. Then, turning his head sideways and giving me a look with only one eye, he says, "If you never been *rabid*, you ain't never lived."

The nerve of him. Like he's some redneck *holy man*.

Get him. He couldn't even work a three-speed mounted on the steering column.

Until that night, he'd never seen *ravioli*.

Dr. David Schmidt (✹ *Middleton Physician*): The little screw-up, that Casey boy, he was presenting symptoms before he bothered to let his folks know he'd been bit. With rabies, the virus is carried in the saliva of an infected animal. Any bite or lick, even a sneeze, can spread the disease. Once you have it, the virus spreads through your central nervous system, up your spine to your brain, where it reproduces. The early stage is called the "eclipse" phase of the disease, because you present no symptoms. You can be contagious as all get-out, but still look and feel normal.

This eclipse phase can last a couple days to years and years. And all that time, you can be infecting folks with your saliva.

Bodie Carlyle: Instead of boosting peaks, Rant wanted to go fishing. He used to say, "My life might be little and boring, but at least it's mine—not some assembly-line, secondhand, hand-me-down life."

Shot Dunyun (ℂ *Party Crasher*): Getting bit by a rattlesnake, that's pretty low-tech.

Dr. David Schmidt: The intolerable aspect was that Buster Casey was a popular boy. He must've been. In the past ten years, we've treated six cases of rabies infection in a male. All six cases being Buster himself. But we've had forty-seven infections in girls, most of those girls he attended school with, and two of those being his female teachers. Out of those, three chose to terminate pregnancies by unnamed fathers at the same time.

LouAnn Perry: Any way you look at it, Buster was a hazard to have around playing Spin the Bottle.

Polk Perry (◯ *Childhood Neighbor*): History is, Rant Casey had rabies more of his life than he didn't. And hatching that much of any bug in your brain had to make him some crazy. Still, there's plenty of folks who find crazy people to be very attractive.

LouAnn Perry: Buster didn't never get me pregnant, but he gave me rabies plenty often. First time, standing under the mistletoe at the school Christmas pageant, fifth grade. One kiss, me wearing my red velvet jumper with underneath it a white blouse, standing in the middle of the front row onstage, and singing "Oh Holy Night," singing notes sweet as any angel, my hair blond as angel hair in curls going halfway down my back, me the picture of sweetness—and I had rabies.
    Courtesy of Buster Casey.

Dr. David Schmidt: In all fairness, I can't blame all the infections on that one boy, but we haven't had a single case of rabies since Buster Casey left town.

LouAnn Perry: Loads of girls went rabid my exact same way. Maybe half our class, freshman year. Brenda Jordan blamed her rabies on bobbing for apples during a Halloween party, taking her turn behind Buster, but fact is—she kissed him.

Buster Casey was for some girls what snakes was for him. A kind of place your folks tell you never to go. But a kind of small mistake that'll save you from a bigger mistake later on.

Mistakes like kissing Buster, most times it's a worst mistake if you don't make them. After a good-looking boy gives you rabies two, three times, you'll settle down and marry somebody less exciting for the rest of your life.

Echo Lawrence: For our second date, Rant wanted to rake up leaves in a park. One of the surefire ways to contract rabies is to mess with bats. Look under enough leaves and you'll find a bat to bite you. Keep *that* in mind the next time you go to jump in a pile of dead leaves.

LouAnn Perry: History is, that boy was very popular. Except maybe with his daddy.

Shot Dunyun: How weird is that? A sexually conflicted thirteen-year-old rattlesnake-venom junkie with rabies—well, it's safe to say that's every father's worst nightmare.

LouAnn Perry: History is, Buster Casey was the kind of mistake a girl needs to make while she's still young enough to recover.

Bodie Carlyle: Us out in that desert, three horizons apart from the rest of the world, Rant's still looking into my eyes, saying, "You feel a heartbeat?"

Me, feeling fur. Petting fur. Underground. Buried. That hand of me still pale as bone. Slippery with the smell of meatloaf grease.

Me in the sun, sunburned, I still nod yes.

Rant smiling, he says, "Don't pull out."

The feel of that fur, soft and warm, until—kah-*pow*—the punch of something pushing through the slack between my thumb and next finger, that web of skin there sunk through with something sharp, and my arm shaking so hard it hammers the tunnel walls already tight around my elbow, far up as my shoulder, me collarbone-deep in pain and trying to pull out.

Rant's hands around my chest from behind, hauling me out of the ground.

The hole in my hand, not two punched marks. Not the little horseshoe of a coyote bite. The blood's pulsing out just one hole, big and straight across.

Rant, looking at the blood and the dripping straight-across hole, he says, "You been bit." He says, "Jackrabbit bit."

Both of us trickling blood out of little holes in our hands and feet, watching our blood leak out in the sand under the hot sun, Rant says, "This here," he says, "far as I'm concerned, this is how church should feel."

10 – Werewolves

Phoebe Truffeau, Ph.D. (⚙ *Epidemiologist*): Among the oldest superstitions practiced by ancient cultures was the warning to never drink from a pool frequented by wolves. Nor did our ancestors scavenge from any game animal—say, a deer or an elk—which had been felled by a pack of wolves. Either of these transgressions—or simply being bitten by a wolf—it is believed would transform one into a legendary half-human, half-canine monster, bloodthirsty and savage: a werewolf.

In the same manner that Old Testament prohibitions against eating pork and shellfish no doubt saved ancients from a miserable death by trichinosis or salmonella, these early wolf superstitions warned them away from any trace of saliva most likely to carry the *Lyssavirus,* a genus of morphologically similar, negative-stranded RNA viruses historically infecting mammal reservoirs worldwide.

Denise Gardner (⚙ *Real Estate Agent*): I can still see Margot stomping out the door to meet her friends. All of them dressed up in black lace and fishnet stockings, like every night was Halloween.

The little creature would be hanging on her sweater like a

furry accessory. A brooch. Those horrible little claws of it, clutching the wool of her black sweater, or some nights Margot would pin up her hair and let the bat nest on top, or swing, alongside her face like a single earring. All her goth friends wanted them . . . Leathery little vermin—I mean the *bats*, not Margot's friends. Bats made the perfect creepy little pet for a vampire teen. All her friends had them. Shame on us, but we didn't know any better. Pet shops couldn't sell them right next to the puppies and kitties if they weren't safe. That's what Sean, my husband, said.

Sean Gardner (○ *Contractor*): Our daughter's name was Margot, but her little vampire friends called her "Monster." She named the bat "Little Monster," then she shortened it to just "Monty."

Phoebe Truffeau, Ph.D.: Prior to the Casey epidemic, the largest outbreak in modern times had been due to an oversight in import protocol. Under the Foreign Quarantine Regulations (42 CFR 71.54), it is illegal to sell bats as pets within the United States. Imported bats are restricted to accredited zoos and research institutions. However, in this one-time incident, a procedural error allowed a shipment of several thousand Egyptian tomb bats (*Rousettus aegypiacus*) to enter the country in 1994 for sale through pet stores.

Sean Gardner: We bought Margot the bat as a Christmas present. Correction: She bought the bat. Her mother and I paid her back. It cost three hundred dollars, from Egypt or some godforsaken place. The food cost another arm and a leg. Bat Chow or Bat Meal. Some ridiculous crap. Her mother wouldn't go near it.

That Little Monty smelled awful.

Phoebe Truffeau, Ph.D.: Of the total humans infected each year, only 20 percent report being bitten or scratched by an animal. A typical case, from March 1995, involves a four-year-old girl in Washington State in whose bedroom a bat was discovered. Because the child reported no contact with the animal, no prophylactic treatment was initiated. Subsequently, both the child and the bat were found to be infected.

Among groundhogs, the disease spreads when one animal simply enters a den previously occupied by a sick animal.

Because the virus is transmitted primarily through saliva, something as minor as a cough or a sneeze can infect those in the immediate vicinity. Certainly within an elevator or an airliner cabin. Mechanically speaking, contracting rabies is as easy as catching a cold. But with a cold you immediately begin to present symptoms.

Denise Gardner: Her teachers complained that Margot acted antsy. They said she seemed fidgety. Distracted. Anxious, sometimes. She was our problem child. All her little goth friends acted the exact same way, always surly and impolite. Just awful. It never even dawned on us. Finally, when Margot brought home a D in her World Civics course, her primary-care pediatrician wrote her a prescription for Ritalin.

Phoebe Truffeau, Ph.D.: Upon contracting the virus, the typical subject will experience a tingling sensation at the site of the exposure, the bite or scratch. If the infection occurs via mucous membrane, that initial site will become hypersensitive. In the event of transmission through oral-genital contact, as appears to be the case with the Rant serotype, the hallmark tingling sensation affecting the genital and perigenital region is reported to be not altogether unpleasant. This pleasurable condition might account for the epidemic's rapid, almost lightning, transmission rate through the population.

Sean Gardner: The symptoms are brooding and antisocial behavior, isolation alternating with fits of hostile aggression. If the CDC treated every teenager that showed those symptoms . . . well, no government has that much money.

Phoebe Truffeau, Ph.D.: Beyond the incubation period, also known as the "eclipse" period, of six to ninety days, the virus replicates in localized tissue adjacent to the infection site. Retrograde axoplasmic flow moves the virus rapidly throughout the central nervous system. It infects neuronal cells of the brain stem, medulla, hippocampus, Purkinje cells, and cerebellum—invading, replicating, and budding within each cell—and in the process causing degeneration of the spinal cord, brain, and axons, and demyelination of the white matter of the brain.

As the viral load increases, the most enervated body tissues are subject to a greater degree, particularly the salivary glands. In the first stage of symptoms, the prodromal phase, the subject may suffer fever, nausea, headache, fatigue, and a lack of appetite.

Sean Gardner: Frankly, the way kids behave these days, who could blame us for not suspecting? Especially the way they dance.

Denise Gardner: Sean blamed her moods on that music they listen to.

Sean Gardner: Well, my wife said it was the video games.

Phoebe Truffeau, Ph.D.: Beyond the prodromal phase, the sensory-excitation phase is characterized by hypersalivation, muscle twitches, insomnia, extreme aggression, and a compulsion to bite or chew.

Once incubation of the disease is complete and the subject exhibits suspect behaviors, there is no treatment. The third and final stage of the disease is paralysis and coma. Subsequent autopsy will reveal antigens when rabies antibodies are applied to samples of brain tissue and examined under a fluorescence microscope.

Denise Gardner: During the worst of it, Sylvia Leonard calls. She's the mother of Dean Leonard, one of Margot's little goth pals. Well, anyway, Sylvia phones and says, hi ho, Dean's pet bat has just croaked. The little fuzzball's been curled up in Dean's underwear drawer, and today it reeks to high heaven. Dead. And Sylvia wants to know: Did Margot's bat get sick? Sylvia wants to know: Did we save the sales receipt, and can she use our receipt to try and get a refund for her dead bat?

We pull the shoe box out from under Margot's bed, and the stink could knock you over. We don't even open the lid. Sean, my husband, Sean just totes the box into the backyard and buries Little Monty with every other gerbil and hamster and kitten and goldfish and lizard, parakeet, guinea pig, mouse, and rabbit that Margot ever begged and pleaded to have. You'd swear, our backyard is *paved* with dead animals.

Phoebe Truffeau, Ph.D.: The word itself comes from the Sanskrit word, used three thousand years before the birth of Christ, *rabhas,* which means "to do violence." By the nineteenth century, the virus was prevalent in all parts of the world, especially Europe. There, people who feared they'd become infected would usually commit suicide.

Those infected, or even rumored to be infected, were often murdered by their peers, out of fear. Or sympathy.

Historically, the virus has moved through a series of mammal reservoirs. In the 1700s, the disease was carried predominantly by red foxes (*Vulpes vulpes*), and gained a foothold in the New World when these animals were imported for British-style fox hunts. During the 1800s, the striped skunk (*Mephitis mephitis*) was so likely to be hydrophobic that the popular slang term for skunks of that period was "Phobey Cats." After the 1960s, the common raccoon (*Procyon lotor*) became the species most likely to be infected. To a lesser degree, the coyote (*Canis latrans*) is responsible for an average of fifty infections annually. Insectivorous bats, an average of 750 infections annually.

Before the advent of the Rant serotype of the *Lyssavirus,* no more than a hundred thousand people died of rabies each year, primarily in tropical or subtropical regions. Despite an annual expenditure of one billion dollars to contain the disease, and a century of vaccinations and public awareness, the infection rate among animals reached a historical peak in 1993.

Due to the epidemic attributed to Buster Casey, human beings are currently the largest mammal reservoir of the rabies virus.

Sean Gardner: As I understand it, you have two types of rabies. There's your "dumb" type, where you never go insane and bite anyone. You only curl up in a ball under your bed and die. And there's the normal kind of rabies, the "furious" type, which 80 percent of folks get. Where you slobber and swear and flail around, smashing everything in your bedroom, including your Dolls of the World collection, and calling your father a "dirty, shit-eating, motherfucking, dick-less dickhead . . ." Well, that's what kind of rabies our Margot had.

Denise Gardner: Shame on us, but I think we started to mourn Margot the day she turned thirteen and first dyed her hair black.

Phoebe Truffeau, Ph.D.: One can argue that all early prohibitions to bestiality were intended to prevent the *Lyssavirus,* or any disease, from jumping to human beings.

Ancient cultures also warned that bastard offspring of a priest would become werewolves. As would any children produced by incest.

Denise Gardner: Shame on me, but when I first suspected, when I had my first inkling that Margot might have rabies, I wrote it off as playacting. Watching Margot and her clique of goth friends, they made such a point to be rude and outlandish. It seemed too much, as if their fondest *dream* was to have rabies. Well, like I said, shame on me.

Phoebe Truffeau, Ph.D.: Once the virus begins replicating and is transported along sensory and motor nerves, the infected subject can remain asymptomatic for months, despite shedding virus and infecting additional subjects. That scenario appears to be the case with the alleged superspreader, Buster Casey.

No, epidemiologists no longer use the term "Patient Zero." Any individual responsible for ten or more infections, we now refer to as a "superspreader." What "Typhoid Mary" Mallon was to typhoid, what Gaetan Dugas was to AIDS, and

Liu Jian-lun was to SARS, Buster Casey would become for rabies.

Sean Gardner: Our Margot, you know what happened. So many of her friends died that we held a group service. Not just Dean Leonard. Except it's different when you bury a goth child. Yes, it's still heartbreaking, only it doesn't look as bad. Actually, our Margot looked better—well, healthier—than she did before she got sick. The viewing, with all of them dressed up and so somber, it looked like her junior prom. But no one was dancing. Or smiling. Or laughing. Everyone gloomy and dressed in black . . .

Okay, it looked *exactly* like her junior prom.

11—The Bees

Echo Lawrence (☾ *Party Crasher*): Get this. Independence Day, one year, the whole Casey clan goes out for a picnic. A barbecue with marshmallows and seared animal flesh. All the aunts and uncles, all the cousins, an acre of Caseys sprawled on blankets or folding lawn chairs, eating corn. Everybody hugging everybody, shaking hands.

Even al fresco, the generation that controls everything, that owns it all, the adults sit at a picnic table. Everyone else, in the dirt. The adults a little shuffled since Esther and Hattie and Bel died, but mostly the same.

That sunny day, first one bee, then another, buzzed the adult table. The old grannies waved them away. Then the table was covered. The adults were coated in bees.

Sheriff Bacon Carlyle (☉ *Childhood Enemy*): The county medical examiner was asking: Did any of the deceased handle bees lately? He's wanting to be told: Did any of them work with beehives? Something he called "swarm attractant" would explain the attack.

From the Field Notes of Green Taylor Simms (ℂ *Historian*): Nasonov pheromones. A plastic vial the size of your little finger exudes the bee attractant equivalent to five thousand honeybees fanning and scenting the air. *Apis mellifera*, the common honeybee, follows the scent and seeks out any cracks or openings in which to create a new hive.

Swatting at these bees will prompt them to exude the "alert" pheromone, which attracts additional bees to attack. Because their primary predators are bears, the attacking bees focus on the eyes, nose, and open mouth of the aggressor—any feature that occurs as a dark opening, including the ears, the bees will swarm. Any carbon dioxide the victim exhales will make the attacking bees more aggressive.

Swarm attractant itself has a pleasant, faint citrus smell. Almost undetectable to humans. Because nasonov pheromones are so potent, the preferred method of storage is to place the plastic vial inside a sealed glass jar, then secure the sealed jar inside a deep-freeze.

Shot Dunyun (ℂ *Party Crasher*): It was like a cloud blotting out the sun, a big black fucking storm. Humming. In the middle of a nice sunny day, it starts to rain. But instead of water, it's raining bee stings. No shit. It's pouring down sheer pain.

Echo Lawrence: People were running for their cars, screaming until their mouths were filled with bees, choking on bees, stung and smothered to death. By the time the county vector control could intervene, Rant's Uncle Clem was dead. So were his Aunt Patty and Uncle Cleatus. His Uncle Walt died in the hospital.

Shot Dunyun: The FBI shitheads who asked about Party Crash nights, after Rant died, those agents loved the bee story. They couldn't take notes fast enough.

Echo Lawrence: Relax. Nobody called it murder. Not yet.

Shot Dunyun: How weird is that? It was like something from the Old Testament: the Killer Bee Picnic, the Mouse Shit Attack, the Plague of Fleas, and the Deadly Spider Hat. The next Thanksgiving dinner, with seven oldsters dead, the rest of that generation stayed home. The oldest Caseys turned over the adult table to their middle-aged kids. Siege ended. Baton passed.

12–The Food

Echo Lawrence (☾ *Party Crasher*): To make time stand still—what sand mandalas are to Buddhist monks and embroidery is to Irene Casey—eating pussy was to Rant. He used to wedge his face between my legs and slip his tongue into me. He'd come up on his elbows, smacking his lips, his chin dripping, and Rant would say, "You ate something with cinnamon for breakfast . . ." He'd lick his lips and roll his eyes, saying, "Not French toast . . . something else." Rant would snort and gobble, then come up with his eyes shining, saying, "For breakfast, you drank a cup of Constant Comment tea. That's the cinnamon."

From just the smell and taste of me, he'd nail my whole day: tea, whole-wheat toast without butter, plain yogurt, blueberries, a tempeh sandwich, one avocado, a glass of orange juice, and a beet salad.

"And you had an order of fast-food onion rings," he'd say, and smack his lips. "A large order."

I called him "the Pussy Psychic."

Bodie Carlyle (☼ *Childhood Friend*): In the time it took most folks to sit around a table, say a blessing, pass their food, and eat it, eat a second helping, help themselves to pie and coffee, then drink another cup of coffee and start to clear the dishes, in that same stretch of time, the Casey family might take only one bite. One bite of meatloaf or tuna casserole, and still be chewing it. Not just eating slow, but not talking, not reading books or watching television. Their whole attention was inside their mouth, chewing, tasting, feeling.

Echo Lawrence: Get real. Most guys are *keeping score* with every lap of their tongue. Every time they come up for air, they're clocking your pleasure. And, lick for lick, you know this had better balance out with the pleasure you give them back. So, lick after lick, you never can relax and get off, not when you know that *meter* is always running. Every lick an investment in getting licked back.

Even guys who hate bookkeeping and doing their taxes, guys who could only shrug if you asked their savings-account or credit-card balance, they'll compute the exact number of laps their tongue's done around your snatch. And the payback they have coming. The sexual equivalent of clock watchers or bean counters.

That's every guy—except Rant Casey. He'd stick his tongue into you and years could pass. Mountains erode.

Edna Perry (☼ *Childhood Neighbor*): Christmas dinner in England, when you find a clove in your food, it means you're a villain. Automatic. If you find a little stick of a twig, you're the idiot. No arguing. And if you bite into something and find a rag of cloth fabric, folks will know you're a slut. Imagine that, being branded a slut, right there at Christmas dinner, but Irene Casey swears she read this in a book.

Echo Lawrence: One time, face planted between my legs, Rant surfaced for air, picked a pubic hair off his tongue, and said, "What happened today? Something bad happened . . ."

I told him to forget it.

He licked me and rolled his eyes, licked again, and said, "A parking ticket? No, something worse . . ."

I told him to forget it. I said nothing had happened.

Rant licked me again, only slower, dragging his tongue through me from back to front, his breath hot, and he looked up, staring, until I looked down at him. Met his green eyes. He said, "I'm sorry." Rant said, "You lost your job today, didn't you?"

My stupid fucking job I had, selling mobile fucking phones.

Like, he could find out anything with his nose, and from the taste of you. That was Rant Casey. Always right.

And between orgasms, I started to cry.

From the Field Notes of Green Taylor Simms (ℂ *Historian*): Every family has its scriptures, but most can't articulate them. These are stories people repeat to reinforce their identity: *Who* they are. *Where* they came from. *Why* they behave as they do.

Rant used to say, "Every family is a regular little cult."

Basin Carlyle (◌ *Childhood Neighbor*): Don't laugh, but in France, Irene says, they bake a metal kind of lucky charm into their dessert cake. Their rule is, the one who bites the charm has to cook the next supper, but folks in France are so cheap they're more likely to swallow the charm. So they won't have to host.

From her reading, Irene says Mexicans bake a Jesus baby

doll into their food. Folks in Spain always throw in some loose change. Irene showed me a little brochure for baking fancy cakes, told all about it. The entire history of cakes from around the world.

Irene Casey (☼ *Rant's Mother*): Near as I recollect, Chet and Buddy didn't start out slow eaters. I trained them that way. It got to be too much, baking a devil's-food cake from scratch and watching Chet and Buddy wolf it down in three bites. Two of them hurrying to choke down one slice, then another, until the cake was nothing left but the dirty plate. Even while they're inhaling my food, they're talking plans about something next, or reading out of a catalogue, or hearing the news on the radio. Always living months into the future. Miles down the road.

The only exception was any food the two of them put on the table. Anytime Chet shot a goose, we sat there, everyone talking up how good it tasted. Or if Buddy caught a string of trout, again, the family spent all night eating it. 'Course, there's bones in a trout. In a goose, you figure to look out for steel shot. There's a price to pay if you don't pay attention to the food you're chewing. You get a fish bone in your throat and choke to death, or a sharp bone stabbed through the roof of your mouth. Or you split a back tooth, biting down on bird shot.

From the Field Notes of Green Taylor Simms: Scripture in the Casey household decrees, "The secret ingredient to anything *tasty* is something that's going to *hurt*."

It's not as if she intended to hurt people. Irene only booby-trapped food because she cared too much. If she didn't give a damn, she'd serve them frozen dinners and call the matter settled.

Basin Carlyle: Don't you forget. The most I saw the Caseys was over church. Seeing them on Sundays at service and after, at the potluck suppers over by the grange hall.

The secret ingredient that made folks really taste Irene's peach cobbler was sneaking in some cherry pits. Could about break your jawbone by accident. The secret of her apple brown Betty was mixing in plenty of sharp slivers of walnut shell.

When you ate her tuna casserole, you didn't talk or flip through a *National Geographic*. Your eyes and ears stayed inside your mouth. Your whole world kept inside your mouth, feeling and careful for the little balled-up tinfoils Irene Casey would hide in the tuna parts. A side effect of eating slow was, you naturally, genuinely tasted, and the food tasted better. Could be other ladies were better cooks, but you'd never notice.

Shot Dunyun (ℂ *Party Crasher*): Rant's father used to go, "If something *looks* like a true accident, can't nobody be *mad* at you."

Irene Casey: Men do have the tendency to rush, always pushing to get a job done.

Echo Lawrence: Here's a single girl's secret—the reason you eat dinner with a man on a first date is so you know how he's going to *fuck* you. A slob who gobbles down the meal, never looks at a bite, you know *not* to crawl into bed with *that* guy.

Bodie Carlyle: Mrs. Casey baked birthday cakes that made you blush out of shame for your own lazy ma. Sometimes, a chocolate-cake locomotive pulling a steam train with one boxcar made of cherry cake and one boxcar made of vanilla, then flatcars and tanker cars, all different flavors, until they ended with a maple-flavor cake caboose. It's good luck, folks say, finding the toothpick stuck inside a cake. But you don't bother tasting her cake and you'd be tasting pine splinters and blood.

Logan Elliot (○ *Childhood Friend*): Truth was, if you didn't chew her food, then her food chewed you.

Irene Casey: The way I figure, as long as food tastes better than it hurts, you're going to keep eating. As long as you're more enjoying than you are suffering.

Basin Carlyle: Potlucks over by the grange hall, you'd expect them to be a social event with folks talking and catching up. Don't hate me for saying it, but anytime Irene brung her chicken bake or three-bean salad, instead of socializing, folks would be too busy picking trash out of their mouths. Her cooking was decent, but it replaced a mess of good gossip. Instead of folks harping on who blacked the eye of his wife, or who was stepping out on her husband, by the end of every potluck, you'd have maybe just a little pile of real trash next to each plate. A trash heap of pits and stones and paper clips. Whole cloves, sharp as thumbtacks.

Edna Perry: Come Christmas, foreign folks have a tradition of baking a cake with a itty-bitty Baby Jesus hid inside. Folks say the person who finds the Christ child will be special blessed in the next year. Just a little plastic baby-doll toy. But Irene Casey used to fold into her batter as much scoops of Baby Jesus as she did flour and sugar. Put a Christ child in every bite. Could be she only wanted more folks to feel lucky, but it never looked right, folks burping up whole packs and litters of naked pink plastic Saviours. Birthing those wet babies out their lips. Big tooth marks bit down and gnawed on our Saviour's smiling face. Christmas potluck at the grange, and folks sitting at long tables with red crepe-paper decorations and those spit-covered Christ babies coughed up everywhere, it never looked all that holy.

Basin Carlyle: The same as how it's not always the good child that you love most—sometimes it's the child that causes you the most trouble—folks only remembered the food Irene Casey brung to potluck. Other food, better food, like Glenda Hendersen's walnut bars or Sally Peabody's baked pear crumble, just because they didn't half choke you to death, you never gave that food a second thought.

Echo Lawrence: This once, after I'd had an orgasm, inside of me is a *pressure*, not a pain, more like that feeling when your tampon turns sideways. Like I might have to take a piss. Rant put two fingers inside and takes out something pink. Bigger than a tooth. Smooth and shiny with spit.

Even naked, we were never touching. Dried sticky or wet slimy, between his skin and mine, you could always feel a thin layer of sweat or spit or sperm.

Still propped on both his elbows, Rant's looking at something cupped in his hand.

As if he's just sucked this *pink* object out of me.

So, of course, I have to sit up and look. But it's a joke.

A little doll. A baby made of pink plastic. And Rant says, "How did *that* get in there?" His *mother's* mantra.

He grins at me, says, "This here makes me the lucky king . . ."

It almost didn't matter that his spit gave me rabies.

13–Sporting

Bodie Carlyle (◐ *Childhood Friend*): Monday mornings, I'd feel wore out from staying plugged in all Sunday night, cramming for Algebra II. Mr. Wyland hands out six or eight hours of homework to boost, and I'd always leave it for the last minute. My eyes closed, I can still hear the voice of the primary witness, the gal who boosted those lessons. Since you can't out-cord thoughts—only sensory junk like taste, smell, sounds, and sights—the primary witness talks through every step of every equation, yakking away, while you watch her hand holding chalk, scratching the numbers on a blackboard.

Her voice saying, "When X equals the cosine of Y, and Y is of greater value than Z, the determining factor of X must include . . ." And by then, I'm asleep. Still boosting, but sawing logs. Monday mornings, all I learned was the smell of chalk dust. The tap-tapping of each time her chalk hit the board to make a new line. Not a Smart Board, not even a whiteboard, that's how cheap: a chalkboard. Decades later, I could tell you that primary witness was right-handed and wore a long-sleeve red sweater rolled back a ways at the wrist. Always, the taste of black coffee in her mouth. A Nighttimer's hand, somebody told me. No tan on the back. The back and knuckles and palm, all the same color.

Only thing that kept me from failing was, Rant Casey knowed even less than shit, and Mr. Wyland graded on a curve. Most Mondays, before daylight, Rant would come knock on my bedroom window. Beyond a couple horizons we'd walk, until Rant found his hole. With one sleeve rolled up and everything to the shoulder of him stuffed underground, Rant would ask me to teach him. Algebra. History. Social studies. He blamed it on the spider bites, the poison, or having rabies, but he complained his port didn't work. He'd plug in but couldn't boost nothing.

Danny Perry (◔ *Childhood Friend*): Rant Casey would go down on his belly in the sand, plant his elbows on either side of a burrow, and poke his nose inside. Just from the stink, sniffing some dirty hole, Rant could tell rabbit or coyote or skunk or deadly spider. Could even tell you *what kind* of spider.

To be Rant Casey's friend was always some test. For guys, you had to shove your hand in his choice of dark hole, far up as your elbow, not figuring what you'd find.

Bodie Carlyle: Us in the desert, watching the light wash up from the horizon, fire colors, I told Rant about the federal I-SEE-U Act and how pale and spooky the algebra hand looked. A hand never out in the sun. The taste of a stranger's coffee still in my mouth.

And Rant says, "Shit." He stuffs his free hand down the front of his pants and grits his teeth.

"Spider-bite boner," he says. "Always happens." And he twists around inside his crotch to hide it.

From the Field Notes of Green Taylor Simms (℃ *Historian*): Chronic priapism is one lesser symptom of a-latrotoxin poisoning. By exploiting his poison-induced erections, Rant was liquidating any collateral he had left in the community. He could never go back home, but he would never *have* to. Something the wealthy know that most people don't is that you never *burn* a bridge. Such a waste. Instead, you *sell* it.

Cammy Elliot (◯ *Childhood Friend*): Our geometry teacher, Mr. Wyland, the same teacher who dogs us through Algebra I and Algebra II, and drags you to stand at the board and demonstrate your limitation to the class, he folds his arms, sucking his tongue to inside one cheek of his mouth, lowers his eyes at Rant, and says, "What seems to be the problem, Mr. Casey?"

And Rant ducks his head, his chin nodding down, he tilts his hips up, points with the gun fingers of both hands at his crotch, where the zipper is tented, pointed, poked out so stiff you can see the silver teeth of the steel metal inside. "Mr. Wyland, sir," Rant says, "I've had a serious erection here for going on two hours . . ."

No lie. A gasp comes, but not from the A-plus rows up front. It's more the B students who believed what they heard. Back in the room a couple rows, some C-minus kid snorted a laugh, lips shut, inside a closed mouth.

"As a fellow matured male, Mr. Wyland," Rant says, "you can appreciate the painful and potentially injurious nature of this situation."

Mr. Wyland, all the air come out of him in one push. One exhale. His folded arms sunk into the collapsed chest of him. His lips peel open, sagging so you can see his bottom teeth, the color of bone shadowed with the brown of tobacco.

"You think maybe somebody should take a look at it?" Rant says on, pulling his eyebrows together, folding worry lines between his eyes.

The geometry equation chalked on the board disappeared, gone from the room. Nothing but chalk-dust chicken scratchings in the same room with the low-down, dirty miracle of a teenage hard-on. Inside his head, Mr. Wyland's super-computing the correct answer. Him stood up to look dumb in front of folks.

Shot Dunyun (© *Party Crasher*): Wyland's beyond trapped. If this teacher slams Rant, merely laughs and tells this punk kid to sit down and concentrate on numbers, the school's looking at a lawsuit. If the kid's got a serious medical emergency, and his dingus turns purple and drops off, the school district will be settling that claim for the next ten million dollars of budget talks. Sure, Rant has a history of disruption. Sure, Rant could've presented the situation in a less invasive manner. But none of that will count for much in a courtroom, while Wyland stands in the witness box and tells a jury why he ridiculed and humiliated a student who was possibly dying of gangrene.

Cammy Elliot: Little flicks of Mr. W's eyes, a twitch of his ear, and a gulp of his Adam's apple, only those signify his brain's at work. His face floods from pale to pink to dark red. His whole face almost tongue red. Like time's stopped.

"Mr. Wyland," a boy's voice says.

Danny Perry sticks one hand up in the air and says, "Hey, Mr. W!" He waves the hand, his fingers flickering fast, and Danny says, "I need the Health Room, too. For the same situation."

Brenda Jordan (○ *Childhood Friend*): From what I recall, Rant only had maybe two shirts. One pair of jeans. Leastways, that's all we saw. The same green-plaid shirt with long sleeves to hide the mess of teeth marks on his arms. And a long-sleeve blue chambray shirt with pearl snaps instead of buttons. You could hear when Casey got nervous, because he'd snap and unsnap the cuffs, popping little snap sounds in the back of the class.

Cammy Elliot: The outline of Rant's boner slung sideways in his jeans, almost pulsing with his heartbeat, he went to the office. His shirt cuffs snapping loud and fast as popcorn.

Silas Henderson (○ *Childhood Friend*): The oldest female excuse out of any class is claiming you have "cramps." Nothing but code for a chance to take a couple aspirin and skip the trigonometry midterm. Compared to that, a fellow's got nothing.

Lowell Richards (○ *Teacher*): A clear corollary formed between sunny weather and the number of boys suffering from painful penile erections. At issue wasn't the penises, but the failure to occlude them while in their turgid state. Furthermore, the district's legal counsel advised that a dress code requiring constraining, modest, fully binding undergarments would be impossible to enforce and serve the negative purpose of drawing increased attention to the issue.

Our chief effort intended to deal with the issue of engorged phalluses obliquely and indirectly. Legal counsel advised no direct condemnation of erections on school property. No district representative was to acknowledge or attempt to mask or resolve any obvious erections.

Cammy Elliot: The biggest secret in Rant's life was his clothes. At home, he had a closet full of shirts and pants and jeans and vests. The hangers packed together so close the closet rod sagged in the middle from the weight. The trouble was, Irene Casey couldn't not be creative. She wouldn't *not* express herself. She was always trying some new skill, embroidering sunflowers and ivy leaves. Smiling half-moons and stars. Trying iron-on patches or colors of glitter paint. Chrome rivets. Batik and tie-dye. Mrs. Casey would sit up half a night, hunched over and stitching herself blind in bad light, trying to make regular clothes into something special.

Wouldn't hurt Rant's pride to wear rainbow glitter and embroidery to high school, but he couldn't tolerate what kids said about his ma's work. Kids saying she was a terrible artist. Saying she had no kind of talent. He wasn't wearing his heart on his sleeve. It's more like she'd sewed her own heart on Rant's sleeve.

Logan Elliot (☼ *Childhood Friend*): Casey had the crowd of us whipped into a frantic. Shouting equal rights for hard-ons, saying how we're oppressed, and burning jock straps in the school parking lot.

Leif Jordan (☼ *Childhood Friend*): Rant advocating for us, our demands included a therapeutic, all-hours lunchroom, since it's a known impossibility to eat food and maintain a woody. We asked for nothing short of equal recognition of our biological . . . But the next word stumped us. Should we say "obstacles"? "Handicaps"? "Disabilities"? This last word, we tortured over.

We finally settled on the word "burden," asking for "full and equal recognition of the burden inherent in the male anatomy." Hearing how "burden" sounded fine and noble.

Bodie Carlyle: Not much in all his dry years of algebra had trained Mr. W to deal with a potentially life-threatening emergency boner situation. Being displayed as a geometry idiot, or sporting wood in class—either way, you were trading away your dignity. At least this way it was Rant posing the tough problem and Wyland forced to sweat out the figuring with all those eyes waiting on him.

Leif Jordan: We'd maybe talk some doctor into calling it "chronic boner syndrome."

Mary Cane Harvey (◎ *Teacher*): Rant Casey told me himself: "This here's my inoculation against ever being embarrassed and humiliated in geometry, ever again."

Cammy Elliot: Had kids, politelike, raising their hand to say, "Beg pardon, Miss Harvey . . ." Saying, "I'd enjoy nothing more than diagramming that lovely sentence, but I'm suffering a chunk of pig iron so beet red it's starting to pain me . . ."

Cross my heart. Kids said, "Could be, if I got myself a breath of fresh air . . ." Until half the class was outside.

Lowell Richards: Instructors hesitated in prompting full participation from male students out of the anxiety that students required to stand might exhibit inappropriate arousal, generating classroom disruption and undermining the instructor's authority.

Sheriff Bacon Carlyle (◎ *Childhood Enemy*): If we were talking about naturally sprung boners, that would be another kettle of fish. But these here were store-bought, chemically engineered woodies sprouted on purpose to disrupt the peaceful classroom environment.

Lowell Richards: Though it was widely rumored that certain students abused medications designed to treat erectile dysfunction, legal counsel advised that no just cause existed for requiring that students submit urine for drug testing. Legal counsel cautioned that, though some tumescence may result from illegally obtained prescription drugs, the majority of genital arousal was naturally occurring and thus protected under the Americans with Disabilities Act. On advice from the school district's legal counsel, the administration organized a presentation exclusively for male students in the affected peer groups.

Dr. David Schmidt (◌ *Middleton Physician*): My slide show consisted of color photographs documenting penises suffering extended priapism and the resulting gangrenous injury. For the purpose of this lecture, I selected the most extreme examples, members on which the foreskin, glans penis, and engorged corpus carvenosa had discolored to a purple-black or iridescent dark green, typical of advanced necrosis in oxygen-deprived tissues.

Silas Hendersen: Some kids would take a shoelace and tie it off. Other kids brung a cucumber. Tying off something full of blood could hurt, but keeping track of a cucumber took all your concentration. God forbid, but you'd see guys limping halfway to the bathroom for readjustment, and a cucumber or zucchini squash slips out the cuff of their jeans.

Kids called it "Sportin', Spottin', or Stuffin'."

Spotting was, you'd take a fingertip of cooking oil or shampoo, something too greasy to dry out, and you put a dark spot on your front. Fake peter tracks.

Lowell Richards: The district's strategy remained only marginally successful.

Cammy Elliot: Rant Casey wore those same two shirts to school because he couldn't bear to have kids make fun of his mom. Even he figured the embroidered rainbows and the ivy she'd stitched up the legs of his blue jeans, they looked pretty sad. So he brung home two secondhand shirts and a pair of plain jeans, and kept them hid in the barn, where he could change clothes on his way to or from school.

He was double-trapped. If he wore the clothes his mom monkeyed with, he'd hear jokes about her until they broke his heart. But if Rant told her to lay off decorating his stuff, then *he'd* be breaking her heart.

Danny Perry: History is, a week into spring term, and Rant sat down to negotiate our demands with the school board. Behind closed doors, in the teachers' lounge, they talked while the rest of us waited in the hallway.

Bodie Carlyle: The teachers' lounge being off-limits to us, nobody knowed it had an outside door. After our long buttsit in the hallway, the school administrators come out. But no Rant Casey.

Danny Perry: History is, Rant skedaddled out that secret door leads to the outside, sidestepped us, took with him a check for ten thousand dollars and a certificate saying he's graduated early.

Logan Elliot: No lie. Rant left us standing there with our boners, taking a political stand with our dicks on the line, and he goes kiting off, paycheck in hand from the school district. Folks is still branded him the Boner Benedict Arnold.

Silas Hendersen: Without him, the Erection Revolution kind of lost steam. Gone limp. Left us just dumb kids with vegetables stuffed down our shorts and rubber bands wrapped around our wieners.

Trusting Rant Casey was our mistake.

Rubber bands was a bigger mistake. Nothing hurts more than snipping a rubber band, snarled and tangled, all mangled up in your short hairs.

Lowell Richards: The trade-off gave Rant a new school record, awarding him a 4.0 grade-point average and top honors, plus a letter in every sport. Rant Casey, who never kicked a ball or ran a step in his life.

But if he ever showed up at a class reunion, there's men in Middleton who'd wait in line to kill him.

Bodie Carlyle: A paycheck at school graduation—instead of just a diploma. Both them, just paper folks agreed mean more. Being in agreement the big step from a lie to reality.

Rant sawed how reality was something you could build. Same as the Tooth Fairy money. If enough folks believe a lie, how it ain't a lie no more.

Mary Cane Harvey: Even all these years later, I'll discover "Rant Casey Got Out of Here" carved in a desk in my classroom.

Leif Jordan: Sure, some folks never forgave Rant for his betraying us. But most guys, we just shrugged. We shook the carrots out of our pants and got on with life.

Irene Casey (☼ *Rant's Mother*): We could only afford the plainest things, but I dressed them up with embroidery or rivets. Boys love lots of shiny chrome. Sometimes, I'd sew on special trims or rickrack. I know Buddy loved those clothes. He wore them to school and kept them so nice.

The night he left home, Buddy packed up the lot of them to wear in the city. He was so proud.

14–Going Away

Bodie Carlyle (☼ *Childhood Friend*): It took the both of us
to haul off Rant's clothes. A night before he left home, he
only pretended to pack them in his suitcase. Got garbage
bags and filled those instead, folding those shirts and pants
just so. Half his mom's life wasted in embroidery-ing. The
young part of her life spent punching rivets and sewing extra
trim on regular blue jeans. Rant, he'd hold each shirt tucked
under his chin, petting the wrinkles smooth against his chest,
then folding the sleeves. He'd button all the buttons. He
piled all the folded pants and shirts into the black plastic
bags.

Over the horizon, beyond the windbreak of Russian olives,
three horizons off from the Casey farm, we walked, until we
almost got to morning. Getting to nowhere, Rant fished a
shirt out from a bag. Holding the collar with one hand, Rant
shook a cigarette lighter in his other hand. Rant sparked a
little flame and stood there, looking at the bright tie-dyed
colors in the weak light. His mom's masterpiece. That shirt
looked brighter and brighter, until Rant had to let go, let it
fall, flaming, to his feet. In the firelight, little snake bites of

yellow stood around us, dog and coyote and skunk eyes flickering, scavengers, watching, all having sunk teeth into Rant's skin.

Echo Lawrence (ℂ *Party Crasher*): The first time you met Rant, the first part you met was his teeth. Instead of chewing gum, him and his redneck friends, they used to pinch up clean tar from the county roads. In summer, black tar oozed up from cracks in the blacktop, and they used to chew it. Teeth they sold to the Tooth Fairy were pitch-black.

Bodie Carlyle: Rant used to carry his radio out, nights, into the desert. He'd walk, monkeying with the dial to pick up traffic reports from all over the world. Car crashes and whatnot. Holding that radio to his ear, Rant used to smile and listen. Eyes closed, he'd say, "It's always rush hour somewheres."

From DRVR Radio Graphic Traffic: Northbound on the 417 Freeway, at Milepost 79, look for a totally cherry Dodge Monaco, maybe the heaviest coupe ever in mass production, four thousand pounds of Winchester Gray powered with a 175-horsepower V8. Very nice hidden headlights. Word from the officer on the scene is, the driver of the Monaco apparently hit a slick patch and went sideways in the right lane. The driver was a thirty-one-year-old female with the dicing injuries typical of shattered safety glass.

Echo Lawrence: On Party Crash nights, Rant used to talk about leaving Middleton. How, on his last night at home, he was chewing tar. That night, Rant sat out with his dad on the gravel shoulder of the highway, down the road three mailboxes from the barbed-wire fence at the edge of their farm. The sun going flat-tire against the soft, wheat-field horizon. Chester Casey, squatting on his cowboy-boot heels in the dust smell of the gravel. Rant, butt up on a cardboard suitcase heavy with gold and silver coins.

Bodie Carlyle: Rant's old suitcase he had was full to busting with Tooth Fairy money.

From DRVR Radio Graphic Traffic: The Monaco was T-boned by a Continental Mark IV that's really worth crying over: California Sunshine Yellow with a cream leather interior, the first model of American automobile to feature "loose cushion" upholstery. The meat-wagon boys called to say the Monaco suffered predominantly left-side injuries, including lacerations of the liver, the spleen, and the left kidney. Immediate cause of death looks like transection of the aorta.

Echo Lawrence: Rant's chewing tar that last night of his childhood. His suitcase packed and dragged to the shoulder of the highway, father and son waiting next to the metal bus-stop sign shot Swiss cheese with bullet holes. The wind twisting the sheetmetal sign a hair, side to side. With the wind whistling through those rusty holes, Rant says, "I got a secret I needs to tell."

And Chester Casey says, "No." He says, "No, you don't. You ain't got no secrets from me." A hand pushing down on the top of each thigh, Chet Casey stands up from squatting. Arching and twisting his spine until it pops, Chester kicks the pointed toe of one cowboy boot, just tapping the side of the cardboard suitcase printed to look like leather. His toe tapping the brown cardboard, Rant's father says, "You ain't never told me as much, but I knowed you're packing nothing but cash money here."

Echo Lawrence: The future starts tomorrow, and Rant needs to say this before the bus pulls up. This moment, it's something his dad won't want to know. This here, Rant says, is the fact that starts a new future. Or a brand-new past. Or both.

Rant slapping flies, cupping wind and sand away from his face, he says, "Just so you know," he swats a bite on the back of his neck and says, "I'm never getting hitched."

A star blinks on the edge of the world, getting bright, blinding bright, growing so fast it goes past before you can hear the sound, the wind and dust of it—only a car, already come and gone. The headlights fading over the far side of the world.

And Rant's dad, he says, "No." He squats in the gravel and says, "You only figure that way to put a fright in me." Chester Casey says, "Soon as you meet a girl name of Echo Lawrence, you'll figure otherwise."

The wind bowing every weed and clump of cheatgrass in the same direction. Shaking every sagebrush. On the wind, you can smell the smoke of embroidery silk and smoldering denim. Chrome rivets.

Look here. It's impossible Chester Casey could've known my name. We'd never met. At this point, I'd never heard of Middleton or Rant.

Logan Elliot (☼ *Childhood Friend*): The only worst part of the Casey house, when you visited, was how his ma used to listen outside the bathroom door. No lie. The first time I was over, I opened the door, and she stood there blocking the way, telling me, "I would appreciate it, upon future visits to this household, if you would urinate from a seated position . . ."

It didn't matter I didn't know the word "urinate."

Echo Lawrence: That night, waiting for the bus, Rant and his dad squinted as a new star blinked on the horizon, getting big, blowing by in a gust of wind and diesel smoke, the star exploded into white headlights, yellow running lights, red taillights. A cab, sleeper box, double trailer. Then—gone.

Rant says, "I'm meeting some girl?" He says, "How do you figure that?"

And his dad says, "Same as I knowed an old man pulled up and talked to you before you come running about your Granny Esther." Chester says, "Old man in a Chrysler, told you that he was your for-real pa."

Spitting black, a sideways stream into the gravel, Rant says, "What model of Chrysler?"

And Chester Casey says, "Same as I knowed your Granny Esther screamed at the sight of him, called him the Devil, and told you to run."

East of the bus-stop sign, the real stars come on. Straight overhead, more stars blink on. Flicker, and stay bright.

Scratching at bug bites, rubbing away goosebumps, Rant says, "Supposing that's the truth," he says, "what else did that old man tell me?"

Cammy Elliot (☼ *Childhood Friend*): At the Casey house, if you used their peanut butter, Mrs. Casey wanted for you to smoothe what was left in the jar. So it always looked fresh store-bought.

Echo Lawrence: Chester Casey tells his son, "That old man told you he was your real pa, he told you to come find him in the city, soon as you was able." Chester's cowboy boot, the pointed toe taps the cardboard suitcase, and he says, "And that old man told you where to find all this cash money."

And Rant spits black tar, close enough to splash the side of the suitcase. Rabies-infected saliva. Black spattered on the brand-new of the cardboard. Rant just sits there, shaking his head no.

Chester Casey says, "That old man, he told the truth about being your for-real pa."

Sheriff Bacon Carlyle (◎ *Childhood Enemy*): Don't ask for my feeling sorry. Your average city's nothing except different levels of pervert. Rant only told that story to fit in. Him and Mr. Casey, they just took their pissing matches a little more far than your average father and son.

Echo Lawrence: At the edge of the world, another star pops up.

Rant says, "You're only lying so I won't get homesick . . ." He shifts his ass on the top of that cardboard suitcase full of gold.

In the city, Chester tells him, Rant will find his real father, and his grandfather. Rant will discover his true nature. "First thing," Chet says, "soon as you meet Echo Lawrence for the first time, you give her a big kiss for me." He says, "Let her know, does her cholesterol taste too high."

Brenda Jordan (◯ *Childhood Friend*): Don't say I told, but Rant showed me a gold twenty-dollar coin his mama gived him for his going away. Dated 1884. Mrs. Casey told how Chet Casey weren't Rant's real daddy, but she'd never tell how come she had that coin she gived him for good luck.

Echo Lawrence: And his dad, whether it's good night or goodbye, Chet Casey leans over the top of Rant's hair. His face bent over the skin of Rant's forehead, where the wind combs the bangs back, that bare spot, his dad bumps. His lips press and bounce off.

Chester says, "Tell Shot Dunyun not to let his little-bitty pug dog, Sandy, drink out of the toilet."

Another impossible piece of advice. Shot had never met Chet Casey. Even I didn't know the name of Shot's little dog.

The next new star gets big. The headlights of the bus, one bright spot breaking into two separate stars. As those lights come closer to Rant and his dad, the headlights spread farther and farther apart.

"Soon as you discover your true nature," Chester tells his son, "you hightail it back to Middleton."

Irene Casey (◯ *Rant's Mother*): Anytime anybody in Middleton opens their mouth, you need to ask: "Why are you telling me this?"

Shot Dunyun (☾ *Party Crasher*): How weird is this? But the last words Rant's old man says to him, while Rant's waving from the window of the bus, is Chet Casey yells, "Find the truth and hurry back, and maybe you can save your ma from getting attacked by that crazy-insane lunatic . . ."

Echo Lawrence: Chester Casey, both his thumbs hooked in the front belt loops of his blue jeans, he says, "Don't think on this any too hard. None of this is gonna make sense until it's close to, just about, almost too late."

Rant's father shouts, "It pains me, I'll never put eyes on you again."

15—Boosted Peaks

Shot Dunyun (☾ *Party Crasher*): How's this for bullshit? At this shop, for our top all-time rental, you're talking about *Little Becky's Walk on a Warm Spring Day*. Shit like that, comfort shit, dumb shits come in here, ask to rent it all day long. The reason I got into this business is I love transcripts, ever since I was little, but this is killing me. It's beyond bullshit.

Eight hours every day, renting out copies of *Little Becky's Seaside Hunt for Shells*. Everybody wanting the same mass-marketed crap. Saying it's for their kid, but really it's not. All these fat, middle-aged dumbshits just want something to kill time. Nothing dark and edgy or challenging. Nothing artsy.

Just so long as it's got a happy ending.

A love story strained through somebody's rose-colored brain.

Your basic experience, what people called a "boosted peak," is just the file record of somebody's neural transcript, a copy of all the sensory stimuli some witness collected while carving a jack-o'-lantern or winning the Tour de France. Officially, that's what the primary participant is called: the witness. The most famous witness is Little Becky, but that doesn't mean she's the best. Little Becky is just brain-dead enough to appeal to the biggest audience. Her brain chemistry gives a nice, sweet perception to softball peak experiences. Hayrides. Valentine's Day. Christmas bullshit morning.

She's what a movie star used to be. Your vehicle for moving through an experience. Little Becky is just somebody with a sweet disposition, the ideal serotonin levels, I-dopamine–and–endorphin mix.

You could say I'm a little beyond burned out on all this new technology.

And you'd better believe I've screwed with a few transcripts. You take a copy of *Little Becky's Halloween Pumpkin Party* and you rewitness it through yourself on acid. You hook up for the boost, plug in for all five of the tracks: tactile, audio, olfactory, visual, and taste. Drop a tab of acid. And at the same time out-cord a transcript of you experiencing the Pumpkin Party while on acid.

Then you rewitness *that transcript* through somebody Down's syndrome or fetal alcohol.

Then you rewitness the resulting transcript through a dog, maybe a German shepherd, and you've got a good product. No shit. A peak worth the time and money to boost. Still, weird as this sounds, you put that on the shelf and don't expect to get anything but complaints.

The bullshit truth is, this entire industry sells to dipshits.

The day that *Little Becky's Happy Treasure Hunt* hit the shelves, we had assholes lined up around the block. We moved something like fifteen hundred copies.

Over on the Employee Picks shelf, my faves are covered with dust. Nobody wants to plug in and boost ten hours of *Getting Gun Shot in Wartime* or *Last Minutes Alive: The Final Moments Aboard the World's Worst Airplane Crashes*. That shit, I love. My favorite part is one crash where the witness has just started to out-cord his peak experience. He's just switched to out-cord his transcript, and you can smell the jet fuel the moment before it flashes. You can taste the bourbon still in his mouth. The airplane seat belt is so tight it cuts across your hips. The armrests are shaking under your elbows, and your bones go stiff, all your joints grinding together inside tight muscle. Then, at the end of every boosted death, you get the blip where transmissions stop. This guy's last neural stream, out-corded to his wife's mobile phone.

When you switch your port, in the back of your neck, to transmit a record of your neural stimuli, when you're broadcasting that experience, officially it's called "out-cording."

A "script artist" is the official term for anybody who monkeys with neural transcripts, whether you're booting, boosting, or damping the tracks.

Just don't expect your artwork to sell. No studio is going to pick up a radically mixed peak for mass distribution. Studios have their own marketing lingo. They'll launch *A Tour of Antarctica*, witnessed through a primary like Robert Mason, some totally bland pair of eyes and ears. But even the studios will sweeten that boosted peak by rewitnessing it through a neutered cat, a Catholic priest, a housewife overprescribed with estrogen. What hits the market is sugary, sweet crap. The tracks beyond balanced. It's the junk food of boosted peaks.

Plus, you have the new automatic interrupts. If at any time during a boosted peak your heart rate, pulse, or blood pressure exceeds the federal limits, the plug-in stops. Just a bunch of lawyers trying to cover the industry's collective ass.

Sweetened, mellowed, nuanced, remixed crap makes the perfect gift.

This is so beyond boring, but our top-selling experience for all of last year was called *Cross Country Steam Train Excursion*. No shit. A seventy-two-hour boxed set of plug-ins where you do jack shit except sit on a fucking train and watch the outsides stream past the window. You smell the upholstery, the cleaning fluid. The postproduction people didn't bother to damp out the chemical stink. The witness is Robert Mason, wearing wool pants you feel itch the whole trip. Wearing Old Spice cologne. The highpoint is, you go to the dining car and have breakfast, some greasy ham and eggs.

Me making that transcript, I'd step off the train at every stop. Walk around in places like Reno and Cincinnati and Missoula. I'd rewitness the whole trip through a dog, a perfect old-school trick for heightening the olfactory track. Really make the smells pop. For the taste track, I'd borrow from the best gourmet boosts, then strain that track through somebody on a starvation diet to really beef up each flavor. That's called "sharpening."

Half of the industry is freaks who rewitness shit to amp the tracks. You hire blind folks to build up the audio track. It's so beyond illegal, but you rewitness the tactile track of anything through a year-old baby, and velvet feels like velvet. Granite like granite. No sloppy guesswork about the texture of anything. No calluses to fudge the feel of real skin or hair. No baby needs a boost port stuck in the back of its neck, but you see them around. This industry is full of assholes ready to let you remix your porno peaks through their kid. It's beyond tasteless, but you can tell porn peaks reboosted through a kid's soft, sensitive skin. It's no wonder the real world can't hold a candle to a boosted experience.

Babies amp the touch track. Blind people ramp up the sound. Hunger, the taste track. Dogs, the smells. To ramp the visual track, some production techs swear by rewitnessing through birds. Hawks. You know, birds of prey. In school, kids I knew used to rewitness through deaf people, saying it gave the final visual track the best resolution. You take all these rebooted tracks, mix them, and you have a train ride worth taking. My point is, if you're going to sell a crap experience, at least the quality should be the best.

My point is, this seventy-two hours is coming out of someone's life. This boost will replace something real a person might do, so it should be decent. Hell, it ought to be beyond decent. If some asswipe's handing over his time, he should get the train trip sweetened by having the whole mess rewitnessed through a Playboy Bunny on heroin. Morphine at least. Watch those boring, bullshit mountains roll past while zonked on opiates and fondling your own set of love-a-luscious titties. You want to wish the old man a happy Father's Day, that would be my gift suggestion.

In school, after all the film schools switched over, after the entire film industry switched over to neural transcriptions, I did my best work by getting it rebooted through junkies. Hang around any transcription program and you'll meet needle freaks who'll sweeten student work for the extra cash. Or speed freaks who'll let you boost a boring peak through them to amp the pace. If you only need some soft-focus, hook up with a codeine fanatic, run your final mix through him for out-cording, and your edges will look a little relaxed. Very damped.

In transcription school, the programs have random piss-testing. That's why you rewitness through some outsider. If you're financing a hundred thousand to get your M.F.A. in neural transcription, you don't want to piss hot and get booted out of school. Before you can boost anything for the industry, you need to learn how to identify a marketable peak. Then how to choose the right primary participant as your witness. How to structure that experience. If it's a sixteen-course meal or a hot-air balloon ride over Holland, you need to deliver the payoffs at regular intervals. Plus, you need to keep your focus; if this is a boosted peak about swimming the English Channel, you don't want to get distracted by muscle cramps or a headache. Nobody is going to buy a bullshit feature-length headache. Even boosted through an OxyContin high, it's beyond impossible to remove a headache from your tactile track. Trust me.

About going professional, a solid method is to boost for the consumer-product market—you know, those boosted peaks where you're always drinking a Coca-Cola and wearing Nike clothing, always looking straight at the logos and brand names of the products. Eating stuff that tastes so incredible, so drool-inducing, that you know the taste track had to be rewitnessed through some starving tribesman in some famine-ravaged nowhere.

How weird is this? But for fifty bucks' worth of rice and canned milk, somebody's rebooted the entire taste track through so many human skeletons that you can hardly get through the peak without interrupting, you're so hot to buy a soda. A doughnut. A hamburger. Old Spice cologne.

In transcription school, you learn all about effective pacing, so you don't overwhelm your user. You learn all the legal criteria for the production codes and rating system. What distinguishes a G-rated peak from a PG-13. Classifications based on the physical reactions, the electrolyte balance and hormone levels, pulse and respiration of a test audience. A good way to flatten a peak—say, lower it from an R rating to a PG, is you rewitness through a dope-smoking stoner. An easy fix.

To graduate, we each had to produce a feature-length peak experience. For my thesis, I had a great concept. We're talking three to six hours of marketable sensory content. My idea I had, it was so great. I threw a party. Invited one Asian friend. One Jew. One black. One queer. One hot lesbian. One straight cheerleader girl. One Native American. One redneck hillbilly. One Hispanic guy. An Irish. An Eskimo. You get the idea. One of everything. They didn't know, but I was boosting while I played host, spending almost exactly ten minutes talking with each person. The cream on my idea was, I'd ask each guest back, to rewitness the party. Each guest would meet themselves and see, hear, smell, and feel themselves for those ten minutes we'd talked.

Splicing all the boosts together, I made it so the whole four-hour peak was tinted by each person meeting him- or herself. The Hindu meeting the Hindu. The Quaker meeting the Quaker. Shit like that, for hours.

Another student in my same class, he boosted the birth of his first kid, then rewitnessed it through himself while he held the kid on a sunny day. Four hours of sentiment, tinted with Percodan. You can tell by the slight halo effect you get boosting through somebody on painkillers.

The Percodan guy, the faculty committee said his thesis peak was extremely commercially viable. And they gave him 360 points out of a possible four hundred.

My thesis, the committee didn't like so much.

It went beyond a disaster. Nothing sharps the contrast like adrenaline. Each guest got so tweaked, seeing how they occurred to strangers, it made the boost almost unbearable to stay plugged into. Beyond bitter. Boosting the peak, you'd sweat so hard it kept interrupting the feed. Some faculty members couldn't stay plugged in past the second hour.

My concept was, I figured people would love to meet people just like themselves. Like, why most French people stay living in France. Why all the Southern Baptists go to the same church. You know, birds of a feather.

What totally wipes ass is, the committee withheld my degree.

The bunch of dipshits.

These days, every month, when I have to send the school a payment on my loans, at the bottom of the check, where it says "For . . . ," in that blank I always write, "Thanks for the best rim job ever!"

To make those dipshit payments, I work here. Renting out copies of *Little Becky's Easter Egg Hunt* to people who just want to get through another awful night, alone. These people, boring themselves to death.

How weird is this? But inside me, in secret, I know that thesis didn't wreck my life. Not by much. Even saddled with a hundred grand in student loans to pay, I can't get too upset. I learned something, maybe not about boosting peaks, but about people.

Whatever the blessing, the talent, or technology, we can still find some way to fuck it up. The other day, the Percodan guy who graduated with top honors after his boosted birthing experience, he comes in here to rent a peak, still lugging around that baby. He tells me, he just lets it slip, that he's got Robert Mason under contract to boost an upcoming white-water raft trip. Such a bullshit big-name fucking player he's turned into. Such an industry hotshot.

It's not even a year old, and he's already stuck a little black port into the back of his kid's neck.

16—The Team

Echo Lawrence (℃ *Party Crasher*): Every Honeymoon Night, I'd wear the same lucky veil. Different nights, I'd wear a long or short wedding dress. A night in late August, driving in a car with no air conditioning, I don't want to be wearing a thousand layers of tulle with heavy silk on top of that. You can't find the stick shift in all your petticoats. But wintertime, if you drive into a snowdrift, Party Crashing on icy streets, that same tulle can save you from freezing to death.

Shot Dunyun (℃ *Party Crasher*): The night in question, the team was Echo, driving; Green Taylor Simms was her shotgun; I was Right B-Pillar Lookout. A girl named Tina Something was Left B-Pillar Lookout, but she keeps kicking the back of Echo's seat, telling her where to turn to find some car that might have a flag up.

Backseat drivers are bad enough. But from somebody riding Left B, that's too much. Un-asswipe-acceptable. Echo pulls over, and Green says, "Enough."

This Tina Something says, "Fine." She throws open her door and gathers up the skirts of her pink bridesmaid dress in both hands. She says, "Even boosting a Little Becky beats being your slave."

Green and me, we look so swank in our tuxedos, wearing black bow ties, with fake carnations glued to our lapels. We have "Just Married" written down both sides of the car with tubes and tubes of white toothpaste. Those Oreo cookies, twisted in half and stuck on. We have cowbells and tin cans roped to the rear bumper—a clear violation of the I-SEE-U Noise Limitations, but even Daytimers will cut slack for young marrieds.

Cowbells bouncing and white streamers flying from our antennae, we pull up to the curb, and some guy's standing there with his hands stuffed in his pockets. Tina Something throws her bridesmaid's bouquet in his face, saying, "Hey, dude." She yells, "Catch!" The girl's silk flowers hit him in the face, but he catches them. He's quick. He's a quick guy, and we're short one lookout. How weird is that?

I yell, "You!" To the guy, I say, "You got gas money?"

It just so happens that guy is Rant Casey.

Echo Lawrence: Listen up. Getting onto a car team is like the starting position in any sport. If it's an established team, you'll start on the lowest rung. That's Left B-Pillar Lookout, meaning backseat behind the driver. The number-three position is Right B-Pillar Lookout, the backseat behind the shotgun. Number two is riding shotgun in the front seat. Being driver is the same as playing quarterback, center, pitcher, or goalie. The number-one position. The glamour spot.

Tina Something (ℂ *Party Crasher*): My old car—I called her Cherry Bomb—she got scored into the gaddamn junkyard, tagged to death. That happens, and chances are you'll start at that bottom position, behind the head of some other

driver with her wheels still intact. Somebody like Echo
Lawrence. Don't think I hate Echo. It's just that she lies. Ask
Echo what she does for a living; if she tells you anything
except sex work, it's a lie.

Echo Lawrence: Pay attention. "Tag Teams" are crews put
together on the street. A "Shark," a lone driver needing a team
for help or protection or company, he'll cruise around before
the "window" opens, looking to draft players off the curb. If
you don't have a car, just stand on some corner with your
thumb out. A car will pull over and ask, "Are you playing?"
   You say, "What you got open?"
   They say, "Still need a Left B-Pillar Lookout." They say,
"You got gas money?"
   Some teams looking for a member, they'll ask you to show
can you turn your head around fast and smooth with no popping sound. No point in having a lookout with whiplash or
cervical damage from some past crack-up. Having gas money
isn't a must, but it shows your level of commitment.

Tina Something: Gimps with fused vertebrae, losers known
to be night-blind or farsighted, you'll see them on the curb
all night. Maybe some team will take pity and give them a
nothing position. In a big car, a loser might get what people
call the "mascot" position, the middle of the backseat, where
you can't do much but talk to keep up the mood. Otherwise,
they're totally Misfit Toys.
   You have a short neck or bad eyes and you'd better bring
lots of gas money and pray for a nice team with a big backseat. Cultivate your jokes and people skills.

Echo Lawrence: The "window" is the determined time a
game begins, until the time it ends. You might have a Satur-

day four-hour window. Or you might play a Monday all-night window, from eight to eight.

Shot Dunyun: The night we met Rant, he'd escaped some voucher hotel, waiting for assignment to transitional Nighttimer housing. In a city where most people are either working jobs or boosting peaks, for a guy without work, a guy whose port won't boost shit, it's no wonder he wandered at night.

Rant climbs into the car and gives me a quarter. How lame is that? An asswipe quarter for gas money. Except it's gold and dated 1887. I don't know what that coin was, but Echo dropped the car into gear, and we slipped into the traffic stream. Rant climbed into our backseat like he'd been waiting on that corner, waiting his whole bullshit life for us to pull up. And Green, twisting to reach back, he says, "Might I have a closer look at that coin?"

Echo Lawrence: A good driver shouldn't have to look anywhere but forward. Good backseat lookouts shouldn't look anywhere but backward and sideways. It's not their job to see where the car's headed. A good shotgun handles his side and half the windshield.

You're not just looking for cars to hit. You're looking for cars headed to hit you. You're looking for cars already on someone's tail. You're looking for police. Not just during a chase, but all the time, parked or baiting or trolling. Or stalking. "Baiting" means to steer something cherry, virgin-perfect, clean, and polished down the middle of the boulevard, the "field" or "route" or "maze." You see a showroom two-door purr bright red down that center lane, flying a game flag: just-married cans or soccer-mom paint—to prove they're playing, and you'd be a fool to chase after.

Not to say a lot of rookies don't—peel off for a piece of that fresh red paint.

The veterans, teams that know "bait," they'll wait a second look. A block back always come the shadow cars, spread out in a wide dragnet, the teams in league with the bait car, ready to slam the rookies flushed out. Next time you hear a Graphic Traffic report about a plague of bad drivers, this is the shadow cars scoring on rookies.

From DRVR Radio Graphic Traffic: Lions and tigers and bears, oh my! Whatever your team mascot, watch out for a flood of soccer fans this evening. It seems every proud parent is driving a crew around with their team colors flying. Go, Cougars! At the Post Circle, along the north side, watch out for a six-car pile-up. No telling who the winner is, but they all appear to be amateur sport teams. No injuries, but the traffic cams show a lot of people arguing in the breakdown lane.

Echo Lawrence: Next time you come across a bad pile-up, you look forward enough, fast enough, and you might see the bait car, that still-pretty redster, disappear around a side corner way, way up ahead.

Tina Something: Your really light kind of tagging, we call that "flirting." You just nudge somebody's rear with your front wheel well. And if the target looks and likes you, if he likes what he sees, you drive away and he comes after you. Your average person will Party Crash so she can be around other people. It's very social, a way to meet people, and you sit around telling stories for a few hours. You could sit at home, but even boosting a party is still being alone. You come to the end of a party boost and you've still spent all night by yourself.

Even Party Crashing can get boring if you can't find another team flying the designated flag, but at least it's a communal boredom. Like a family.

From the Field Notes of Green Taylor Simms (ℂ *Historian*): Party Crashing appeals primarily to people too poor or too rich to be engaged in the middle-class pursuit of monetary success. Mr. Dunyun and Miss Lawrence didn't consider they had anything to lose.

Shot Dunyun: We're not two bullshit blocks before our car jerks forward, the tires bark, pushed across pavement. A Shark's bitten paint-deep into our seven o'clock, ready to repeat-tag our left rear quarter-panel.

Still holding his bouquet of silk flowers, Rant whips around, saying, "Fella hit us!" Shouting, "He *hit* us!"

Into her rearview mirror, Echo says, "Why'd you *let* him?" She says, "Mind your field *fucking* quadrant . . ."

Green holds the gold quarter between two fingers, just touching the edges, saying, "Where did you acquire this extraordinary coin?"

And Echo hits the gas, throws us around the next right, the Shark still chewing our paint.

Tina Something: Everybody knows a full moon means a Newlywed event. A Honeymoon free-for-all. Doing this every month for a couple years, you pile up racks of wedding gowns. Racks. Ruffled shirts and penguin tuxedos. My favorites are pretty sherbet-pink bridesmaid dresses. But it's wedding gowns most Party Crashers wear: the big full skirt, the poofy veil. Half the time, one team plows into the back end of another team, and between the two cars eight brides pile out to scream at each other in the emergency lane. Some brides with hairy arms and Adam's apples jumping under their square, stubbly chins. The knuckles of one hairy hand holding the train of a dress, to show greasy work boots underneath. All the teams in gowns and veils, black people, white people, women or men, all brides look alike.

Echo Lawrence: The full moon is the best night for starters. The flag is so easy to spot. You write "Just Married" in shaving cream down the car doors and across the trunk and hood. You tie some white streamers to the top of the radio antenna and put on your best Sunday clothes. A starter team is out ten dollars, tops, to get into the game.

Veteran newlyweds, they have to count back on their fingers. Toyota, Buick, Mazda, Dodge, Pontiac. Red, blue, silver, black. This month, this honeymoon might make a vet's fifth car, ready to get pounded with dents.

Shot Dunyun: Any Honeymoon Night, you'll see another "Just Married" car in every block. Brides stand on street corners, looking for loose grooms. Grooms wait on curbs, wearing top hats, hoping to wave down a bride with her own wheels.

From the Field Notes of Green Taylor Simms: A crucial aspect of dressing for any Honeymoon Night is to fasten your boutonniere with a portion of double-stick adhesive tape. In the event of a car accident, you do not want a long straight pin stuck anywhere adjacent to your heart.

Echo Lawrence: Another piece of advice: Scotchgard your seats. Before Tina Something, we had a newby lookout in the backseat during the pulse. A Shark plows into us, tags our right rear corner so hard we're spun sideways, traffic and headlights coming at us from every direction, horns blaring, and this newby lookout, she takes a leak. Damage from the tag was nothing Bondo won't fill. But we were sponging that girl's piss out of the backseat for weeks.

Shot Dunyun: The Shark still tagging our ass, he's some asswipe in a Maserati Quattroporte Executive GT painted Bordeaux Pontevecchio. Craning around, I watch out the back window, and he's not a lone Shark. Riding shotgun is a cloud of pink. A bridesmaid. Our Tina Something we ditched. Her teeth make a round oval, her mouth's that wide open. Tina's laughing that hard as the Shark's bumper clubs our ass.

Still holding Tina's bouquet of fake flowers, Rant's twisting inside his seat belt, trying to see, and says, "Why's he after us . . . ?"

Echo Lawrence: After you're tagged out, the brides and grooms, the best men and bridesmaids, they all fake their anger. Fake-screaming and pop-eyed. Fake-fighting for the people slowed down to watch. The rubberneck effect. Passing traffic slows to a crawl to watch the spectacle. The police never stop, not for a fender bender.

The wedding parties, they're just trying to milk out the moment their life gets slow. The pulse when two cars come together.

These are regular people watching their lives squeezed down into dollars, all the hours and days of their life compressed the way the crumple zones of a car get sacrificed. The total hours of their waiting tables or sorting mail or selling shoes, it gets screwed down until they have enough money to pool and buy some wheels. A wedding dress. String some tin cans and buy some shaving cream.

The next new-moon night, these people are cruising or getting cruised. They're driving and waving to the rest of us not in the action. They're watching in every direction for a Shark, listening for the clatter of enemy tin cans, until another team of "Just Married's" see them and give chase. A swerve and black tire marks, one car darts after another so fast the tin cans stop touching the road. One red light and— that's the moment time explodes. What automotive crash-test engineers call "the pulse."

From the Field Notes of Green Taylor Simms: Beginning with Santa Claus as a cognitive exercise, a child is encouraged to share the same idea of reality as his peers. Even if that reality is patently invented and ludicrous, belief is encouraged with gifts that support and promote the common cultural lies.

The greatest consensus in modern society is our traffic system. The way a flood of strangers can interact, sharing a path, almost all of them traveling without incident. It only takes one dissenting driver to create anarchy.

Echo Lawrence: When a back car hits a front, brides get thrown against their seat belts, their veils whipped forward so fast your face gets a rash that players call "lace burn." That moment, time slows down. All the hundred years of every boring day—they explode to fill that half-moment. That pulse.

Here's time squeezed down until it explodes into a slow-motion moment that will last for years.

Your car you saved to buy, it's punched down, smaller, but your life's pumped back up. Bigger. Back to life-size or beyond. The brides on the side of the road, throwing white rice to hurt, they're just trying to make that moment stretch. Milking the pulse.

Shot Dunyun: Tina and the Shark get bigger in our back window, laughing and leaned forward so hard their breath fogs the windshield. Their bumper pushes our five o'clock, squeaking our springs and shocks. Their front tires spin so close that Echo's parking alarm starts to beep. Beeping faster. Beyond close, the Shark's wheels bite off one of our dragging tin cans, pinching each can flat and snapping the string. So close that Echo's parking alarm goes to sounding one long beep.

Rant leans forward to pat Green's padded tux shoulder and says, "By the way, congratulations."

And, still looking at that gold quarter, Green says, "For what?"

From the Field Notes of Green Taylor Simms: Perpetuating Santa Claus and the Easter Bunny breaks ground for further socialization—including conformance to traffic laws which allow the maximum number of drivers to commingle on our roadways. In addition, insisting that the journey is always a means to some greater end, and the excitement and danger of the journey should be minimized. Perpetuating the fallacy that a journey itself is of little value.

Shot Dunyun: Tina and the Shark bite off another can, bump us again, drop back. Laughing. Rant says, "You . . . ," and he hitches a finger between Green and Echo, saying, "You got married . . ."

Green says, "New team at two o'clock."

And Echo says, "Find me a hole!"

Echo Lawrence: With both my feet I'm standing on the gas pedal, already planning to blind that Tina Something with a handful of raw rice. I can see my wheels in some junkyard still smeared with "Just Married" toothpaste.

From the Field Notes of Green Taylor Simms: The activity casually referred to as Party Crashing rejects the idea that driving time is something to be suffered in order to achieve a more useful and fulfilling activity.

Tina Something: At the next gaddamn police impound auction, I'll be bidding against Echo. In less than one odometer click, we'll both need new wheels.

Shot Dunyun: And the bullshit Shark drops back.

Echo Lawrence: Tina's slammed against her headrest. Her tits and pearls thrown up, high, around her neck. Veil burn. Steam rises behind them, and their six o'clock's been tagged. Taken out.

From the Field Notes of Green Taylor Simms: Our Shark has been preyed upon by someone else. The Maserati has been slaughtered amid a litter of cowbells, shattered glass, and tin cans.

Shot Dunyun: Echo pitches us around a corner, into a dark alley. She shuts off the headlights and taillights, letting the motor idle. She parts her veil to take a better look at Rant, and Echo says, "Get your Day Boy ass out of my car!"

Offering the gold coin to her, Green says, "Do you know what this is worth?"

And Rant Casey, he touches the backseat and sniffs his fingers, saying, "That girl who peed, three, maybe four weeks back"—Rant looks at us—"she ate bell peppers that day."

Rant grins his tar-black teeth at us and says, "Any of you folks know a fellow by the name of Chester Casey?"

17—Hit Men

Lynn Coffey (ℂ *Journalist*): The poet Oscar Wilde wrote, "Each man kills the thing he loves . . ." Each man except the smart ones. The ones who don't want to serve time in prison, the smart men used to hire Karl Waxman.

Tina Something (ℂ *Party Crasher*): How'd I know what Wax was up to? I couldn't know. The first night he Tag Teamed me, that Honeymoon Night when Echo ditched me, Wax pulled over to the curb in a Maserati Quattroporte Executive GT. Painted dark red, Bordeaux Pontevecchio. Rosewood panels in the dash. The headliner is sewed out of Alcantara suede, and the heated seats actually give your butt muscles a constant Swedish massage.

Wax buzzed down the electric window on my side. I'm still standing on the curb in my pink bridesmaid gown, and Wax waves something floppy and white at me. That's how Wax introduced himself.

"Before you touch anything, baby," he tells me, "you put on these."

It's latex gloves.

Lynn Coffey: It's tragic. Young people seldom purchase these exotic sports cars, certainly not professional basketball or football players. They could never fit in the bucket seats. No, almost all such cars go to older-middle-aged or elderly men who seldom drive them. These Maseratis and Ferraris and Lamborghinis sit garaged for years, like lonely mistresses, hidden from direct sunlight.

Jarrell Moore (ℂ *Private Investigator*): As per my investigation, nobody's 100-percent sure who runs Party Crashing, but it can't be any single individual. That guy would have to keep track of fouls for every player. Anybody calls three fouls on you inside of two months, and you stop getting notified about the next game. Fouls include tagging too hard—figure the impact by the speed of each vehicle. Anything totaling more than twenty miles per hour is a foul. If I'm driving ten, and you're driving eleven, and you swerve to hit me head-on, that's an impact over twenty. I can call the foul on you.

Excess impact is only one foul to call.

Tina Something: Wax could tell you details the gaddamn owners never could. All types of convertibles: the Fiat Spyder, the Maserati Spyder, and the Ferrari Spyder, they're all named after some kind of seventeenth-century horse-drawn coach. With no top and high wheels, this black olden-days carriage looked like a spider.

Wax could work the steering-wheel paddles to shift a Formula I or Cambiocorsa trannie. He saw how Jaguar Racing Green shows up a half-shade lighter than British Racing Green. When you open the door of a Maserati, and only a Maserati, you hear a faint, high-pitched whine . . . Wax could tell you that was the hydraulic trannie pressurizing.

"Nice," Wax would say, gunning the V8 of a Jaguar XJR, painted Winter Gold. Flexing his fingers, he'd say, "They sprung for the *heated* steering wheel . . ." Then he'd drop the J-gate trannie into second gear and butt-ram some rusty Subaru wagon.

Lynn Coffey: In Party Crash culture, Karl Waxman was known as a "Hit Man." A species of paid assassin.

Shot Dunyun (ℂ *Party Crasher*): Me, my focus is providing the music for a perfect night of Party Crashing. But, no bullshit, I'd love to be a Hit Man. A night a while back, I watched some Hit Man scrape every inch of paint off the body of a half-million-dollar Saleen S7. A car with three and one-half inches of ground clearance, and the driver raced it off-road. That's beyond sadistic.

Lynn Coffey: That people hired a Hit Man demonstrated their love for a particular vehicle. An owner might want a Rolls-Royce Silver Cloud or Silver Shadow destroyed, but said owner could never, by his own hand, defile such a beautiful automobile.

Tina Something: One point, a Jaguar X-Type, Wax says, "Can you believe this?" He slams the heel of one hand, bam, on the leather steering wheel, saying, "Can you fucking believe this tightwad! Cheaped out and settled for the *Tobago* wheels, not the Proteus, not even the Cayman wheels." Nailing the gas, Wax popped the right front wheel up on the sidewalk, just long enough to flatten one of those steel-plate mailboxes, exploding sparks and paint chips and white envelopes, before the wheel thuds into the gutter, the speedo never needling below forty.

Lynn Coffey: Among other things, Waxman would accept payment for disposing of luxury cars. Typically, cars about to be lost in a messy divorce decree. Or vehicles the owner could no longer afford to make payments on. Or simply insurance fraud. Or spite.

A certain go-between would pass Waxman the keys and an envelope of cash, typically two or three hundred dollars, then tell Waxman where to find the vehicle. The owner would leave town, establishing an alibi for the two or three days during which Waxman might joyride. By the time the owner returned to report the vehicle stolen, Waxman would've ditched it somewhere it wouldn't be found.

Shot Dunyun: No bullshit, but I've watched people stop in the middle of a funeral, the dead body smiling there in the casket, the old ladies sobbing, and people stop to change the music. Mozart instead of Schumann. Music is crucial.

Beyond no way can I overstress this fact.

Let's say you're southbound on the interstate, cruising along in the middle lane, listening to AM radio. Up alongside comes a tractor trailer of logs or concrete pipe, a tie-down strap breaks, and the load dumps on top of your little sheetmetal ride. Crushed under a world of concrete, you're sandwiched like so much meat salad between layers of steel and glass. In that last, fast flutter of your eyelids, you looking down that long tunnel toward the bright God Light and your dead grandma walking up to hug you—do you want to be hearing another radio commercial for a mega, clearance, close-out, blow-out liquidation car-stereo sale?

Tina Something: Another point, could be our third date, a Dodge Viper, Wax got going about how his clients always wash and wax the car, detailing every inch, before they turn over the cash and keys. "It's like watching those actresses," he tells me, "those women who get their hair done, colored and curled, and their fingernails manicured and their legs shaved smooth and tanned, all that fuss just to appear in a gang-bang porn video."

Wax steered that Viper down a flight of those concrete stairs in the park, leaving a long trail of our exhaust system and suspension, saying, "Baby, I could just cry over those perfect manicured fingernails if they weren't so fucking stupid."

Shot Dunyun: No bullshit. If your car skids into oncoming traffic, and you die listening to The Archies sing "Sugar Sugar," it's your own damn laziness.

Lynn Coffey: Certain Party Crashers you could tell were Hit Men or Hit Women. If their vehicle was always pristine— even a Chevette or a Pinto, always showroom perfect and polished. If their decoration was minimal, nothing except the basic flag. And if they readily drove over curbs, sideswiped concrete traffic barriers. From that you could deduce their wheels had been someone's dream gone awry. A lovely mistress or trophy the owner didn't want another person to ever own.

Jarrell Moore: Other fouls you can call include tagging off-limits areas of the target. No T-boning—that's a head-on impact against the side of your target. No angling to ram anywhere on the sidewalls between the front and rear axles.

Tina Something: For Rant and Wax, it irked them both that ancient mountains and forests were being sliced up to provide affordable granite countertops in tract houses, or Peruvian-rosewood dash panels in luxury cars no one would drive.

At some point, Wax mentioned how appalling it seemed that those brilliant minds who could invent miracle medicines and nuclear fission and dazzling computer special effects, they had such a complete lack of imagination when it came to spending their money: granite countertops and luxury cars. Talking about that stuff, Wax driving, the madder he got, you could watch the speedo creep up past eighty, ninety, a hundred.

Lynn Coffey: With Hit Men, perhaps with all Party Crashers, we're describing a self-directed road rage.

Certain men may claim to adore women; they'll marry a dozen times, then drive each wife to suicide with abuse. Karl Waxman felt that same way about those stolen luxury automobiles. He loved to speed along at seventy, all those jealous eyes turning to follow him, but he resented the fact he needed a Jaguar or a BMW to gain such recognition. That the automobile didn't even belong to him was the ultimate insult. The supreme manifestation of all his self-perceived shortcomings.

Shot Dunyun: No bullshit, but I never leave the house without a mix for anything: Falling in love. Witnessing a death. Disappointment. Impatience. Traffic. I carry a mix for any human condition. Anything really good or bad happens to me, and my way to not overreact—like, to distance my emotions—is to locate the exact perfect sound track for that moment. Even the night Rant died, my automatic first thought was: Philip Glass's Violin Concerto II, or Ravel's Piano Concerto in G Major . . . ?

Jarrell Moore: The way I figure it, the head individual in Party Crashing would have to tally fouls. Plus, keep track of teams by their license plate. Plus, name the flag and window for each game. Yeah, and notify all the players about upcoming events. If that's only one guy, it's a safe bet he's pretty damn busy, and not just some thug. He'd need to be pretty damn bright.

Tina Something: Didn't matter was it a Lexus or a Rolls-Royce, at the finish of every Party Crash date, Wax and me ended up at the top of the Madison Street boat ramp, the place where the ramp's angled, steep, into deep water. Trailed behind us, cotter pins and U-joint needle bearings, crankcase oil, brake fluid, and maybe slivers of carbon fiber. And smoke, gaddamn fog banks of black or blue smoke. Our drivetrain barely still functional.

I'd climb out and watch while Wax shifted down to first gear. With the engine still running, some nights, if nobody was around, he'd press the panic button on the alarm. What a gaddamn noise. The sirens and whatever lights we hadn't already busted, they'd be flashing on and off. With the Mercedes or Lamborghini still flashing and screaming, Wax would step out and slam the door shut. The car already rolling down the boat ramp, nose-first, into the black water. Like watching an ocean liner sink. The *Titanic*. White and amber lights, horn blaring, even as the car settled deeper, under water, that trashed relic of somebody's dream would keep wailing, flaring, fainter and fading, until it settled onto some secret mountain of wrecked dreams—Jaguars and Saleens and Corvettes—that people had hired Wax to murder.

18–The City

Todd Rutz (◯ *Coin Dealer*): The kid who died. The kid comes in with a sweat sock tied in a knot, starts undoing the knot with his teeth. Nothing inside that old yellow sock should be worth my time to look. My permit says I can stay open four hours past the night curfew, long as I don't leave the shop. Past curfew, I lock the door, and anybody comes I buzz them inside. This kid with the dirty sock, I almost didn't buzz him. You can never tell with Nighttimers.

But even I can tell, this kid's a convert. His suntan he hasn't even lost yet. So I took a chance I'd make some money. Look at New Orleans, 1982, some bulldozer doing construction work downtown at lunchtime, businesspeople walking around dressed in three-piece suits. The dozer scrapes the dirt and busts open three wood cases of buried 1840-O Liberty Seated quarters. Not gold, mind you, but coins worth in the range of two to four grand apiece. Those bankers and lawyers wearing suits and dresses, they jumped into the mud and wrestled each other. Biting and kicking each other for a handful of those Gobrecht quarter-dollars.

My point being, you just never know where a hoard of treasure will surface.

Edith Steele (℃ *Human Resources Director*): We interviewed Mr. Casey for a position as a nighttime landscape-maintenance specialist. He was referred to our firm through the I-SEE-U labor help line. On the occasion of his third failure to arrive for work, claiming his fifth injury due to a non-work-related traffic accident, Mr. Casey was removed from our payroll.

Todd Rutz: The Baltimore Find of 1934, two little boys were goofing around in the basement of a rented house and they discover a hole in the wall. On August 31, 1934, they pulled 3,558 gold coins out of that hole, all of them pre-1857. At 132 South Eden Street in Baltimore, Maryland. A fair number of those coins, we're talking "gem condition." At the very least, perfect uncirculated or choice uncirculated.

Lew Terry (℃ *Property Manager*): If it was up to me, I'd never even rent to Nighttrippers—those Daytimer kids who switch over. It's just to irk their parents, they convert. Those delinquents feel compelled to live into every negative stereotype they have about Nighttime culture—loud music and boosting drug highs—but the housing statute says a minimum of 10 percent of your units you have to make available to converts. Casey moved in with nothing, maybe one suitcase, into Unit 3-E. You could go look, only the door's still sealed with police tape.

Todd Rutz: The kid with the sock, he's chewing at the knot with his teeth, and inside the toe you can hear coins clinking together. My point being, that sound makes me glad I buzzed the kid inside. I can tell the sound of silver from copper and nickel. Running my shop so long, I can hear coins rattle and tell you if they're twenty-two- or twenty-four-karat gold. Just from the sound I hear, I'd chew on that stinking, dirty sock with my own teeth.

Jeff Pleat (℃ *Human Resources Director*): According to our records, we engaged Buster Casey for two weeks in the capacity of dishwasher. By apparent coincidence, during the brief span of his employment with us, some sixteen dinner guests encountered foreign objects in their food. These ranged from steel paper clips to a buffalo nickel dated 1923.

Todd Rutz: The kid slides an arm inside the sock, all the way up to his skinny elbow, and he drags out a fistful of . . . we're talking *impossible* coins. It wouldn't matter how bad they smell. A 1933 gold twenty-dollar in gem condition. A 1933 gold ten-dollar, uncirculated. An 1879 four-dollar piece, the Liberty with the coiled hair, near-gem condition.

Jarrell Moore (℃ *Private Investigator*): My statement for the record is, Buster Landru Casey, aka "Rant" Casey, did contact me via the telephone and did arrange an appointment to discuss my services toward locating a missing biological father. At that time, I informed the potential client that my base fee was one thousand dollars per week, plus expenses. Said potential client assured me the expense would not be an issue.

Brenda Jordan (☼ *Childhood Friend*): If you promise not to tell, another thing Rant Casey told me was that the old man who showed him about the coins, the stranger who drove up the road from nowheres, said he was Rant's long-lost, for-real pa from the city.

Todd Rutz: Dealing with a kid like that, believe me, I looked for obvious counterfeits: any 1928-D Liberty Walking silver dollars. Any 1905-S gold Quarter Eagles. Blatant fakes. An 1804 silver dollar or Lafayette dollar. I put a Confederate 1861-O half-dollar under a lens and look for coralline structures and saltwater etching, "shipwreck effects" that might tell me more than the kid's letting on. I check for microscopic granularity that might come from sea-bottom sand.

We're talking coins that haven't been whizzed and slabbed. Raw coins. Some with nothing except bag marks.

Allfred Lynch (ⓒ *Exterminator*): Vermin control is not your chosen field for most, but Rant Casey took to it like a roach to cat food. The kid would crawl under houses, into attics, didn't matter if the job was vampire bats. Snakes, bats, rats, cockroaches, poison spiders—none of it made Rant Casey break a sweat.

Funny thing, but his physical exam came back positive for rabies. No drugs or nothing, but he had rabies. The clinic took care of it and updated his tetanus booster.

Todd Rutz: Believe me, I was only pretending to check the blue-book values. I tell him, the Barber Liberty Head half-dollar he's got, the 1892-O, when Charles E. Barber first minted it, newspaper editors wrote that the eagle looked starved to death. The head of Liberty looked like "the ignoble Emperor Vitellius with a goiter." While I'm feeding the kid my line, really I'm going over the stolen-property bulletins for the past year.

The kid's looking out my front window. He's shaking the sock to jiggle the coins still inside. He says his grandmother died and left these to him. Offers that as the only pedigree for his collection.

Allfred Lynch: Only single problem I ever had with Rant Casey was, every month or so we do random lunchbox checks. As the guys are headed home, we ask to look inside their lunchboxes. Our guys are alone in people's homes, sometimes with jewelry and valuables sitting around. A random check keeps everybody in line.

Never found Rant stealing diamonds, but once we popped open his lunchbox and the insides was crawling with spiders. Black widow spiders he's supposed to been killing that day. Rant says it's by accident, and I trust him.

I mean, who'd smuggle home a nest of poison spiders?

Todd Rutz: The deal ended up, I paid the kid fifteen thousand out of petty cash. Gave him every bill I kept in the safe. Fifteen grand for the 1933 gold twenty, the 1933 gold ten, and the 1879 four-dollar piece.

When I ask his name, the kid has to think, look around at the floor and ceiling, before he tells me, "I ain't decided yet."

Believe me, it didn't matter if he lied. Didn't matter that he refused anything except cash payment. Or that the kid's teeth he used to untie the sock, his teeth are stained black. Jet-black teeth.

My point being, just that 1933 gold Saint Gaudens Double Eagle, that's an eight-million-dollar coin.

19—Student Driver

Shot Dunyun (ℂ *Party Crasher*): One Student Driver
Night, Rant asked Green Taylor Simms to take a picture, a
photo of Rant standing next to me. Rant handed Green one
of those throwaway paper cameras, and, holding one hand
stiff, chopping at his own knees, he goes to Green, "From
here up."

Green drove his car that night, his big Daimler, and we'd
pit-stopped at a drive-in for something to eat. Rant stands
next to me, reaches an arm around my shoulder. He fingers
the knob of my port, where it comes out between the Atlas
and the Axial at the back of my skull, and Rant goes,
"What's this like?"

He tells me how, because of rabies, his port won't boost.
His fingers still pushing, rubbing the skin around mine. His
fingers warm, as if he's been holding a cup of coffee. Fever-
warm. Hot.

A port is like having an extra nose, I tell him, only on the
back of your neck. Only not just a nose, but eyes and a tongue
and ears, five extra ways to see. Sometimes, I say, it's bullshit.
You're supposed to control a port, but sometimes you get a
whole-body hunger for a Coke or potato chips, stuff you'd

never eat, so you know the corporate world must broadcast peaks or effects that enter the port even when it's unplugged.

Green's standing, leaning against the driver's door of his car, holding the camera to his face, going, "Tell me when." Cars drive past, behind him, some cars with "Student Driver" signs. Some Party Crash teams, slowing to see if we're flying a flag.

Rant cups the back of my neck in his hand, going, "Now."

For example, tonight, I wasn't hungry until we drove past this fast-food place. My drool, it's real. But the bacon-cheeseburger taste in my mouth is a boosted effect.

Green Taylor Simms goes, "Say 'cheeseburger.' "

And, Rant's hand gripping my neck, he twists my face toward him and plants his mouth over mine. When the camera flashes, Rant's other hand is dug between my legs, spread and thumbing between the buttons of my fly.

The crazy asshole. His tongue hot in my mouth, his saliva on my lips, fast as spit can transfer rabies. The camera flash comes twice before I push Rant Casey away, and he goes, "Thanks, man." He takes the paper camera from Green and says, "My dad won't believe I bagged me such a good-looking boyfriend."

How bullshit is that?

And me, I'm just spitting and spitting. The hot taste of cheese and bacon and rabies. Spitting and spitting.

From DRVR Radio Graphic Traffic Reports: Bad news for those of you westbound on the 213 Freeway: A four-door hardtop has sideswiped the inside divider and flipped, trapping the driver and one passenger inside. The ambulance boys say the driver is a thirty-five-year-old male, losing blood from a compound fracture of his femur; his pulse is weak, and his blood pressure is falling rapidly. His current prognosis is cardiac arrest due to exsanguination, with another update on the quarter-hour. This is the DRVR Graphic Traffic Report: We Know Why You Rubberneck . . .

Shot Dunyun: On Student Driver Nights, the flag is one of those signs that warn: "Caution—Student Driver at the Wheel." You have to make two good-size signs and wire one between your taillights, across the back of your trunk and rear bumper. You wire the second sign across the front of your hood, but so it won't block ram air into your radiator. Beginners, teams that expect too much from their viscous fan clutch and coolant pump, they'll make a sign that blocks the whole grille, and you'll see them overheated at the side of the road.

Echo Lawrence (ℂ *Party Crasher*): Party Crash rules require all the teams use some form of "Ajax Professional Driving School" sign since a few seasons ago a real student driver wandered into the course, during the window. That guy's a legend. The poor student, the story goes, six different teams serial-tagged his car, chased him for blocks, gang-banging his rear bumper until his muffler dropped. People say the student and the instructor just bailed, drove up onto a curb and left the front doors hanging open and the motor running.

From DRVR Radio Graphic Traffic Reports: Here's another update regarding that rollover accident on the 213. Driver extrication continues, but we're already looking at signs of a cerebral subarachnoid hemorrhage and pneumocephalus caused by the driver's forehead contacting the windshield-mounted rearview mirror. That's all there is to see on the westbound side. We'll have another update on the quarter-hour. This is the DRVR Graphic Traffic Report: We Know Why You Rubberneck . . .

Shot Dunyun: Party Crashing might sound exciting, but most of it consisted of sitting, talking, and driving in circles. Cruising around, watching for another car flying the correct flag for that time window. The flag announced on the phone call or e-mail or instant message that went around. Some windows, you'd see a team without a clue, dressed for a Honeymoon Night with wedding shit on their car. Or you'd see a team wearing the wigs and driving a car painted with "Go Team" shit, perfect for a Soccer Mom Night. If your flag is wrong, you look like assholes. Or worse.

Teams with the wrong flag up, people say they're police trying to break the game. Or they're teams that tagged too hard, rammed other cars in the side or some other verboten spot. You commit enough fouls and people start to call the Party Crash Hotline and report you. Enough fouls go on your tally and you stop getting notices about the next flag and window.

From DRVR Radio Graphic Traffic Reports: Here's a quick look at the rollover on the 213. The meat-wagon boys tell me the driver exhibits bursting lacerations of the pericardium—that tough little bag that holds your heart. Early word is, localized impact appears to have driven the heart against the vertebral column, resulting in a contusion of the posterior wall of the interventricular septum. Dead means dead, and drive time means an update every ten minutes. This is the DRVR Graphic Traffic Report: We Know Why You Rubberneck . . .

Shot Dunyun: That Student Driver Night, I'm riding shotgun, with Rant covering the backseat. The field looks pretty thin. With my window rolled down, I'm spitting outside, telling Rant, "Even if you give me rabies, I'm not your butt boy." I spit and say, "Especially if you give me rabies."

Normally, Rant smells like a glass of clean water, but not tonight. Every place he touched me, I smell gasoline. "What's that stink?" I ask him.

And Rant goes, "Dimethylcyclopropanecarboxylic acid." He's turned around, watching our five o'clock, out the rear window. Rant says, "Supposed to kill spiders."

From DRVR Radio Graphic Traffic Reports: This just in from the 213: Further treatment of the driver reveals a lateral compression fracture of his right femur, resulting in lateral fractures of the pelvic rami, disruption of the sacroiliac joints with impaction, and fractures of the acetabulum. For those of you on the North Side, the northbound exit from the 614 to the eastbound Helmsberg Freeway is slow, due to a Student Driver stalled on the right shoulder. For Graphic Traffic, this is Tina Something.

Shot Dunyun: Green's lurking us behind a student driver, trailing, weaving through traffic for a better angle, hoping to split the target onto a side street where a solid tag won't soak up too much attention. Maybe police attention. Green's keeping a van, a taxi, a bus—anything big and bright—between us, so the target won't see our flag flying.

Watching for Sharks, I ask Rant if he's looking for a boyfriend.

And Rant goes, "Nah." He'd screw a German shepherd, Rant says, if it would make his folks love him less. Save them from pain.

"Part of my strategying," Rant goes, his head turning to cover two quadrants, our three to nine o'clock. "The worse my folks think of me," he says, "the less they'll hurt about me being gone."

The bus driving next to us, it brakes, drops back for a stop. We're exposed for the time it takes Green to say, "Gentlemen, brace yourselves," and the Left B-Pillar Lookout in our target is staring back, straight at our flag.

The target dives around the next right turn, down a dark lane of parked cars, and Green throws us past the bus in pursuit. Two student drivers, leaving rubber and smoke.

From DRVR Radio Graphic Traffic Reports: This update just in from the meat wagon, en route with our earlier 213 rollover: We won't know for sure until the autopsy, but it looks like another minor laceration of the proximal jejunum with communication with the peritoneal cavity. Inside word is, just two thousand milliliters of purulent material leaks into your peritoneal cavity and the ambulance driver shuts off those sirens and fancy lights. Something else to keep in mind as you hurry through your commute today.

Shot Dunyun: Our target's cruising slow, too close to parked cars for us to make our tag without costly collateral damage. Putting a dent in a game car is fair, but denting an innocent bystander, you have to fess up. Pay for repairs. Our target banks on this fact and tucks close beside parked cars, staying safe until he can lose us around a quick exit. An alley. Or a cop.

Keeping an eye on my game quadrant, I ask Rant if he's queer or not.

That's the night Green Taylor Simms started calling him Huckleberry Fagg.

And Rant goes, "Truth is, I won't never be a doctor. Don't even ask me to do long division." He goes, "I can't do much to make my folks proud . . ." And he leans forward, reaching into the front seat to turn up the radio. Tina's yakking. Her taking calls from paramedics and traffic cops and pasting together her rubberneck deal.

"But," Rant goes, "if I get my folks' expectations low, and pester them with the worry they messed me up, then just the simple miracle of me getting a girl in trouble—that will bust them open with joy and relief."

From DRVR Radio Graphic Traffic Reports: One last report from the boys in the meat wagon, regarding the fatality rollover on the 213: The song they died hearing was "My Sharona" by The Knack. And that makes Brian Lambson our newest Death Song winner. Brian, if you're listening, call in the next hour to accept your prize. This has been Tina Something for Graphic Traffic: We Know Why You Rubberneck . . .

Shot Dunyun: As Rant reaches into the front seat, to fiddle with the radio controls, written on the back of his hand in blue ballpoint pen it says: P295/30 R22 . . . P285/30 R22 . . . 425/65 R22.5. Obviously tire sizes. Big tires.

Nodding at the blue numbers, I ask him, "Been car-shopping?"

And Rant goes, "How good do you know Echo?" He sits back.

Good enough, I tell him. Pretty good.

Green Taylor Simms feathers the gas pedal, patient. The target car almost touching-close. Almost brushing the line of parked cars. Our two cars moving first-gear slow. The smell of insecticide. The flavor of rabies.

And Rant goes, "Figured maybe I'd get her a present . . ."

Echo is off, working, tonight. Doing some bullshit I don't want to explain here. Complicated shit.

Rant goes, "Really truly with her whole entire heart, does Echo hate somebody?"

I go, doesn't Rant mean "love"?

And Rant shrugs and says, "Ain't it the same thing?"

20 – Junkyards

From the Field Notes of Green Taylor Simms (ℂ *Historian*): For sheer spectacle, the peak of Party Crash culture had to be Tree Nights. The idea, as always, was to choose a flag that the unaware public could dismiss as ordinary, normal— or, at worst, an accident.

Among the accident type of flags were coffee cups and sack lunches. Crash teams utilized these flags on Ooops Nights: For example, during an Ooops "Coffee" game, participants indicated they were in the game by bolting or gluing a large travel mug to the roof of their vehicle. The actual coffee was optional. In the event of an Ooops "Brown Bag" game, teams glued a brown-bag "lunch" to their roof. To the general public, these flags occurred as silly accidents, and unaware drivers might pull alongside laughing and pointing, attempting to get the driver's attention and help resolve the misplaced item.

The "Baby on Board" events used another type of mishap flag. Understandably, public reaction was somewhat less jolly at the sight of a speeding car weaving through traffic with an infant carrier and baby seemingly forgotten on the roof.

Shot Dunyun (© *Party Crasher*): The auctioneer starts the bidding at fifty dollars, saying, "Do I hear fifty? Who wants to give me an opening bid of fifty dollars for Lot Number One?"

This is Sammy's Towing, so this must be Tuesday night. The Wednesday police impound auction is at Radio Retrieval. How organized is this? On Fridays, we'd be at Patrol Towing to preview the cars. Police crime impounds. Abandoned cars. Cars seized in drug busts or for unpaid parking tickets. Cars towed out of pay lots and never claimed, they all go for chump change to the highest bidder.

To find a car you can drive for a few days, paint and glue shit all over, and ram into another junker car, here's your market. Marked with neon-bright grease pencil, yellow or orange, in the windows of some cars you can read "Brken Tming Blt." Or "Eng Mnts crakd." In one big four-door, still messy with "Just Married" toothpaste and hanging tin cans, Auction Lot 42, written on the windshield it says, "Cam lobs scord."

The car up for bid right now, dented and crumpled, you'll find dried blood and hair still caked on the dashboard.

From the Field Notes of Green Taylor Simms: The infant doll and the carrier were, of course, bolted in place. Most teams used the same drilled hole and carriage bolts each week, switching the baby carrier for the coffee mug for the bag lunch. Other teams, as their vehicle accumulated dents and scratches, becoming less attractive as a target, these teams would expand on the basic theme. Instead of a coffee mug, they might bolt an espresso machine and a tray of demitasse cups and saucers to their roof. A basket of *pain au chocolat*. A silver bud vase with a single red rose trembling in the slipstream.

Shot Dunyun: The auctioneer's chanting, "Seventy-five, seventy-five, who'll give me eighty? Who'll bid eighty dollars? Do I hear eighty dollars . . . ?"

Rant and Echo are still poking around the lot, looking under hoods. Echo pointing at bashed, rusted minivans still decorated with shreds of crepe paper and poster-paint words that say "Go Team! Tigers Go to State!" The seats and floor littered with snacks and fast-food wrappers left when the team bailed on a Soccer Mom Night.

Echo opens the driver's door of a coupe, a faded artificial Christmas tree still tied to the roof. With one finger, she punches a button on the stereo, but nothing happens. She punches it again, hard, and a disk pops out. "My favorite chase mix," she says, waving the disk for Rant to see. Echo goes, "I thought I'd never hear it again."

From the Field Notes of Green Taylor Simms: Approaching Thanksgiving, the simple misplaced-coffee-cup theme would expand to include papier-mâché turkeys, painted and varnished to a glossy brown. Sloshing stemmed goblets of red wine. Salt and pepper shakers. And tall white candles in brass holders, their flame bulbs glowing, battery-powered. A display of this extent usually signaled the last event in which a team planned to drive a particular automobile: Mounting dishes of yams and green beans required drilling dozens of holes through the roof and headliner.

For these elaborate vehicle send-offs—known as Funerals or Final Runs—teams arrived at the event grid, or field, no less than an hour before the window. Until the play officially began, these cars would parade and model their decorations, bidding one final, grand farewell before the night's play would leave them in a junkyard.

Shot Dunyun: The script artist inside me still looked for events worth out-cording. I'd reach back and touch my port, ready to switch it. Maybe out-cord an interesting moment of my awareness. The way a rusted car looked. Or the way Rant smiled at Echo when it's just her ass end stuck out from under a half-open hood, her voice muffled by grease and sheetmetal, saying, "This butterfly valve is *fucked*."

A few wrecks away, a bashed hardtop sits up to the rims in mud. Written across the trunk lid in bright-pink paint, sparkle-pink fingernail polish, it says "Cherry Bomb III." Next to the wreck stands Tina Something.

When Tina's fingers curl into fists and she starts stomping through the mud, advancing on Echo's ass, I switch my port to out-cord the carnage.

From the Field Notes of Green Taylor Simms: As I've mentioned, for sheer spectacle nothing surpassed Tree Nights. At those rare events, cars old and new arrived early to show off. The original idea had been to tie an evergreen Christmas tree to the roof of your vehicle, as if you were a happy family bringing it home from the corner lot or the forest. But, like the simple coffee cup that evolved into the feast, soon a plain green pine tree wasn't sufficient.

Teams used artificial trees, of course, tied lengthwise, usually with the stump looming above the car hood and ropes holding it secure to the bumpers. Beginning with the original Tree Night, teams draped their branches with silver tinsel. Teams wired bright stars to the crown that hung and bobbed above the car's trunk. People glued or wired shining ornaments among the needles. As early as two hours before a Tree Night window, Party Crashers will parade; atop their cars, their trees twinkle with colored lights, and a cord trails through a window to their cigarette lighter or vehicle wiring harness. Christmas carols will boom from every car stereo.

The moment the game window opens, those Christmas lights go black. The parading cars go silent. Teams scatter, and the real hunting begins.

Shot Dunyun: The auctioneer is saying, "Forty dollars. Do I have forty dollars? Come on, folks, it costs more than that to fill a gas tank. Do I have thirty dollars . . . ?"

Echo's still leaned over, with both arms buried up to the shoulders in engine, her face cheek-to-cheek with a valve cover, when Tina Something comes to stand behind her, saying, "Hey, whore!"

Rant's planted both elbows on a front fender, peering under the hood at Echo.

The auctioneer's saying, "Do I hear twenty-five? Twenty-five dollars . . . ?"

And Tina says, "You, stop calling bogus fouls on me." Talking to Echo's butt, Tina says, "You foul me out and I'll phone in fake shit on you."

From the Field Notes of Green Taylor Simms: With their Christmas lights extinguished, the Tree Cars become black, shaggy, scratchy . . . monsters. The soft tinkle of swinging glass and crystal drops, a faint clue. A team might drive past any dark hedge or bush only to see it blaze into a hundred colors in their rearview mirror. A squeal of tires, and that mass of sparkling light and color will sideswipe their vehicle and again vanish into the night.

Shot Dunyun: The auctioneer is saying. "Twenty dollars? Can we start the bidding at twenty . . . ?"

And from inside the engine compartment, her face still

against the firewall, Echo says, "Forget you. I don't even know your current plate." Still giving Tina nothing but ass, Echo goes, "How do I call fouls on you if I don't know your plate?"

The auctioneer says, "Twenty! I got twenty. Do I hear twenty-five? Who wants to bid twenty-five . . . ?"

Rant watches Echo, still propped on his elbows, leaning into the fender. Me, I'm still watching, out-cording so I can live this at home later.

Tina says, "Hey, Day Boy . . ." To Rant, louder, she says, "You, with the black teeth! *Day* Boy!"

Rant looks up. His shirtsleeves rolled back to show the bite scars on his forearms.

And Tina says, "Has your girlfriend told you what she does for work? How she makes the cash she spends on wheels?"

Rant says nothing. Just from habit, I spit. Spit again.

One of Echo's arms pulls back, out of the engine compartment, the elbow bending to show a hand. The hand stuffs an adjustable crescent wrench into one back pocket of her pants.

And to Echo's ass, to the wrench poking out of her pocket, Tina Something says, "Your girlfriend you like so much, she fucks for money." Tina crosses her arms over her chest, leans back, and yells, "Your little girlfriend is a gaddamn whore."

From the Field Notes of Green Taylor Simms: The day following a Tree Night, the streets sparkle. They gleam. Gold and silver strands of tinsel flicker and flutter in the wind. Shattered glass ornaments crunch under passing tires.

Shot Dunyun: The auctioneer is saying, ". . . I have twenty-three. A bid of twenty-three dollars. Going once . . ."

Echo steps back, stands, and turns to look at Tina.

And Rant says, "Is that true?"

The auctioneer says, ". . . going twice . . ."

Echo twists her head to both sides until her neck pops, and she says, "Is what true?"

Rant says, "What she said." He says, "Are you really my girlfriend?"

And the auctioneer says, "Sold!"

21—Echo

Canada Mercer (☉ *Software Engineer*): My wife and I
hired Echo Lawrence after a dinner party. A couple we knew,
the Tyson-Neals, had just given birth to their first child, and
the baby's needs kept interrupting the meal. After the mother
had disappeared to tend it for the umpteenth time, the father
remarked, "I'm glad we experimented with three-ways *before*
we started a family." With a newborn, he said, they'd never
have the time and privacy necessary to experiment with
bondage and vibrators and police uniforms. But now all of
that was behind them, so they had no regrets about this baby.
They seemed very happy.

As we left that dinner party, Sarah and I felt so far
behind the curve. Here we were considering a child of our
own, and we'd never even tried anal. We'd never even discussed a three-way. A few days later, we phoned the Tyson-
Neals and asked how they'd met a woman who'd consider
intimacy with a couple. They knew a young lady who
worked with no one except couples our age. A Nighttimer
girl who'd be happy to come to our apartment after the
curfew.

Echo Lawrence (☾ *Party Crasher*): Forget it. The police never found the fucker that smashed into my family. The last I remember of my parents, we were driving. We were always driving. My mother always drove a gray car that came with her job, so covered with dents it looked like tinfoil someone had balled up and then tried to press smooth. As an infrastructure engineer, my mother always lectured me on service flow rates: Level of Service E versus K. She'd stop in the middle of an overpass so we could look at the roadway below with the traffic passing under us, and she'd quiz me about Hourly Volume and the Peak-Hour Factor of measuring traffic flow.

I was asleep across the backseat of that gray car when someone smacked into us, head-on.

Sarah Mercer (○ *Marketing Director*): When she arrived, the young woman had what I'd call a withered arm. One of her elbows was crooked, bent a smidgen, and that hand seemed stunted. The fingers curled into the palm, and she never used them to grasp or lift anything. Her leg on that same side was shorter, and she seemed to swing it from her hip with each step, walking into our living room with a pronounced limp.

She would've been very pretty if it hadn't been for a palsy or paralysis that seemed to leave the left side of her face slack and immobile. The poor dear, she'd come to the last word of a sentence, then stop with her mouth gaping open, clearly trying to force out the exact word. It was agony, the effort it took to not jump in and finish her every thought. After a glass of Merlot, she told us her handicaps stemmed from a single brain injury, caused when her mother had struck her in the head.

Echo Lawrence: I do. I tell people that. My mom did hit me. So did my dad, but not the way I let people imagine. Well, technically, I hit them. At the pulse of the car accident, I came rocketing out of the backseat and hit them both in the back of the head. The officer at the scene never put this on paper, but I broke both their necks. My head slammed against my father's so hard it compressed my right temporal lobe. The tiny arm I have now is the arm I had when I was eight. My leg's grown, a little. The aphasia, when I struggle for words, that's a little put-on. I'll pretend the last word in a sentence is almost choking me to . . . and I'll pause . . . death. Like I can't quite force out the right . . . word. That tension makes people really listen to me.

The car that hit us was another gray sedan owned by the county traffic division, exactly like the one my mother drove. Dinged and dented all over. A head-on collision, and they never found the other driver. Sounds . . . wait for the word . . . fishy.

Sarah Mercer: The girl had grown up an orphan, dating anyone who asked. One of her boyfriends escorted her to a private swingers' club where people do their business in front of each other. He convinced her to have intercourse standing in the center of this club. Entered her from behind. She's the first woman to arrive that evening, so they have plenty of unwanted attention. To endure this, she shuts her eyes, tight. The entire time, her boyfriend holds her withered hand, whispering *"Meine kleine Hure . . ."* in her ear.

Secretly, she's flattered by all the attention, dozens of strange men bothering to watch. When the ordeal is finished, she finds her skin running with something more than sweat. She's awfully glad she kept her shoes on, because she's standing in a little puddle. All their sperm is dripping off of her. Grotesque as it sounds, apparently that evening did wonders for her self-esteem.

Until then, she didn't even know that particular boyfriend spoke German.

Canada Mercer: The subject of venereal disease came up, and she insisted it wasn't a problem. The Lawrence girl, she explained that sex workers regularly perform oral sex as part of foreplay. She told us the true purpose of the act is to routinely test a client for illness. Syphilis, she said, tastes like curried chicken. Hepatitis tastes like veal with capers. Gonorrhea, like sour-cream-and-onion potato chips. HIV, like buttered popcorn. She looked at my wife and said, "Let me lick your pussy and I can tell if you've been exposed to venereal warts, and if you're at risk for developing cervical cancer." Most forms of cancer, she said, taste similar to tartar sauce.

Echo Lawrence: As an adult, I found riding the bus made my hands sweat. Riding in a taxi, I could hardly take a deep breath. Driving, my heart would pound in my ears, and my vision would lose any awareness of colors. I'd get *that close* to fainting. I was so sure I'd be rammed by another car. On an unconscious level, my memory of the head-on collision was controlling me. It got so bad I couldn't cross the street for fear that a driver might run a red light.

My world kept collapsing down, getting smaller and smaller.

Sarah Mercer: Canada will tell you. We had this dear, sweet crippled girl here, and she'd brought along a black leather shoulder bag that she set on the dining-room table. At some point in the evening, she set down her glass of Merlot and

went to the bag, unzipping it and unpacking these . . .
things. Long thick pink rubber things that were so worn in
places that you'd be terrified of them breaking in half inside
of you. Pink rubber that looked stained and smudged. Brown
stains that might've been old blood. Black deposits, where
the batteries had leaked. Things, I couldn't say what they
were. Handcuffs and blindfolds. An enema bag with a nozzle
that didn't look any too clean. Latex gloves. Some horrible
spring-loaded things that looked like jumper cables—she
called them "tit clamps." Everything just reeked of chlorine
bleach.

All these horrors, this girl was putting on my polished
Drexel Heritage dining-room table, right where we set the
turkey at Thanksgiving. And a speculum, oh Lord, so old it
had a crack in the clear plastic. I remember her saying, "You
can do any of these things to me . . ."

Echo Lawrence: My routine—where I talk about tasting
people for hepatitis or gonad warts—I was saying that long
before I met Rant Casey. The fact he could actually do that
trick, it was un-fucking-believable. He licked me one time
and told me to lay off eating whole eggs. From the taste of
my pussy, he said my cholesterol was too high. Later, the
blood work came back that he was dead-on.

Canada Mercer: This girl, Echo, she took out a thick white
candle and lit it, telling us to let the wax melt so we could
pour it onto her bare breasts. She shook out the match and
told us, "I don't want you to torture me just because you *feel
sorry* for me. I want you to really *enjoy* hurting me." She said,
"I want tonight to be about *you*."

The young lady said she despised what she called "*Pity
S & M.*"

Echo Lawrence: Get this. The ideal therapy came to me: If I could just stage an accident and survive it, then I might start to get past my fear. If I could just bump my car into another car and cause a fender bender, then I'd see that fatality accidents are so rare they're not worth the worry. So I started stalking other drivers, looking for the perfect car to bump. The perfect accident. Just one perfect, controlled accident.

A certain car might look perfect, but when I drove close enough to smack my fender, I'd see a baby seat in the back. Or the driver would be so young you knew an accident would destroy their insurance rates. Or I'd trail someone until I could tell they had a terrible minimum-wage job and the last thing they needed was a sprained neck.

Nevertheless, the role reversal helped my nerves. Instead of waiting to be killed by another reckless driver, I'd become the predator. The hunter. All night, I'd be looking. You can't count the number of people I shadowed, trying to decide if I should plow into their car.

Canada Mercer: No, we never did have three-way sex. The girl never took off her coat. A week later, I came home to find Sarah sitting in the kitchen drinking tea with the girl. We paid her two hundred dollars, cash, to drink tea for an hour. Sarah kept telling her how pretty she looked. The week after, I came home and Sarah was washing the girl's hair in the kitchen sink. Sarah gave her a permanent wave with blond highlights, and paid two hundred dollars for each of the three hours it took.

If Sarah could boost her self-esteem, we hoped the girl might find a new career. Talking to her, praising her, we lost track of our plan to have a child of our own. The girl cost so much and took up so much of our free time, I couldn't afford to buy a dog. To this day, we still see her every week. And I do think we're making some headway.

Echo Lawrence: My perfect accident turned out to be some guy with a dead deer tied across the roof of his car. Some fucking Bambi-killer, a guy wearing a camouflage jacket and a hat with ear flaps. He's driving a fuggly four-door sedan with the dead deer roped lengthwise, its head laying at the top of the windshield.

In the city, a dead deer's not something you can lose sight of very easily, so I keep my distance and track him through neighborhoods, biding my time, looking for the perfect spot to nail his killer ass. Somewhere an accident won't block traffic or endanger bystanders.

Get this. I'm hunting him the same way he stalked that poor four-legged creature. Waiting to get my best shot.

I mean, I'm really getting off on this. I'm so fucking excited. I scoot through yellow traffic lights, staying a field of cars behind him. I slow and drop back when he turns, then make the same turn. I let cars slip between us so he won't notice how long I've been in his rearview mirror.

At one point, I lose the fucker. A light goes red, but he runs it and cuts a right turn around the next corner. All my months of tracking, and my perfect accident's escaped. The light goes green, and I sprint to find him, turn the same corner, but he's gone. Down another block, I'm scanning my way through intersections, hoping for a glimpse of that deer corpse, that poor, sad murdered deer, but there's nothing, fucking *nada*. Nobody. My watch was ticking toward morning curfew, and the last thing I needed was a fucking five-hundred-buck ticket for getting caught outside in the daylight.

Sarah Mercer: We called the Tyson-Neals, and they admitted to never having sex with the girl, either. The reason they'd finally decided to have a child was because it penciled out as cheaper than seeing Echo every week.

Echo Lawrence: Listen up. I'm driving home, at least happy that I won't get a past-curfew ticket or be facing some redneck hunter over his crushed quarter-panel—when I see the dead deer. The car's pulled off the street, idling in the drive-through lane of a fast-food place. The driver's window is rolled down, and a bearded face is barking at the menu speaker. In the fluorescent drive-through lights, the car looks spotted with rust. The paint, scratched. Most of the car is piss yellow, but the driver's door is sky blue. The trunk lid is beige. I pull over and wait.

A hand passes a white bag out the drive-through window, the driver gives the hand some paper money. Another beat, and the piss-yellow car eases across the curb, moving into traffic. Before he can disappear again, I'm on his tail. I pull my seat belt tight across my hips. A heartbeat before my front bumper should smack his backside, I take a deep breath. I shut my eyes and stomp the gas pedal.

And again, fucking *nada*. The car's jetted ahead, darting between other cars so fast the deer's dead ass waves its tail back and forth in my face.

Chasing him, I forget I have a bum arm and leg. I forget that half my face can't smile. Chasing him, I'm not an orphan or a girl. I'm not a Nighttimer with a crummy apartment. The deer's ass dodges through traffic, and that's all I see.

Up ahead, a light turns red. The piss-yellow car, its brake lights flare red as it slows to turn right. For a blink, the deer's gone, until I follow it around the curve. And there, on a quiet side street, without bystanders or police, I shut my eyes and . . . kah-*blam*.

The sound, that sound's still recorded in my head. It's time frozen solid. My only wish is that I'd out-corded the chase and attack, but I'll still never forget it.

My front end is buried so deep in his trunk that the dead

deer's swung loose. The ropes broke, and the deer's busted open. At about the belly, the carcass has torn into two pieces. And inside, instead of blood and guts, the deer is—white. Solid white.

The driver throws his door open and climbs out, bearded. His camouflage jacket quilted and huge. The ear flaps of his hat flapping with every step toward me.

I say, "Your fucking deer . . ." I say, "It's fake."

And the guy says, "Of course it's fake."

I say, "It's . . . Styrofoam?"

The deer, turns out it's a life-size deer target for bow hunters to shoot at.

And the hunter, he goes, "Where's your damned flag?" Walking around to the back of my car, looking at my license plate, he says, "You better believe I'm calling fouls on you— no flag, way too much impact—multiple fouls."

Canada Mercer: We never did get around to experimenting with bondage and police uniforms. For Christmas, we asked Echo what she wanted Santa Claus to bring her, and she told us a "fisting dildo." Instead, we chipped in with the Tyson-Neals and a few other couples and bought her a car. It would seem she's a terrible driver.

Echo Lawrence: Those fucking blond highlights, I couldn't wait for those to grow out.

Sarah Mercer: To this day, I still have no appetite whatsoever for tartar sauce.

22–A History

From the Field Notes of Green Taylor Simms (ℂ *Historian*): For myself, personally, my reason for participating in Party Crash events is quite simple: I hold my life as precious. I adore my friends and family. I treasure my health and the myriad capabilities of my aged yet healthy body and mind.

I consider myself to be enormously gifted with good fortune, but accidents do happen. Annually in this nation, approximately sixteen thousand people are murdered. During the same period of time, approximately forty-three thousand die in motor-vehicle accidents.

Every time I operate a motor vehicle, all of what I treasure can be taken. Stolen in an instant without due process. When you're aboard a motor vehicle, death passes within a finger's length every few moments. Anytime a vehicle passes mine in the oncoming lanes, I could be subjected to torture more violent and painful than anything the world's dictators would ever stoop to inflict. Perhaps another driver has eaten nothing except hamburgers for his entire life, and as his car approaches mine on the freeway, his clogged heart fails. Blind with pain, he clutches his seizing chest. His automobile veers to one side, colliding with mine, and forcing me into another car, a gasoline tanker truck, a guardrail, over a cliff.

Despite my lifetime of declining rich desserts, my evenings spent jogging, regardless of all my careful moderation and self-discipline—I'm trapped, wadded inside a shell of steel and aluminum. My body, violated in countless places by fragments of broken glass. My low-cholesterol blood rushes to abandon me in hot, leaping spurts.

Despite all my care, the heart-attack victim and I will both be just as dead.

Accidents do happen.

Echo Lawrence came to Party Crashing to help resolve her personal history. Mr. Dunyun, to experience an actual event after his life spent boosting other people's recorded adventures. And I'd speculate that Rant Casey simply enjoys being among other human beings. I came to Party Crashing because accidents happen. People you love will die. Nothing you treasure will last forever. And I need to accept and embrace that fact.

Irene Casey (☀ *Rant's Mother*): I recollect, come about this time we got a letter from Buddy. Tucked in the same envelope was a snapshot of him kissing some strange boy. I didn't know what to think of that. In one photo, Buddy looked dressed up in a shirt and tie for a friend's wedding, so Chester said there was still hope. Buddy wrote us that he was working for a bug exterminator, and he had his own apartment. He wrote about going to a dentist. A girl he met was teaching him yoga. A girl, thank God.

We wrote back to say Cammy Elliot had asked after him at church. She'd just got her last round of rabies shots. In case he got hungry with his new friends, I sent him a batch of fudge. The kind he likes best. With plenty of chopped walnuts and thumbtacks.

From the Field Notes of Green Taylor Simms: Prior to the inception of the Infrastructure Effective and Efficient Use Act—the I-SEE-U Act, as people refer to it—when transportation engineers endeavored to make the system carry more vehicles, their first tactic was to study the ways traffic flow fails. What was the chain reaction that starts with a sideswipe and backs up vehicles to the horizon in every direction? Much of this you'll have to swallow on faith. No Freedom of Information paperwork is going to confirm something this confidential. There exists no official mention of the mercenary Contractor Cars. On paper, the government refers to the project as "Incidence Event Prompting."

Irene Casey: Some of the other snapshots Buddy sent, they showed his new best friends. Another snapshot showed a girl who didn't look healthy. Her one arm was, oh my, like a skinny praying-mantis arm. Just a itty-bitty arm, with the hand pulled up to her chest. The little fingers held one end of this pink baseball bat, so long that the top of the bat rested on her shoulder. She was sitting cross-legged on the carpet, and her other, regular hand looked to be rubbing the baseball bat with a square of sandpaper. In other photos, the girl is rubbing smudges of shoe polish on her pink baseball bat. That girl wouldn't be doing messy work like that, not on my carpet.

From the Field Notes of Green Taylor Simms: Incidence Event Prompting boiled down to trans-staff engineers requisitioning old, unmarked pool cars and intentionally colliding with each other on busy arterials during peak traffic times in order to study the effect. The project killed two birds with one stone: First, obsolete four-door sedans went to the scrap heap to better serve humanity. That, and the traffic engineers accumulated video documenting how drivers react to an accident in their immediate presence.

None of the engineers impacted with enough velocity to hurt their comrades, and none of the events was worse than paint scratches and sheetmetal body damage. Still, on video you see traffic immediately slow to a voyeuristic crawl. The infamous and bothersome rubberneck effect.

Brannan Benworth, D.M.D. (ℂ Dentist): According to our files, Buster Casey made a single visit to our office. I have one hygienist who still talks about his teeth. The worst stains she's ever seen. Mr. Casey was referred by a longtime patient, a favorite among the office staff, a young man named Karl Waxman.

From the Field Notes of Green Taylor Simms: Community busybodies, thin-skinned control freaks, they complain about the traffic reports on DRVR Radio. The Graphic Traffic Updates. That voice announcing the tag line: "We Know Why You Rubberneck . . ." Naturally, the Transportation Department is behind that radio show. The transportation engineers simply wanted to see if drivers would continue to gawk if they knew exactly what they'd see. If a radio personality was telling them the grimmest details, would traffic still snarl?

The transportation agency monitors paramedic frequencies and passes the DRVR announcer the gory facts. A majority of the general public adores that show. People swoon over traffic accidents. A quick peek or a good long gape.

Echo Lawrence (ℂ *Party Crasher*): Yeah, I wanted Rant to do yoga before Party Crashing. Everybody should, just to stay limber and avoid getting hurt. Yoga and stretching. I showed him the Down Dog pose and the Rabbit. We were practicing the Archer when he asked me about the hit man Tina Something goes around with, her boyfriend, Karl Waxman. Rant really admired the asshole's teeth.

Tina Something (ℂ *Party Crasher*): I don't give a gaddamn what the police say. Wax did not kill that hillbilly.

From the Field Notes of Green Taylor Simms: Long before modern Party Crashing, the traffic engineers were running each other down. The videos show them, four geeks in each gray car: one engineer steering, one in charge of documenting with the camera, two engineers on lookout for other gray pool cars covered with dents and scratches. Each car the same government issue: four-cylinder, automatic-transmission, three-point seat belts, and a big "No Smoking" sign riveted to the dashboard.

The pool-car boys loved to hunt each other. Those gray pool sedans were so easy to find, especially after bankers' hours ended. With full-coverage health insurance, driving a car not their own, with complete permission and encouragement to crash—and getting paid overtime wages, to boot—the infrastructure teams treasured their work.

Jarrell Moore (ℂ *Private Investigator*): Our firm was able to locate one likely candidate who fit the client's vague description for a biological father. An individual by the name of Charles Casey. That's the good news. That Charles Casey, aka "Charlie," attained Nighttimer status and housing under the I-SEE-U recruitment program. He did work a variety of city-government jobs while enrolled in college.

From the Field Notes of Green Taylor Simms: Event Prompting was so exciting that when the study window ran out and manpower was reassigned to flow studies and traffic-light timing, these traffic geeks couldn't give it up. Even without a paycheck attached, and forced to wreck their own cars, those original engineers kept up their games. Naturally, outsiders caught on. No matter how diligently you keep something a secret—accidents do happen.

Jarrell Moore: The bad news is, the Charles Casey we found has been missing and presumed dead for almost sixteen years. He'd been a traffic-flow engineer for the city and died in a work-related car accident. It seems he'd requisitioned a car from the department motor pool, then ran it head-on into another car, driven by a female co-worker. The woman and her husband were both killed. Their daughter, who'd been asleep in the backseat of their vehicle, was left handicapped by the accident.

Charles Casey's body was not recovered at the scene. The couple he killed, their names were Larry and Suprema Lawrence.

Irene Casey: By the last snapshot that Buddy sent home, you can tell that crippled girl, she's not sanding and refinishing a baseball bat. That thick pink club she's rubbing on with sandpaper and steel wool, and staining with shoe polish and old tea bags, it looks exactly like some giant's sex thingy. A girl like that, with a gimp arm, making herself a dirty, big-man thingy . . . It's a stretch to see that girl as the mama of my future grandbabies.

From the Field Notes of Green Taylor Simms: Strange as it sounds, emergency service personnel continue to channel Tina Something the gory details of each drive-time accident. Everyone with a government letterhead will deny this, but it's true.

It's all connected. The I-SEE-U Act. Team slamming.
Night versus day. Graphic Traffic. Our tax money was the
springboard for what eventually became the Party Crashing
culture. The pool-car boys, those unsung engineers, their
study recommendation split this country into day and night.
And they brought us the number-one-rated daytime radio
program in this market.

Echo Lawrence: Yes, fuck, yes. The name on my dad's tomb-
stone is Lawrence Lawrence. That's not funny. But Waxman
did kill Rant. Sure, he's got great teeth, but the man's evil.

Shot Dunyun (ⓒ *Party Crasher*): Beyond evil.

23—Love

Shot Dunyun (€ *Party Crasher*): The minute Rant comes to me asking what model car has the biggest backseat, I could tell where he was headed. My advice was, I told him to get a car with dark upholstery.

Echo Lawrence (€ *Party Crasher*): Forget it. Our first time alone, I asked Rant what he *really* wanted from me. Did he plan to go around with me, then take me home as a fugly club to beat on his parents? Was dating a deformed cripple his last act of teenage rebellion? A surefire way to freak out the folks down on the farm?

Or was I some erotic fantasy? Was sex too boring with normal girls, people with two arms and legs that matched, mouths that could kiss back? Was fucking me some one-time goal in the great scavenger hunt of his sex life?

Or was I just the only girl he knew in the big, bad city? His mentor. A guide into the Nighttimer life. Was sex his way of clinging to me because he was too afraid to be alone in this scary new world?

Sitting in the backseat of that Eldorado, I really let Rant have it with both barrels. We'd parked next to some bushes, away from streetlights, but it's never totally dark in town. I can remember Rant wore his blue bug suit, and smelled toxic. None of this sounds very romantic.

Shot Dunyun: Part of my job, renting bullshit peaks to idiots, is to boost a few myself and stay familiar with the various current titles. For that couple weeks, all we got from the distributors were defective transcripts. I'd be boosting a dessert peak, and the taste track would cut out. A thick slice of chocolate cake would become a mouthful of sticky, greasy pulp. It smelled like chocolate, but in your mouth the cake was nothing but gummy texture. Trapped at home during curfew, one day I boosted my favorite porno peak, and none of the vaginas smelled like anything. The transcripts weren't the problem. My brain was the problem.

Echo Lawrence: Sitting in that Eldorado, Rant looks at me until I stop talking. He waits about two traffic lights' worth of silence, then he says, "What did you eat for breakfast yesterday?"

No cars go past. The street's empty. Rant's eyes float in the shadows. His black teeth, invisible.

Yesterday? In my kitchen, I have frozen waffles, but when I go out to Tommy's Diner I order the hash. I tell Rant, "Cereal." I say, "No, wait. French toast. No . . . cinnamon toast . . ."

Rant's hand slides across the seat until his fingers touch mine. He lifts my hand to his face, his lips touching my knuckles, he sniffs, eyes closed, and says, "Wrong." He says, "Yesterday, you had rolled-oat granola with maple sugar and pumpkin seeds, vanilla yogurt, and dried cranberries . . ."

And of course he's dead-on.

Shot Dunyun: Most boosted peaks are bullshit compared to even the slowest night spent Party Crashing, spending time in a car with people and music and snack food, always in a little danger. On a secret mission to meet more strangers. Real people. A road trip to nowhere.

Nonetheless, I'd been boosting peaks since I was in diapers. My parents used to port me to infant-enrichment peaks. Half my childhood I spent plugged into babysitting peaks. As a transcript artist, not being able to plug in would make me the equivalent of a blind painter or a deaf musician. Beyond my worst nightmare.

Echo Lawrence: Rant lifted my hand toward me, saying, "Smell." And I leaned forward to smell, nothing but my skin, my soap, the plastic smell of my old nail polish. His smell of insecticide.

With my head bent down to meet my hand, Rant leans close to put his nose in my hair, his lips at the side of my neck, under my ear; he sniffs and says, "What was for supper two nights ago?"

My fingers still tangled with his fingers. His breath against my neck. With his lips and the warm tip of his tongue pressed wet on my pulse, the heartbeat in my neck, I say, "Turkey?" I say, "Lasagna?"

And Rant's warm breath, his whisper against my ear, he says, "Taco salad. White onions, not yellow or red." He says, "Shredded iceberg lettuce. Ground chicken."

My nipples already getting hard, I ask, "Light or dark meat?"

Shot Dunyun: A head cold can distort how a peak will boost, the same way food never tastes the same when you're sick. It must be I was catching a cold. But a week later, with no runny nose or sore throat, I still couldn't plug in and boost a good peak. By then, I was picturing a brain tumor.

Echo Lawrence: Kissing my eyelids, Rant whispered, "You should throw out those roses . . ."

He had never been to my apartment. Back then, Rant didn't even know where I lived. I asked him, "What roses?"

"Were they from a boyfriend?" he says.

I asked him to tell me the color of the roses.

"Were they from a girlfriend?" he says.

I asked if he'd been stalking me.

And Rant says, "Pink." Still kissing my forehead, smelling and tasting my skin, my closed eyes, my nose and cheeks, he says, "Two dozen. Nancy Reagan roses mixed with baby's breath and white little-bitty carnations."

They were a gift, I tell him, from a nice middle-aged couple I sometimes work for.

Shot Dunyun: The doctor at the clinic calls me a week later—really just a lady from the clinic calls—and says I need to come back at my earliest convenience. She won't go into any details about my blood work. They get that bullshit smile in their voice, and you know it's not good news. The billing department just really needs full payment before you croak. So I go, and the doc says—it's rabies. No shit, rabies. He gives me the first of the five injections. He won't promise that I'll ever be able to boost another peak.

Right from the clinic, from the pay phone in the waiting room, I phoned Echo and told her to never, never, ever let Rant Casey put his mouth on hers.

Echo Lawrence: Kissing my mouth, Rant tells me my showerhead is brass instead of chrome. From the smell and taste of me, he says I sleep on goose-down pillows. I have a coconut-scented candle I've never lighted.

Lew Terry (℃ *Property Manager*): The only occasion I entered Mr. Casey's apartment was with our standard twenty-four-hour notice to enter premises. Rumor was, he kept pets. My first look around, I didn't see nothing. A mattress on the floor. A telephone message machine. A suitcase. In the closet, hanging, are those blue coveralls that were the only clothes you ever saw him wear. Clean or dirty, Casey smelled like poison.

If somebody says I took anything, there was nothing to take.

Echo Lawrence: I didn't let Rant kiss me because he smelled my food. I kissed him after seeing how gentle he treated this huge fugly spider. As we sat there in the backseat of the Eldorado, he unzipped the pocket of his coat and reached one hand inside. He opened his fingers to show me the biggest monster spider. Slowly turning his hand over, he watched the spider crawl from the palm to the back, perched on the big veins.

Both of us looking at this monster spider, I say, "Is it poisonous?"

Shiny, not hairy. Legs thin as eight jet-black hypodermic needles, the spider bends all eight knees, lowering itself to touch Rant's skin.

This spider looks as ugly as I feel.

And Rant says, "I call her Doris."

Lew Terry: It's there, in the back of Casey's closet, lined up on the floor, I find the jars. Different sizes of mayonnaise and pickle and spaghetti-sauce jars, clear glass and washed out. At first they look empty, but I unscrew one lid. There's nothing inside, but when I go to put the lid back, on the underneath side of each lid sits a huge black spider. Huge, grizzly bastards.

No matter what anybody says, I didn't take anything. Not money or anything.

Echo Lawrence: Our breath fogged the car windows, but, watching that spider, neither of us could breathe out. The moment Rant breathed, the spider had bit him. He inhaled, and I inhaled, and Rant said, "Roll down your window."

I opened the window.

Leaning across me, Rant stuck his hand into the night air. Shaking the spider into the bushes next to the car, he said, "Good night, Dorry."

Leaned across my lap, his hips pressed into mine, I could already feel the effects of the black widow spider venom.

Todd Rutz (◎ *Coin Dealer*): About the same time the Casey kid was selling me coins, I met Lew Terry. Terry used to bring me a few good specimens. If I recall, a 1910 Indian Head quarter in extremely fine condition. A 1907 Liberty Head quarter in AU-50 condition. Nothing spectacular, but I bought them. It wasn't until the police interviewed me that I found out Terry and Casey lived in the same apartment house.

Echo Lawrence: As Rant's lips move down my throat, I challenge him to smell what type of birth control I'm on.

As his lips move down my chest, Rant says, "None. You had your period thirty-four—no—thirty-six hours ago."

When I said "down my throat," I meant on the outside.

Todd Rutz: This Lew Terry character, it's obvious he's a born Nighttimer. Pale. His face and hands clear as the skin he was born into. Always he wore the same oily-brown trench coat and a knitted kind of brown stocking hat pulled down too far.

Echo Lawrence: "Besides," Rant says, "why would a virgin use birth control?"

Todd Rutz: One night in my shop, this Terry character offers me the Liberty Head and the Indian Head and tells me he needs to see fifteen hundred dollars out of the deal.

Echo Lawrence: Of course I was a virgin. With this twisted little branch for an arm. Half the time I couldn't tell, but I'd be drooling out one corner of my mouth. The palsy side. With my job, I'd made a cottage fucking industry out of being as unappealing as possible. Do you think I could just vamp it up? Snap my fingers, and go from sideshow freak to sex kitten?

Todd Rutz: Time passed, and the Casey kid would turn up with lesser and lesser coins. Buffalo nickels. Wheat pennies. Nothing worth remembering. His stash had to be running low.

Echo Lawrence: The next night, Rant sent me two dozen red fucking roses. And the keys to a Galaxie 500.

Shot Dunyun: Those bullshit rabies shots took forever. It didn't help that I kept reinfecting myself with my own tooth-brush. By the end, my port went as dead as the knob on the back of Rant Casey's neck. Beyond dead.

Lew Terry: The only other detail I remember from Casey's apartment, stuck on the wall next to his bed, I found all these little lumps. Round and dark, like bugs. Soft, like little balls of hashish. Except they didn't taste like hash.

Echo Lawrence: Our first night alone in the Eldorado, all I could think was: Thank God the leather seats are dark burgundy.

24–Werewolves II

Vivica Brawley (☾ *Dancer*): See how, my one foot, the skin looks smooth and white as a bar of soap? Before the attack, I used to have beautiful feet. Tons of men said so. Didn't matter was I naked, all I needed to do was slip off my shoes and some customers would fork over their tip money.

Phoebe Truffeau, Ph.D. (☉ *Epidemiologist*): At the height of the Peloponnesian War, in 431 B.C., Thucydides wrote of a plague that spread north from Ethiopia, through Egypt and Libya. In Athens, the citizens suffered fevers, sneezing, and a violent cough. Their bodies glowed red with lividity, until thousands threw off their clothing, and an unquenchable thirst drove them to drown in the deep, cool water of public wells and cisterns. The city-state was demoralized, its navy crippled. This is how measles destroyed the civilization of the ancient Greeks.

In the first century B.C., a virulent strain of smallpox drove the Huns west from their homelands in Mongolia, toward Rome. For Napoleon's Grand Army, the ultimate foe would be the bacteria *Rickettsia prowazekii*, otherwise known as typhus.

Our greatest civilizations have always been destroyed by epidemic disease.

Carlo Tiengo (ℂ *Nightclub Manager*): Viv? Mind you, back then all the dancers boosted some effect to stay high, at least while they were performing. Most our dancers indulged in an opiate effect the club knew to provide.

Not exactly legal, mind you, but easy to make. Somebody gets high—an actual, primary high, shooting or snorting—then they boost some packaged episode, let's say a Little Becky transcript. They out-cord their experience, then we run a subtraction equation on that script to strip out the original Little Becky. What's left over is pure opiate effect. A wireless high. Just a rush we can narrow-cast on the stage, looping it so the effect never lets up. A dancer steps into that feel-good spotlight and she won't have a care in the world.

Phoebe Truffeau, Ph.D.: In 1347, England was a nation of grain farmers, cultivating and exporting corn. That year, Italian traders arrived in Genoa with the Black Plague, and by 1377, one and one-half million English were dead, as much as a third of the population. Because agrarian labor was in such short supply, the entire economy switched from producing corn to raising sheep, and the English feudal system had been destroyed.

Vivica Brawley: Bernie was working the door. It's horrible what happened. Them tearing him apart the way they did, before the cops came around.

Carlo Tiengo: The customers, mind you, they're a different matter. Our business is, we sell a one-time, primary experience. We catch anybody transcribing or out-cording their experience in the club, and they're eighty-sixed.

To protect our product, we made it policy to broadcast a scramble effect. Renders any active port inoperative. Jammed. If we didn't, you'd have script artists sitting ringside, out-cording every dancer, and dumping her on the Web. One out-corded lap dance can wreck the career of some poor girl. The first shitheel pays to be with her, but everyone after him gets her for free.

Phoebe Truffeau, Ph.D.: During the Great Plague of London in 1665, the weekly death rate fluctuated between one hundred and four hundred persons until July 1. By the middle of July, the weekly death rate had risen to two thousand. By the end of July, sixty-five hundred were dying each week, and by the end of August, seven thousand. Though the common source of bubonic plague had been fleas carried by the European black rat (*Rattus rattus*), the explosion in new infections arose from a change in disease transmission. Instead of bites from fleas, the causative organism, *Pasteurella pestis*, had begun spreading from person to person via droplets of saliva and mucus ejected in coughs and sneezes.

Carlo Tiengo: It's the rabies, why we had so much business lately. These perverts come down with it, and they can't boost their secondhand smut off the Web. They're forced to come downtown and pay for a primary experience. Mind you, I should've known. Any Tuesday night, we see more than six fellows in the audience, that's a warning sign. The night we lost Bernie, there had to be fifty Droolers around the stage. Twitching. Spit looped in long strings out the corners of their lips. They squint, even in the dim light. All those tendencies, obvious rabies symptoms.

Phoebe Truffeau, Ph.D.: Beginning in 1490, a new epidemic spread across Europe and Asia. The first symptom was a small ulcer at the site of infection, which disappeared after three to eight weeks, leaving a faint scar. Within a few weeks, the victim appeared free of infection. The Chinese called it the "Canton disease." The Japanese, the "Chinese disease." To the French, it was the "Spanish disease." And to the English, it was the "French pox." The modern name is derived from a shepherd imagined in 1530 by Girolamo Frascatoro in his poem "Syphilis sive Morbus Gallicus."

Vivica Brawley: One of my regulars, this balding Nighttimer, he didn't look so good. He's sitting with both elbows propped on the padded edge of the stage, drooling, drool running down his chin, real shiny. The rule is, no touching, but he reaches out a five-dollar bill, folded long-ways, like he's going to slip it between my toes. He's a Teamster, if I remember.

Used to be I always had a French-tipped pedicure, back when I still had ten toes. These days, if I took off my shoes in a salon, the girl who does the nails would run screaming.

Phoebe Truffeau, Ph.D.: In its late latent stage, tertiary syphilis weakens the walls of blood vessels, leading to death by heart failure or stroke. The disease also enters the central nervous system, damaging the brain. Symptoms include personality changes marked by a manic optimism and increased excitability, which ends in general paralysis of the insane (GPI). This hyperactivity, in tandem with the disinhibitions caused by said brain damage, can also spur the infected individual to seek the pleasure of compulsive, casual sexual activity, further spreading the disease, and earning syphilis the common moniker of "Cupid's disease."

Carlo Tiengo: Viv's poking her toes the way she does to accept tips. The Drooler's just some perv who stops in after work on his payday. He stands up from his stool and leans over the edge of the stage. Viv's sitting, leaned back on her hands, pushing one foot into his face, the ways pervs like. Then she's screaming.

Vivica Brawley: See here, on my right foot, where the three little toes should be? That's how much he crammed in his mouth. The bald Teamster. He grabs both hands around my ankle and bites down, and I'm screaming for Bernie. Carlo's behind the bar, doing nothing. With my other heel, I'm kicking the Teamster in the forehead, in the eyes. That's when Bernie grabs him by the shoulder from behind and spins him around.

The sound of his teeth coming together, the "click" is still in my head. Since the moment I heard that click, my foot's looked how it does.

Phoebe Truffeau, Ph.D.: Prior to 1564, Ivan IV, the first Tsar of All the Russias, had allowed freedom of opinion and speech. Ivan accepted petitions from all classes of his subjects, and even the poorest citizen had access to him. Of his three sons, one died at six months, one was lethargic and dim-witted, and the third joined his father as the elder gradually earned the nickname Ivan the Terrible.

All three sons suffered from congenital syphilis. As their father's cerebral syphilis progressed beyond 1564, he subjected thousands to execution by burning and boiling. In the city of Novgorod, the Tsar and his son spent five weeks flogging prisoners to death, roasting them alive, or drowning them below river ice. On November 19, 1581, the Tsar stabbed his son and namesake to death with a steel-pointed spear.

Carlo Tiengo: Benjamin Searle, people called him "Bernie," he was huge. Easily three hundred pounds. Played professional ball for one season with the Raiders. Bernie spun the psycho around. Pried his jaws off Viv's foot and spun him around, and the psycho sinks his teeth into the side of Bernie's neck. The vein they got there. The juggler.

Phoebe Truffeau, Ph.D.: Among those crippled and killed by syphilis was England's King Henry VIII, as well as France's Charles VIII and Francis I. Artists include Benvenuto Cellini, Toulouse-Lautrec, and the writer Guy de Maupassant.

In the Paris of 1500, a third of the citizens carried syphilis. Among the French nobility, those who were not infected, Erasmus reported, were condemned by their peers as being ignorant and crude. By 1579, the surgeon William Clowes reported that three-quarters of Londoners carried the disease.

Vivica Brawley: Weird what you remember, but I looked at my foot, and I see wire sticking out. Silver wire and pink plastic. And for one crazy second I think, I'm a robot, some kind of an android. And I'm only just finding out . . . But not really. I'm stoned on the boosted effect, and I'm bleeding and in shock. But I'm no android.

The wire is, the bald guy wore a partial upper, a partial upper denture, and the two teeth of it are still stuck in my foot. His real teeth are dug into Bernie's throat.

Phoebe Truffeau, Ph.D.: As with bubonic plague, the transmission rate of syphilis exploded due to a change in the nature of the causative organism. Rather than being imported from the New World, it's more likely the disease was originally the African skin infection known as yaws, which was primarily spread by body contact among children playing nude. Bacteriologically, the two diseases are identical, although yaws is spread by any physical contact involving skin eruptions. Because of the clothing needed in the colder climate of Europe, yaws emerged as a disease spread through the predominant method of greeting: a mouth-to-mouth kiss. Only as syphilis became epidemic did Europeans abandon the kiss for the handshake, and the disease assumed its current venereal form.

Carlo Tiengo: It's the sight of blood or something, but every Drooler and perv in the club piles on top of Bernie. Viv and the other girls lock themselves backstage. The bartender and me, we're locked in the office, calling to get the cops. The door is solid oak, thick as a telephone book, and we can still hear Bernie bellowing for help.

Phoebe Truffeau, Ph.D.: It would not be unrealistic to assume that—like bubonic plague and syphilis—the current rabies epidemic is due to casual contact, becoming a zymotic disease common to crowded cities. Like syphilis, the disease brings the subject to an agitated state where he is more likely to seek out and infect others. Additionally, the damage caused by the *Lyssavirus* to the central nervous system prevents the sufferer from "boosting" or otherwise enjoying the solitary entertainment of neural transcripts. This inability increases the likelihood the infected individual will seek amusement outside his home, indulging in risky social interaction such as "Party Crashing" and casual sex.

Vivica Brawley: Poor Bernie. After the cops shot everybody, they had to autopsy their stomachs to find all the bites people took. Bernie's ears and nose and his lips. The surgeons at the hospital showed me some toes in a pan of salt water and offered to reattach them. The toenails still had their nice white-tipped French pedicure.

But I just looked at those toes all chewed up by a Teamster and half digested, and I told the doctors, "Don't bother."

25–The Patsy

Irene Casey (☉ *Rant's Mother*): Depends on if you believe that deformed girl or you believe the police, but their first night together was the same night Buddy was supposed to have killed that lady. The one owned the little pet store, that Libby woman.

Shot Dunyun (☾ *Party Crasher*): What's to love most about Party Crashing is how close it matches real life. I mean, a drunk driver doesn't care that you've been painting for years and your first gallery show opens next week. How bogus is that? The fifteen-hundred-pound elk, the one standing in the shadows at the edge of the road, ready to jump, it has no idea that your baby is due next week.

The greasy brake lining or the cell-phone talker . . .

The loose lug nuts or drowsy truck driver . . .

It doesn't matter for crap that you've got three years of sobriety or that you finally look good in a two-piece bathing suit or you've met that perfect someone and you've fallen deeply, wildly, passionately in love. Today, as you pick up your dry cleaning, fax those reports, fold your laundry, or wash the dinner dishes, something you'd never expect is already stalking you.

Officer Romie Mills (ℂ *Homicide Detective*): Edith Libby, the victim, was five-foot-eight, 128 pounds. Her body was discovered during the morning curfew sweep in an area bordering on both Nighttimer and Daytimer districts. The cause of death wasn't readily apparent. Nor were any injuries evident. The location in question was not surveyed by the existing system of street cameras.

Shot Dunyun: That bullet or drunk driver or tumor with your name on it, the way I tolerate that fact is by Party Crashing. Here's one night when I control the chaos. I participate with the doom I can't control. I'm dancing with the inevitable, and I survive.

My regular little dress rehearsal.

From the Field Notes of Green Taylor Simms (ℂ *Historian*): Any idea of Progress depends on not looking at the past too closely. It's undeniable that the streets are less crowded than they were before the inception of the I-SEE-U curfews, but society will always have to manage a certain amount of resentment among people who feel short-changed by their immediate circumstances.

Lynn Coffey (ℂ *Journalist*): You study any pretty democracy, from the ancient Greeks forward, and you'll see that the only way each system functions is with a working class of slaves. Peons to haul the garbage so the upper crust can campaign and vote. Nighttimers had become that—an effective and efficient method to sweep the slave class out of sight.

Forgive me, but after two decades of reporting on local

politics, I guess I've earned the right to finally tell the truth. And the truth is, no Nighttimer has ever been elected President.

Officer Romie Mills: Wade Morrison was another story. Age: twenty-four. A born Nighttimer. Middle of one night, he collapsed, just as dead as the Libby victim. Granted, we weren't treating these deaths as homicides per se, not until they began to form a pattern.

Lynn Coffey: It's still segregation, only not by space—the backseat of a bus or the balcony of a movie theater. It's segregation by time. Go ahead, call it a social contract, like speed limits or building codes, but it's still living on the graveyard shift. One clock tick past that curfew, and you'll find out just how equal you are.

The fallback argument is that Nighttimers can always leave an urban area and live in a rural district not subject to the I-SEE-U Act. But that takes money. Plus, the majority of jobs and education opportunities are in cities.

Officer Romie Mills: With the Morrison killing, we had testimony that the victim had been subject to mood swings and aggressive outbursts. In a typical outburst, the deceased had been denied service by a Daytimer after the morning curfew. A key method of curfew enforcement is to levy fines against businesses that serve or sell merchandise to people who prove to be out of their domiciles in violation of their time status. In the case of Wade Morrison, a clerk at a corner grocery asked to see his status card. When Morrison turned out to be a Nighttimer, the daytime clerk refused to sell him cigarettes, and witnesses report Morrison made verbal threats and left the store.

Irene Casey: While all this went on, Buddy's squiring that girl with her lopsided face.

Oh, they had his fingerprints recorded, the government, from when he sent in his application to go be a night person. They knowed every detail they needed to set him up as a patsy. A boy like that, somebody coming from nowhere and nothing, they needed to find themselves a nobody, and that's what happened.

From the Field Notes of Green Taylor Simms: Among the protest elements of Nighttime culture, my favorite is the faction that seeks to outlaw the sun. They market clothing and bumper stickers emblazoned with their slogans. For example: "Ban the Sun." Or "Moonlight Is Enough Light." Unfortunately, I can see how this might worry the powers that be. The last ordeal this nation needs is a civil war pitting night against day.

Another common bumper sticker says: "Take Back the Day!"

One man's joke can very easily become another's call to arms. Historians speculate that *Mein Kampf* was created as a rather cunning satire, a parody that the general public interpreted far too literally.

Lynn Coffey: It was Thomas Jefferson who warned us that any nation would always need a frontier as an escape valve or a place to store the perennial tide of lunatics and idiots. That's not anywhere in the official propaganda, but nighttime is the big trash bin for your mental defectives. Your angry loners. Your cripples. Nighttimers get free health care. It's part of the incentive program. The clinics are shitty and crowded, but they're free. The housing is subsidized. The jobs are more likely to be low-skilled, but they offer a wage differential of a couple bucks over the same dead-end job in the daytime. It's no surprise the misfits of society wash up as Nighttimers.

From the Field Notes of Green Taylor Simms: In hindsight, we had no idea of the events taking shape. Naturally, one read about the deaths in the newspaper, but I never gave them a second thought. We were far more concerned about preparing for the next Honeymoon Night, or decorating a Christmas tree for the upcoming Tree Night. An ominous shadow was falling over Rant, and we were debating whether to hang white or multicolor lights on our tree. Pontiac versus Dodge? Pine or spruce?

Officer Romie Mills: The third victim died in the same manner as the first two. An autopsy turned up encephalitis and myelitis of the brain, including Negri bodies in the pyramidal cells of the hippocampus, and Purkinje cells of the cerebellum. The short and sweet version of that is rabies. All three of the victims died of undiagnosed, untreated rabies.

Irene Casey: Buster wrote to us, saying he was so in love and courting somebody. His dad and me, we only prayed it was the girl, not the boy.

Officer Romie Mills: According to the Centers for Disease Control, the most recently diagnosed case of rabies in the area had been a twenty-six-year-old male named Christopher Dunyun.

It was during our preliminary investigation that the fourth victim collapsed and died of previously undiagnosed rabies-related encephalitis. Our fear was that the disease might be spreading exponentially. We could be looking at a hundred or ten thousand people unaware they'd been infected.

Shot Dunyun: It could've been an earthquake that got Rant Casey. Or a fire. Or a bullshit strain of some killer flu.

It's comforting to know, after all the Party Crash accidents I've survived, that, the day I finally meet Death, the two of us will be old, long-lost friends.

Me and Death, separated at birth.

26–In Denial

Shot Dunyun (ℂ *Party Crasher*)**:** How weird is this? The last night I go out with Rant Casey, we waste our whole window Mercy Crashing. The more front-end damage your car has, the better you look in Party Crashing. Teams I know, they'll take a sledgehammer to the bumper and front fenders of any new ride, just whale away on their headlights and grille so they won't look like newbies.

The opposite of status is rear-end damage from getting tagged. First, because it marks you as a loser, you've been nailed so many times. Second, because after too much damage nobody bothers to even stalk you. The damage Sharks inflict, they want it to show. Any team looks for something pristine to ram into. You might take half the night to stalk a battered car, but if something with a perfect paint job and a showroom body drives by flying the flag, you'll go for the cherry.

Neddy Nelson (ℂ *Party Crasher*)**:** In Party Crashing, you know what a For Sale Night means? You know the flag is to write big prices painted in white across your windshield and rear window? To keep the flag exclusive, you know you have to always make the price thirteen thousand dollars and fifty cents? Can you imagine the mess if the flag was just any price?

Shot Dunyun: For one Dead Deer Night, we're cruising with our Styrofoam deer tied to the roof and a bullshit Park Avenue charges out of nowhere. It slams into our right head-light, breaks a radiator hose, and our coolant goes down a storm drain. The Park Avenue backs off with nothing but body damage. Even with their windows rolled up, you can hear them laughing. Rant climbs out of our backseat, walks over to the team in the other car. Mr. Money Bags, he leans into the driver's window, and out of his back pocket he pulls a wad of bills. They signed over their pink slip, and took their dead deer home on the bus. We moved our deer to their car, and played the rest of the window in that Park Avenue.

Bodie Carlyle (○ *Childhood Friend*): In a letter Rant wrote to me, he said, everybody being inside cars, you couldn't tell women from men. Black from white. If you asked him, the tough teams to beat were always the gimps. Gimps or queers. You put them in a car on a level playing field and you'd see some pent-up frustration. Nobody drove as hard as paraplegics with hand controls. Or skinny, hundred-pound girls.

From the Field Notes of Green Taylor Simms (℃ *Historian*): The night in question, our last together, was a Mattress Night. Foremost in my memory of the evening is Rant Casey unbuttoning his blue uniform coveralls in a brightly lit parking lot while we drank coffee. I remember his chest was riddled with hundreds of extra nipples, countless raised, round welts. "Hobo spiders," he told me. "Found some at work." He said he'd tried to smuggle them home by dropping them inside his open collar.

Shot Dunyun: Certain game windows, if you don't tag anything all night and nobody tags you, just so you don't go home disappointed you might slam into some trashed old Shark. Any game window, you'll see beater cars rattling around, each in its own cloud of blue smoke, their rear ends balled up into shivering, creaking sheetmetal. Rolling scrap. You get your hit, and that beater Shark feels like part of the game.

If you smash into some clunker out of pity or desperation, that's what we call Mercy Crashing.

Echo Lawrence (ℂ *Party Crasher*): Come on. Dunyun was all, "Don't!" Don't mix with Rant. Don't fall in love. Dunyun kept tugging me aside, all, "Can you still boost anything?" Going, "Rabies!"

I'd let Rant ride in my backseat for months.

Shot Dunyun: Our last game as a team, we're playing a Mattress Night. Certain people will spray-paint their mattress black to make it harder to see. You want my advice, crack your side windows and loop the rope through the inside of your car. Tie down your mattress, leaving the slipknot on the inside. That way, if the police come sniffing around, you can yank the slipknot undone and ditch the mattress. It slides off, taking the ropes with it, leaving you just another innocent car on the city street.

Our last Mattress Night, every sputtering, rattling old rust bucket with a stained mattress roped to the top, Rant says, "Give them a bump." He goes, "Smack 'em, and make their night."

Echo Lawrence: Check this out. Rant was such a romantic. It's one thing to buy a girl roses she can watch wilt and rot. It's a much nicer thought to give a girl a fully equipped Skylark she can total. One Honeymoon Night, my sweetheart handed me the keys to a white Lincoln Continental with power everything. A very solid set of wheels. A ride so smooth, with a stereo so loud, at some point a Jetta rammed us from behind, hooked its front end under our rear bumper, and we didn't even notice. We drove around half the game, dragging this little car full of angry people.

Shot Dunyun: Now, how bullshit is this? In Mercy Crashing, the second you pull your bumper out of some pockmarked, saggy, rusted rear end, you regret not just going home without making any tag. You can feel so dirty and sad, you don't bother to get out and yell. You just nail and bail. Nail and bail. The rules of Party Crashing call that a foul, but chances are a junk heap will be too grateful to call you on it.

What's worse is you can picture yourself after a few more years of Party Crashing, dragging your crumpled rear end around, hoping somebody's bored or desperate enough to nail you. A big reason you nail and bail is, it's sad seeing the beater car, but it's unbearable to see the driver. Somebody wearing a cervical collar, walking with a cane, stiff and limping. Most likely that's you in a few more years.

Echo Lawrence: Let me think. Rant bought me a LeSabre I couldn't total fast enough. He bought me a Cavalier that I rammed into the back of someone's Audi. Then he bought me a Regal that I swerved to trash the side of a Taurus. No, wait, there was a Grand Am in there somewhere. A Grand Am and a Cougar and a Grand Marquis. Oh, and the Lebaron that we caught on fire, trying to eat fondue during one game. Maybe that car shouldn't count.

Shot Dunyun: We're stopped at a red light when a scrap heap rolls, coughing and shivering, from a block behind us, heading to tag our rear end. You can hear the engine tappets knocking from a block away, the springs squeak, and the headlights flicker. The fan belt's squealing, and a stained mattress quivers on its roof. This monster creeps closer, but we're trapped in traffic, waiting for a green light.

The light goes green, and this monster behind us still drags itself along, crawling toward our bumper. Echo starts to gun the engine, but Rant tells her, "Wait."

From the Field Notes of Green Taylor Simms: Young Rant was committing the most kind and gracious act of generosity.

Shot Dunyun: We sit through that green light, another red light, and half a second green before this sputtering, trembling old clunker—it just nudges our bumper and dies. Dies dead. The fan belt whimpers and goes quiet. Steam boils up through the grille, and the loose sheetmetal and chrome trim stop banging. The old car seems to sag down onto its axle stops, and the driver gets out. A kid, maybe sixteen years old. No shit. A kid by the name of Ned . . . Neddy . . . Nick, I forget.

Our car was a Caddy Seville. We had the room, so Rant offers the kid mascot position in the middle of our backseat.

We were the first tag this kid ever made; I remember he was smiling so wide.

From the Field Notes of Green Taylor Simms: Another pleasant aspect of Party Crashing was the piñata aspect. We project the worst aspects of ourselves into the vehicles around us on the road. The drivers dashing past us, we imagine them filled with arrogance. The slow drivers we're trapped behind, we imagine them as controlling or infirmed.

The joy occurs when, with one nudge or scrape, that enemy vehicle bursts open to reveal stamp collectors, football fans, mothers, grandfathers, chimney sweeps, restaurant cooks, law clerks, ministers, teachers, ushers, ditch diggers, Unitarians, Teamsters, bowlers, human beings. Hidden inside that hard, polished paint and glass is another person just as soft and scared as you.

Shot Dunyun: With every Mercy Crash, Rant would try and not hit too hard. A bump here. A ding there. Flirting kind of hits. I remember he said his money had run out, and he couldn't buy us another car. He said the car we were driving, that Caddy, it would have to last for one more big Tree Night.

Echo Lawrence: Earlier, when I say I let Rant "ride in my backseat," that's not a euphemism.

Neddy Nelson: You know how great Rant was? You know what he did when they dropped me off at my building, just before curfew? Anybody tell you Rant flips me a gold coin, saying, "For your next wheels . . ."? Can you imagine my surprise when the coin shop offers me ten grand for that 1884

Liberty Head dollar? Was there ever a guy so generous? Without Rant Casey, you think I'd be driving another car so soon?

From the Field Notes of Green Taylor Simms: That, I believe, was the squandered remainder of Rant Casey's Tooth Fairy fortune.

Echo Lawrence: When Shot said "rabies," I thought he'd said "babies." The results came back negative, thank God, but I think I asked for the wrong test.

27–Tree Night

From the Field Notes of Green Taylor Simms (ℂ *Historian*): Following enormous deliberation, we chose to use a real tree. We decided on a noble fir. Festooned in blue lights, and crowned with a glowing blue star. Fastened lengthwise along the roof of the Cadillac Seville, the tree resembled a blue comet: the big star bobbing above the windshield, trailing hundreds of dazzling blue sparks behind it.

Neddy Nelson (ℂ *Party Crasher*): Do you think I'm an idiot if I say the best part of Party Crashing, what makes it best, is it's like this breaker? A circuit breaker? How about if your mom is yelling, calling you a lazy fuck, and you lost another job, and your friends from school, they have everything going, and you don't even have a date? What if it's a total toilet in your head, but out of nowhere—slam-bo!—somebody crashes into you, and you're better? Isn't it like a gift, somebody slamming you? Don't you get out of the car, all shaky and shocked? Like you're a baby getting born? Or a whole relaxing massage that happens in one-half a second?

Isn't Party Crashing like an electroshock treatment for your depression?

From the Field Notes of Green Taylor Simms: The night Rant died, he wore a blue denim shirt embroidered quite enthusiastically, if not expertly, with a variety of rainbows and flowers. The shirt was quite a departure from his usual blue coveralls which reeked of insecticide. I seem to recall columbines, or a similar native flower species, stitched in purple, circling the collar. On the chest pocket, over his heart, an emerald-green hummingbird hovered, feeding from a yellow daffodil.

Lew Terry (ℂ *Property Manager*): The only other occasion I entered Casey's apartment was, one day I go down to the basement to clean out the recycling bins, and dumped there in the clear-glass bin is those jars I seen in his closet, only empty. No spiders. On the top of each jar, Casey's put the name "Dorry" or "June." On every jar, a girl's name.

The company where Casey worked, the exterminators said he'd quit. He wasn't so much killing bugs as he was just relocating them. Seeing how this was a vermin issue, I'm allowed to use my pass key and take a look. Was nothing left on the premises but his empty suitcase and those little dark lumps on the wall above the bed, no bugs or rats, nothing. The only thing out of the ordinary was a plain white egg, set in the middle of his bed pillow. And if anybody's saying I took that egg, it was the police detectives who took it. Since then, the county threatens to fine us, we have so many poison spiders. The crazy bastard must've set loose his whole friggin' collection.

Echo Lawrence (ℂ *Party Crasher*): Picture it. We'd mixed hours of Christmas music to blast. For two hours before the ten o'clock window, teams cruised around, showing off their trees. Parading cars, streaming with silver icicles. Cars shaggy with gold tinsel and shaking off glass balls that popped in the street. People stood on every corner, wearing red hats with white fur trim, waving for places on a team, shouting and flashing skin to get a spot in any car really done up in lights and decorations. Hundreds of Tag Team wannabes dressed as Santa Claus.

Shot Dunyun (ℂ *Party Crasher*): How weird is this? You'd cruise past a Santa Claus standing on some corner, and jolly old Santa would flash you his rack. Her rack. Tits on St. Nick. That's the kind of carnival that Tree Night turns into.

Echo Lawrence: There's no team loyalty for the two hours before the window. As everybody parades their decorations, people are climbing in and out of cars. Pit-stopping. Teams come together and dissolve. Just this mingling, mixing party that takes place in a milling sea of lit-up cars.

Shot Dunyun: About a minute before the window opens, every car kills its Christmas lights and scatters. Beyond instantly, we're back to being enemies.

Echo Lawrence: All I remember is Shot was all: "No mistletoe! No kissing! No rabies!"

From the Field Notes of Green Taylor Simms: Pit-stop culture developed as an offshoot of Party Crashing. Teams stopped in order to refuel, members used the public bathrooms and bought food and coffee. Initially, teams completed their business as quickly as possible and rejoined the game, but occasionally teams would linger at a gas station or a convenience-store parking lot. Pit-stop culture is perceived as a safe resting place or refuge during any Party Crashing event.

The Tree Night in question, we'd stopped at a gas station. Rant told us he'd refuel the car while Echo, Shot, and I went inside for provisions.

Echo Lawrence: Standing there, pumping the gas, Rant asked for pork rinds. Rinds and root beer.

Shot Dunyun: Corn dogs with mustard for me. Corn chips. Microwaved nachos.

From the Field Notes of Green Taylor Simms: My weakness, I confess, is for Red Vines licorice.

Shot Dunyun: And beef jerky.

From the Field Notes of Green Taylor Simms: It's fortuitous we seldom drove the same vehicle for more than three weeks. One has so many possible ways to wreck a car, from either the outside or the inside. Nacho cheese can destroy resale value faster than any rollover accident.

Shot Dunyun: I walk out of the store, and Rant is gone. Nothing but a big puddle of gasoline where the Caddy had been parked.

Echo Lawrence: The car was gone, and way down the street you could see this blue comet flying along. Spread out behind the Seville, a rolling forest of dark, dead trees are chasing after him. A total wolf pack. Rant's left the Christmas lights on, and every car in the game is out to tag him.

From DRVR Radio Graphic Traffic: This just in: A police pursuit is in progress along the Landover Parkway. According to reports, the suspect vehicle is a white Cadillac Seville which failed to stop for a traffic light at the intersection of Winters and 122nd. At this point, the Seville is westbound on the parkway, and the latest sightings put a lighted Christmas tree on the vehicle's roof. No kidding. A tree covered in blue Christmas lights is roped to the roof of the fleeing car. Three police vehicles are in pursuit, with a helicopter expected to join the chase. Also, an unusually large number of looky-lous seem to be following the Seville, coasting in the path cleared by the cops' lights and sirens. Reporting for DRVR Graphic Traffic, this is Tina Something . . .

Echo Lawrence: Fuck me. I flagged a team and jumped in their car. I just told them, "Go!" Some bunch of stoner kids. I pointed down the street, where you could barely see Rant's blue lights through the forest of dead trees, and I said, "There!"

From DRVR Radio Graphic Traffic: To give you an update on that police pursuit, at the Highland interchange we had a vigilante car, driven by a private citizen, cut in from a side street and ram the blue Christmas tree. The blue tree is now speeding, eastbound, on Waterfront Avenue. And how's this for a coincidence? The driver who attempted to stop the fleeing car was also driving with a Christmas tree on the top of her car. 'Tis the season, I guess. For DRVR Graphic Traffic, this is Tina Something . . .

Shot Dunyun: I'm standing there with my hands full of shit food, Red Vines licorice and shit, and Echo just bails. Green goes to the curb and hails a cab. They're both beyond vanished. Rant's gone, and I'm left on the sidewalk holding microwaved nachos and a bullshit root beer.

Symon Praeger (ℂ *Painter*): My car, we'd parked at Pump Three. That man, Casey, at Pump Seven, he yanked the gas nozzle from his car. It was no accident. He hosed the Christmas tree on top of his car. Soaked every branch. Had gas just dripping off his rocker panels.

From DRVR Radio Graphic Traffic: Police and emergency-dispatch officials have requested that private citizens refrain from interfering with the suspect vehicle. At this point, at least six private cars have rammed the escaping car, all of them also carrying Christmas trees. Police blame this flurry of accidents for the suspect's continual escape.

Police helicopters now report the primary suspect is northbound on the Greenbriar Thruway. Next update as it happens. For DRVR Graphic Traffic, this is Tina Something . . .

From the Field Notes of Green Taylor Simms: Forgive me for falling victim to the excitement of the moment. My intention wasn't to abandon Mr. Dunyun. I acted instantly, engaging a conveyance and giving chase. The moment felt very much like a hunt—the plethora of lights and sirens—as if we were a pack of hounds baying after the same fox.

Any memory I might have of Mr. Dunyun at that stressful moment includes his mouth hanging slack, his uncomprehending tongue slathered in orange cheesefood. I stepped into the back of a cab and simply told the driver, "Follow the blue Christmas tree . . ."

From DRVR Radio Graphic Traffic: The police pursuit of a white Cadillac Seville has reached the West Side of town. At last estimate, some two hundred vehicles have formed a wave of traffic sweeping along behind the Christmas-tree car—which some witnesses report has sustained at least twelve intentional collisions from bystander vehicles. To date, the Seville seems to have lost its rear bumper, its exhaust system, and, judging from sparks, at least one rear wheel is running on the rim. We'll let you know if the gas tank explodes. For DRVR Graphic Traffic, this is Tina Something reporting . . .

Shot Dunyun: How lame is this? We really believe a strip of paint down the middle of the road is going to keep us safe. That a white or yellow line is some kind of protection. I can tell you this, Rant Casey will never be one of those old Sharks, dragging his ass, hoping for someone kind enough to ram him. No shit, there's worse ways to be dead than dying.

From DRVR Radio Graphic Traffic: What started as an attempted traffic stop for failure to obey a red light has snowballed into one of this city's most dramatic police standoffs. Despite police protest, bystanders continue to ram, sideswipe, rear-end, scratch, and dent the escaping vehicle. More on this continuing story as is happens. This is Tina Something for DRVR Radio Graphic Traffic . . .

From the Field Notes of Green Taylor Simms: If you'll ponder the thought, no one ever closes a thoroughfare due to the death of an individual. You can still drive over the spot on which James Dean died, or Jayne Mansfield, or Jackson Pollock. You can drive over the spot where a bus drove over Margaret Mitchell. Grace Kelly. Ernie Kovacs. Death is a tragic event, but stopping the flow of traffic is always seen as the greater crime.

From DRVR Radio Graphic Traffic: The police chase of our renegade Christmas-tree Cadillac has reached the Barlow Avenue Viaduct.

From the Field Notes of Green Taylor Simms: All of my automobile accidents have felt similar, like swimming through amber or honey. A moment unspools for years, time almost stops, in the same manner that one can dream for hours or days in the seven minutes between hitting the snooze button and the next alarm. In a car accident, you slow down to dream time. Time jells or freezes until you can recall every moment of every moment of every moment, the way Rant could taste your entire life in any single kiss.

From DRVR Radio Graphic Traffic: The police chase of the Christmas-tree car is headed up the East Side ramps to the Barlow Avenue Viaduct.

From the Field Notes of Green Taylor Simms: Common to almost all spiritual beliefs is the idea of Limnal Time. To ascetics, it can be the moment of greatest suffering. To Catholics, it's the moment the Communion wafer is presented to the congregation. The moment is different for each religion or spiritual practice, but Liminal Time itself represents a moment in which time stops passing. The actual definition is a moment "outside of time."

That moment becomes the eternity of Heaven or Hell, and achieving even an instant of Liminal Time is the goal of most religious rituals. In that moment, one is completely present and awake and aware—of all creation. In Liminal Time, time stops. A person is beyond time.

Being involved in an automobile accident has brought me

closer to that enlightenment than any religious ritual or cere-
mony in which I've ever participated.

From DRVR Radio Graphic Traffic: Our latest word is
that the Christmas tree atop the escaping Cadillac has burst
into flames, becoming a speeding, blazing bonfire, plowing
along, leaving a trail of blue smoke and sparks.

The police have closed the west end of the Barlow Avenue
Viaduct. A police roadblock is in place.

Shot Dunyun: It's beyond typical, but every tag I've been
involved in, time slowed. Slow as stroboscopic photography,
where you see the bullet creep through the air, pressing the
side of the apple, tunneling inside, gone a second, then
bulging out the far side, splitting the apple's skin, and coming out.

From DRVR Radio Graphic Traffic: Here in the news-
room, we've confirmed a telephone call from the driver of
the burning Cadillac, and producers are patching the driver
through. Do we have the line patched? Do we still have
reception?

Echo Lawrence: It's funny, what you remember about a
person.

From DRVR Radio Graphic Traffic: With its blue Christmas tree still shining, the still-blazing Cadillac has flipped,
police report, and is now sliding toward the north edge of the
Barlow Avenue Viaduct at its highest point above the river. If
we're lucky, the next voice you hear should be that of the
unidentified driver . . .

Echo Lawrence: But anytime Rant had an orgasm, or the moment after we'd been rammed by another team, right when he blinked his eyes and seemed to realize he wasn't dead, he'd smile and say the same thing. At that moment, Rant would always smile, all dopey, and say, "This is what church should feel like . . ."

Rant Casey on DRVR Radio Graphic Traffic: ". . . I love you, Echo Lawrence, but I got to try and save my mom."

Shot Dunyun: Off the record, but, weeks ahead of that night, I'd been dosing Echo's root beer with that Plan B, morning-after abortion pill. Just in case. I can't say how many little Rant Caseys I made her poop out.

Rant Casey on DRVR Radio Graphic Traffic: ". . . What if reality is nothing but some disease?"

28–Embedded Commands

Wallace Boyer (○ *Car Salesman*): Remember, car buyers will fall into one of the three learning styles: visual, auditory, or kinetic.

Talk to Echo Lawrence, for example, and her eyes are rolled up, looking at the ceiling. Every other sentence out of her mouth is "The way I see it . . ." or "Watch out for that bitch Tina Something . . ." To pace Echo, you only have to look up when you think. Do it subtly, but bunch up the fingers on your left hand to mimic hers. Speed up until your breathing is forty, maybe fifty breaths per minute. Blink your eyes at least thirty blinks every minute.

Always remember: The person asking the questions is the person in control. The way to get that huge, impossible yes is to pile up a mountain of small, easy yeses. A good salesman starts by asking what're called tie-down and add-on questions; these are questions such as "Do you want to make your wife happy?" or "Is your child's safety important to you?" Ask questions people have to answer with a surefire "yes." Ask: "Is gas mileage important to you?" and "Do you want a reliable car?" Just keep piling up those small yeses.

The more any customer says yes, the more "pliable" they become.

Another kind of questions are called "control questions," such as: "Do you like light colors or dark colors?" Or "Are you looking for a car or truck?" Control questions include the only answers the customer can give. You're limiting the answers to the options you give. Two-door or four-door? Convertible or hardtop? Do you want leather or cloth seats?

And when a person says, "Hold on," or "Listen up," that's called an "embedded command." To sell cars, you use embedded commands all day long. For example:

"Would you just look at the two-tone paint job on that beauty?"

"Treat yourself. Just feel that leather upholstery."

"Wow, would you listen to that stereo!"

If you pay attention to Echo Lawrence, half of what comes out of her mouth is embedded commands.

Control questions, tie-down questions, and embedded commands—that's how a good salesman coaxes you to open up. You pace Shot Dunyun by wiping your lips with the back of your hand while you talk. Cross your arms over your chest and flop your head from one shoulder to the other. Say "What I heard is . . ." and "Word on the street says . . ." Convince Shot you're an auditory learner. Listen for him to introduce "doors": those little glimpses into his personal life. His dog, for example. His pug dog. And remember, he'll look side to side as he thinks about how his dog died.

But if Shot Dunyun looks at his right ear—he's lying.

For now, remember: Echo Lawrence is visual. Shot Dunyun is auditory. Neddy Nelson is kinetic.

In that last sentence, the word "remember" is an embedded command.

To repeat, the way you get to the huge, impossible yes is, you start collecting a lot of easy, small yeses.

29—Werewolves III

Neddy Nelson (℃ *Party Crasher*): Did I ever tell you about the longest day of my life? The day I almost died?

Jayne Merris (℃ *Musician*): If you ask me, at first it was hilarious. Droolers, my friends called them; anybody with end-stage rabies couldn't give a damn about curfew. Droolers weren't even aware they had rabies. Most infected people just felt a little more pissed off every day. Always edgy or grouchy. They'd take anger-management courses and serotonin reuptake inhibitors. They did meditation at Zen retreats, or cognitive talk therapy, to deal with their growing anger. Junk like deep breathing and creative visualization. All this junk, until, one day, they woke up not just on the wrong side of the bed but actually twitching, their throat spasming, maybe their legs partially paralyzed—a Drooler. Next thing, you'd see them staggering down the street, on the traffic cameras, violating the eight o'clock morning curfew.

Phoebe Truffeau, Ph.D. (☉ *Epidemiologist*): A historical precedent had existed. In 1763, during the British war against the French for territory in North America, the vast population of Native Americans sided largely with the French. In a gesture of seeming good will, the British provided the aboriginals with blankets that had been used in hospitals treating smallpox victims. With no natural resistance to the *Variola major* virus, countless Native Americans died.

Galton Nye (○ *City Councilman*): The rabies epidemic was tragic. It continues to be a human tragedy of staggering proportions. My heart really does go out, but you have to understand the need to contain the disease to the night segment of the population. The so-called Nighttimers. Making a limited tragedy into everybody's problem wasn't the answer.

But, please, intentional genocide this was not.

Neddy Nelson: Are you sure I didn't tell you already? How one game window, right at the tail end of the window, not more than an hour before the morning curfew, some Shark slammed my right rear wheel? You ever been slammed so hard your axle spindle is toast? You know how many hundred foot-pounds of torque it takes just to strip the threads on a hardened-steel spindle? Are you surprised that kind of slam would bounce my head off the steering wheel and black me out for a couple hours?

Galton Nye: We used to hear stories, how radical Nighttimers were plotting to spread the infection across the timeline. Out of frustration, these same political radicals accused Daytimers of engineering the epidemic in order to cripple the Nighttimer birthrate and their so-called inevitable rise to a voting majority.

Jayne Merris: On the traffic cameras, the Droolers used to limp around, dragging one leg, slack-jawed, snarling. People who used to be wives, fathers, and even little kids, now— completely gone berserk, lurking in public toilets and department-store fitting rooms with one goal: to sink their spitty teeth into somebody.

Neddy Nelson: You know the only Sharks who tagged that hard? The only players that brand of stupid? You know what a Drooler is? Can you picture somebody with end-stage rabies, all that bottomless rage, can you believe they'd still be driving and Party Crashing? Now can you get the mess that Party Crashing was turning into?

Phoebe Truffeau, Ph.D.: In 1932, a government study identified approximately four hundred African American men infected with syphilis. Rather than treat the disease, the study officials allowed it to progress for forty years, in order to track subsequent infection patterns and autopsy the men as they eventually died. Known as the "Tuskegee Experiment," this U.S. Public Health Services study ended in 1972, only when a whistle blower leaked insider information to the *Washington Evening Star* newspaper.

Galton Nye: We had to be careful. All the early outbreak clusters had to be confined to the nighttime, and any daytime infection was traced to direct interaction with a Nighttimer. Because so many of these encounters were of a so-called covert nature, mostly involving illegal drugs and sexual contact, the infected Daytimers were slow to recognize and report their symptoms.

Jayne Merris: Before the Droolers, it used to take a minute, tops, to turn over the city at curfew. The curfew sirens blasted—first the ten-minute warning, then the one-minute warning. The curfew bell used to ring, and anybody still on the street, the traffic cameras snapped their picture or their license plate, and the state matching program sent them a hefty bill for the fine. Five hundred or a thousand bucks, depending on your trespass record.

The Droolers turned up, and next thing, the police stretched the old curfew minute to ten minutes, to do walking searches and make sure no Droolers were lurking behind newsstands or parked cars. After a Drooler hid in some bushes and jumped a mess of fourth-graders in the daylight, the curfew minute expanded to a full hour. If you ask me, that's way too long.

Neddy Nelson: You ever wake up with a bloody forehead and your steering wheel collapsed from the impact? You ever wake up to the morning-curfew sirens with blood gluing your eyes shut? Your car toasted? The seat belt almost cutting you in half? You ever get your eyes open just in time to see some trigger-happy curfew squad making the sweep down the street where you're trapped? A posse of spooked vigilantes searching to flush out any bleary-eyed, dazed Nighttimer like you to shoot?

Galton Nye: They became the biological equivalent of suicide bombers, those maniac so-called hydrophobes staggering around at the morning-curfew change.

Jayne Merris: A Drooler could manage the nights. No sunlight. But when the morning sirens blasted, they didn't know anymore to come inside, and if the curfew squads caught somebody hiding or running away, they'd assume the worst and just shoot the person dead.

If you ask me, by then nothing short of a bullet was going to cure a Drooler.

Phoebe Truffeau, Ph.D.: In 1940, four hundred men, prisoners from the Chicago metropolitan area, were covertly infected with malaria in order for public-health officials to test new types of treatments for the disease.

Neddy Nelson: You know how much the daylight sucks? You ever climb from the front into the backseat of a totaled car as a gang of gun-toting hired killers marches your way? You ever hide under the shit in your own backseat, the elastic seat-cover and dirty laundry and fast-food trash, counting your heartbeats to keep from bolting, freaked out, and running down the street in a hail of gunfire?

What's the longest you ever counted your heartbeat? You ever counted heartbeats up to ten thousand? Twenty thousand? How about 41,234?

Galton Nye: My heart goes out, but we had our children to consider. Our own families. Citizens have a personal responsibility to conduct their lives in a way where they minimize their own exposure to dangerous disease. The decent, productive members of any society have a responsibility to protect the next generation.

Our children truly are the future.

Phoebe Truffeau, Ph.D.: Beginning in 1963, officials at the Willowbrook State School, a residence for developmentally disabled children in Staten Island, New York, intentionally infected healthy children with hepatitis in order to test the effects of gamma globulin on the disease. For three years, school officials repeatedly injected the children with viral agents, until public outcry stopped the program in 1966.

Neddy Nelson: Do you know how hot it gets in a parked car with all the windows rolled up on a sunny day? Buried under trash? Hearing a city of people walk past? Knowing how you'd look, a born Nighttimer, never been in the sun more than a total of six hours in your life, how you'd look, your face smeared with blood and sweat, your eyes swoll up and bruised, crawling out of a wrecked car? How fast do you think they'd shoot you dead?

Galton Nye: My heart goes out. I'm not saying anybody deserves to go insane and be gunned down by the curfew police, but please consider how Nighttimers live. The rest of us, who live our lives according to the word of God and common sense, we should not have to foot the bill for their sins.

A person only has to look at how Nighttimers behave. They expect life to be just one big party. Their lives revolve around sex. Crashing their cars, and meaningless one-day stands with strangers. Our minister devoted one entire sermon to describing their lifestyle. It gets hard to feel sympathy for people so reckless with their own health. These so-called victims are people who don't respect themselves. Or respect God.

If they want to thin their own ranks, I say let them.

Phoebe Truffeau, Ph.D.: In the mid-1960s, the American anthropologist James Neel inoculated members of the Yanomami tribe in Venezuela with a virulent strain of measles. Neel and his team of researchers refused to treat the sick; instead, they documented how the disease spread, killings thousands, in order to test a controversial theory of eugenics.

Neddy Nelson: You have any idea how bright the sun looks if you've been raised at night? Have you spent a hundred-something-thousand heartbeats wondering if you're not already dying of rabies? Maybe you haven't boosted in weeks, because you're afraid you won't be able to?

You ever see friends you recognize get machine-gunned by police on real-time traffic cams?

You ever found yourself trapped in a world where you're everybody's worst nightmare?

Jayne Merris: If you ask me, the first sign was finding public bathrooms locked at night. Pretty soon, a lot of public drinking fountains stopped running except in the daytime. Daytimers staked out the bathrooms and restaurants and drinking fountains they wanted, and Nighttimers had to settle for the rest. The segregation only got worse as the rabies epidemic spread.

The twelve hours we spent on the backside of the planet, if you ask me, the night turned into just another kind of ghetto.

Neddy Nelson: Do you have any idea how sweet the sunset looks after you've been sweating and bleeding, pissing yourself, in the backseat of a wrecked car all day? Can you imagine how sweet those sirens sound at evening curfew?

Galton Nye: We used to hear stories in Bible-study group, how these so-called Droolers would try to spit in your mouth.

The way Nighttimers carry on, they only protest so loud so their spit flies in your eyes or into your food. I'm talking about intentional high-risk conduct.

My heart goes out, but I say, sooner or later, the quarantine had to start.

30—In Mourning

Lynn Coffey (ℂ *Journalist*): On the first day after Rant Casey died—an apparent suicide witnessed by thousands of people, millions if you count the television rebroadcast of his car exploding—on the very next day, a curfew officer named Daniel Hammish, age forty-seven, a nineteen-year veteran of curfew patrol, was making his evening sweep when he assaulted a passerby. Hammish bit this stranger, with his teeth, in an unprovoked attack, on the exposed skin of her neck. Responding emergency medical technicians found Hammish delirious and seemingly hallucinating, before he lost consciousness and subsequently died.

Todd Rutz (☼ *Coin Dealer*): The police come into my store, show me a mug shot of the kid who's been selling me his coins, that's the first I know the kid's name is Buster Casey. They tell me he's died in some car wreck, was on the news. Ask, what did I know about the kid, this Casey kid? They ask stuff like, did he ever exhibit violent tendencies? Did the kid ever kiss me? Or bite?

Crazy questions.

Lynn Coffey: In my opinion, there was something a little stagy about Casey's death. First, he was careful to drive the largest, brightest car that night, literally heaping that car with lights, drenching it with gasoline, and driving zigzag through the playing field to attract as many taggers as possible. Plus, the television newscopters and the way he called the radio station and kept talking until he'd burned. Even the way Casey ran that red traffic light, smack dab in front of some cops, seems calculated to give him a full lights-and-sirens escort to his next life.

From the Field Notes of Green Taylor Simms (ℂ *Historian*): How does one compensate for the loss of a peer?

Looking back, I sometimes wonder if we didn't invent Rant Casey. The group of us. If, perhaps, we didn't need some wild, mythic character to represent our own vanishing lives. A marvelous, glittering antihero to be the challenge whom the rest of us—Mr. Dunyun, Miss Lawrence, and I—had survived to tell about. The moment Rant exploded on television, the moment his car burst into flame, he became this fantastic tale we could recount about our reckless Party Crashing past. And, bathed in the flare of his gasoline limelight, we would appear mythic by association.

Shot Dunyun (ℂ *Party Crasher*): How weird is this? It didn't matter a thousand people had Party Crashed over the past few years, getting nothing worse than whiplash. We hadn't really seen what could happen. We didn't realize. When we saw the worst that could go wrong—shit, we could die, we could burn alive—then Party Crashing did start to peter out.

From the Field Notes of Green Taylor Simms: Not to be overly moralistic, but sometimes the death of one person can justify the death of an entire culture.

Lynn Coffey: On the third day after Rant Casey died, the drag boats hooked his car on the bottom of the river channel. Over the better part of three hours, they pulled the scorched shell of the Cadillac Seville—complete with the charred skeleton of a Christmas tree still tied to the car's roof—out of the river at the Madison Street boat ramp.

Neddy Nelson (ℂ *Party Crasher*): Doesn't the government have to make damn sure Rant Casey never turns into our martyr? Haven't oppressed people always gone to church for comfort? There, didn't they meet other oppressed people? Haven't all your major revolutions brewed as people complained together and sang songs and got riled up to take violent action?

Wasn't Party Crashing our church, the way people came together? Like in pit stops, griping together? Weren't we the revolution that every night almost happened . . . almost happened . . . kept almost happening, but instead we just only crashed into each other? If just one leader would emerge— Rant Casey or anybody—the army of us, ready to fight and die, wouldn't we be invincible?

From the Field Notes of Green Taylor Simms: In actuality, we're mourning a thousand vehicles filled with snack food, flirting, and talk therapy. It had been a form of consciousness-raising. Also, connection, dreaming, planning, perhaps even actual cultural change. Every night since that night has become the postmortem of Party Crashing. An autopsy, not of Rant Casey, but of a subculture that some Nighttimers

have come to believe would have improved their quality
of life.

Lynn Coffey: With all the windows rolled shut, the velvet
interior of that torched Cadillac remained largely unsinged.
According to eyewitnesses, the automatic transmission was
still in drive, and the headlights were still switched on,
although the car's battery had long been flooded. Furthermore, that powder-blue interior contained river water, one
blue denim shirt embroidered with flowers, one pair of blue
jeans embroidered with ivy leaves, two Converse high-top
basketball shoes, but not a single, solitary Buster Casey.

In addition, to open the vehicle, the officers at the scene
had to call for a Slim Jim rod. Because all the doors were still
locked. And the keys still in the ignition.

**Reverend Curtis Dean Fields (○ *Minister, Middleton
Christian Fellowship*):** The Bible tells us it will happen in
the twinkling of an eye. The Rapture. Rant was delivered to
Heaven. That's what I stopped by and told Chet and Irene.
You never saw a couple so heartbroke.

Officer Romie Mills (℃ *Homicide Detective*): It's at this
point the department issued a warrant for Buster Casey's
arrest.

31–An Accounting

Irene Casey (☉ *Rant's Mother*): Close as I can figure, the older Carlyle boy went and got himself made sheriff just so he can break bad news to folks. He come up our porch steps, middle of breakfast, the morning after Buddy's car accident, and banged on the screen until Chet come to the door. Bacon Carlyle, he says, "I regret to inform you, but your son, Buster Landru Casey, was killed in a car accident at approximately eleven-forty-three of last night." He read the words from a little white card, looking at the card instead of us. Sounding out each word, slow as if he was in second grade. Then, all respectful, he snatched off his trooper hat, and he turned the card over and read the back side, saying, "You have my deepest sympathies in your time of grieving."

We'd already see'd that part while he read us the first side. Chet asks, "They found a body yet?"

Bacon shrugged, the big idiot. He stuck the white card inside his hat and set the hat back on his ears.

Lew Terry (☾ *Property Manager*): Some farmer in bib overalls shows up, ringing the buzzer, and rolling me out of bed in the middle of the day. Daytimers haven't any respect. He won't leave my stoop, and he's waving an envelope with this building as the return address, claiming to be the Casey kid's father. The father guy comes here all the way from nowhere to collect his kid's stuff.

Of course I gave him my sympathy. The police have already combed the apartment, but they didn't say I couldn't let in relatives. Funny thing is, the layout of this building isn't overly logical. To find the kid's unit, you need to go all the way to the back of the first-floor hallway, take the fire stairs up to the second floor, then walk along an open-porch deal to the end door. I don't tell the father guy this, but when I duck back inside my unit to get the pass key, the guy's disappeared.

One, two, three, the father guy's found his way to the kid's door and gone inside. His boots tracking cow shit all over my floors without a single misstep. Like he's lived here, but I swear he's never set foot on the premises. To open the apartment door, he shows me, you lift the knob and the hinges give, the screws wiggle, so you can trip the latch.

Me standing there with the pass key in my hand, he waves me inside.

But somebody's already beat us there.

Sheriff Bacon Carlyle (◯ *Childhood Enemy*): The coldest folks you'll ever meet. Them's the Caseys. Raised an only son who run off and got himself killed, probably just to pain his old man. Then Chet Casey stood on his own front porch and took the bad news like I was a radio giving the weather report. No emotion on that man's face. None whatsoever. All I can figure is, with a loco kid like Rant Casey, his folks gived him up for dead a long, long time before.

Lew Terry: The father guy's with me in the apartment, but you can hear somebody banging around in the bathroom. A burglar. These sneak thieves, they see an obit in the paper, or they see an article about how somebody snuffed it, and these lowlifes bust in to steal the stereo, the television, the prescription drugs. Seeing how our burglar's in the toilet, it's got to be some junkie ransacking the medicine cabinet.

Meanwhile, the dead kid's father, he doesn't look too concerned. He doesn't look too sad, neither. He's running the palm of one hand over one wall, feeling the paint with the flat of his hand.

The bathroom door busts open, and a girl steps out. One of her arms, it's not right, shriveled up, but in her other hand she holds the top of a black plastic garbage bag. She looks at me and the kid's father and says, "Who the fuck are you?"

And this hayseed smiles. Grinning like an ape, he steps away from feeling the walls and says, "Echo . . ." He says, "It's darned sweet to see you again."

Irene Casey: The morning I drove Chet up to the airport in Peco Junction, on his way to collect Buddy from the city, Chet told me the oddest bit of news. He reminded me about the brown cowboy wallpaper we hung in Buddy's room. He said to pull it down. Steam it soft, and tear it down, he said.

Stuck in the wall, behind every wad of booger that boy pasted there, Chet told me to dig in the plaster drywall. If I did that, he said, I'd never need for money another day in my life. Only, touching the boogers, he told me to wear rubber gloves.

Lew Terry: So this girl with the curled-up arm and the garbage bag, she looks at the father guy and says, "Have we met?"

And Farmer John, he nods at the black plastic bag she's holding and says, "What'd you find worth busting in for?"

"Rant gave me a key," the girl says.

And the father guy says, "I'm sorry. I reckon I forgot."

To me, the girl says, "You know what a 'Porn Buddy' is?" She says that if somebody dies, most times they have a close friend who's designated to hurry over and search their place for drugs and sex stuff. All the junk they don't want their parents to know about them. She swings the black plastic bag in her hand and says, "Everything you don't want to know about your son is inside here."

Shot Dunyun (ℂ *Party Crasher*): We were, all of us, worried about Echo. On my own, I went to visit her. I took her a deli carton of chicken soup one night. I wanted to make sure she was eating. We sat and talked, and I didn't leave until she'd eaten every bite.

Just to tie up any loose ends, I'd loaded that soup with those Plan B birth-control pills. To really flush her out, I mean *beyond* loaded.

Lew Terry: The kid's father has gone back to feeling the walls, touching the soft black lumps that, close as I could guess, were hashish. Still touching the wall, not even looking at this girl with her bag, the father guy says, "Two second-hand skin magazines, some Percocet left over from his one visit to the dentist, a stained vibrator, and a pair of handcuffs lined with fake fur."

The girl looks inside the bag.

"The last two gadgets are yours," the father guy says, "but you're welcome to take it all."

And the girl says, "How the fuck . . . ?"

Officer Romie Mills (℃ *Homicide Detective*): Standard procedure is to stake out the residence of anyone emotionally significant to the suspect. We had officers watching the Lawrence apartment and the suspect's apartment. We were well aware of Chester Casey's comings and goings, and we can confirm that both he and Echo Lawrence were in the suspect's apartment, together, for a period of time with the landlord, Lewis Terry.

Lew Terry: The father guy touches a spot on the apartment wall, tapping the paint, and he says, "Look here."

It's one of those hash bumps.

The father guy reaches inside the chest pocket of his bib overalls and brings out a jackknife; he snaps the blade open and stabs it into the plaster.

And I tell him to just hold on. The damage deposit won't cover him carving up the walls.

With the knife still sunk into the plaster, he's wiggling the blade, saying, "But the money you stole should cover it . . ."

I didn't steal any money. I tell you. I told him, I did not steal anything from this apartment.

"Let's ask the coin dealer over on Grinson Street," the father guy says, and he draws the jackknife blade out of the wall. Where he stabbed and dug, he picks with two fingers. He slides out something and wipes the white plaster dust from it. A gold coin. And he says, "This look familiar?"

Officer Romie Mills: What's less clear is why Echo Lawrence apparently invited the suspect's father to her home, after that meeting. And why she allowed Chester Casey to take up residence in her apartment.

At that point, we had no solid leads on the whereabouts of Buster Casey.

Irene Casey: When I saw Chet onto that airplane, he must've been scared he was going to die. The poor man, he told me, "Reen, you've had a difficult time of this life." He said he was sorry about everything, but that he loved me, he would always love me. The last time he looked at me, from the doorway of going on that plane, Chet said, "You were a wonderful mother."

Shot Dunyun: Boy oh boy, Rant's dad rolls into town certifiably, bona-fide, bat-shit crazy. He shacks up with Echo. Calls that pest-control place to ask for Rant's old job. The first time I meet him, this middle-aged doofus, he grabs my neck with one hand. He gropes me, plants his mouth over mine, and says, "Miss me?"

How weird is that shit?

When I said "mine," I meant my *mouth*.

Lew Terry: Me and that crippled girl, we watch while the dead kid's father goes around the room. Everywhere there's a soft black lump, he stabs in his knife and digs out a gold coin. Looking at the girl, the father guy says, "In your apartment, when you fell asleep, the last night you and Buster were together, he pasted lumps of his snot around your walls."

The cripple, she says, "Rant wiped boogers on my walls?"

Everywhere she finds a lump of snot, the father says, Rant was leaving her some treasure.

She says, "I still don't understand."

He says, "Don't bother getting tested for rabies, just start your treatments."

This girl, she says, "You're not really a policeman, are you?"

32—In Hindsight

Ruby Elliot (☼ *Childhood Neighbor*): I can tell you, getting abandoned at the Junction Airport by her husband is not the worstest event ever to happen to Irene Casey.

Glenda Hendersen (☼ *Childhood Neighbor*): Basin and Ruby and me, we went through school with Irene, and she was always cutting class. Never did seem to matter, how she come into the world without a daddy. Irene was full of grand plans. Talking all the time about college or the army, anything she figured could deliver her out of town. Sad part is, she never did get beyond the ninth grade. The summer we was thirteen years old, her and Basin, Ruby and me, we ran wild, staying out; then Irene quit coming to the phone. Irene quit—well—everything.

Ruby Elliot: Between you, me, and the lamppost, it was no surprise to anybody that Irene was expecting. Three months along, folks say, before she married Chet. Story is, out of the blue, Chester Casey walked up on her porch and asked her ma, Esther, Could he have a word with Miss Irene Shelby? Like him and Irene was total strangers. Nobody hereabouts knew Chester from Adam. He come out of nowhere, no job or family, simply showed up in Middleton, saying, "Good morning, Dr. Schmidt . . . Howdy, Reverend Fields." Calling everybody by his name.

Wasn't until that day Esther even knowed her girl was pregnant.

Dr. David Schmidt (☼ *Middleton Physician*): For better or worse, it was Chet's child. The age Irene was, we wanted to be certain she wasn't making another mistake, only looking for some man, any man, to help her raise a child. Chester must've been nineteen or twenty years old. We ran your standard paternity test, and every genetic marker pointed to the baby being his.

In hindsight, every genetic marker pointed at the baby being *him*. His genes and the child's were so close, the two were indistinguishable.

Reverend Curtis Dean Fields (☼ *Minister, Middleton Christian Fellowship*): My clearest recollection is, during our requisite premarital counseling, the couple waived any discussion of intimacy. It was my assumption that their squeamishness arose from Irene being so far along. A lecture on contraception would have been locking the barn door long after that particular horse had run off.

Whether or not it was due to the pregnancy, I have never seen a couple less physically infatuated with each other. So you know how standoffish they seemed, at their wedding, when I told Chester he could kiss his bride, he kissed Irene on the cheek.

Dr. David Schmidt: Our gravest reservation had been regarding the possibility that Chester Casey had raped thirteen-year-old Irene Shelby, and circumstances were forcing her to marry her assailant. Small towns have a tragic way of trapping young people and making them answer for small mistakes with the rest of their lives.

Ruby Elliot: All the Shelby kin, leastwise the womenfolk, they were born under a dark star. Irene's own great-great-grandmother had been attacked by a man. Her Great-grandma Bel Shelby, when she was thirteen or fourteen years old and walking home after school, a stranger assaulted her. A transient. No sheriff ever caught the man, but Bel Shelby had a baby as the result, and that illegitimate baby was Irene's Grandmother Hattie.

It's as if bad luck stalks after the women in Irene's family.

Basin Carlyle (◑ *Childhood Neighbor*): Don't make me laugh. Don't call what's really loose morals any "attack." Women in the Shelby family have always run around. No curse settled on the Shelby women, except maybe the curse of promiscuity.

Ruby Elliot: But soon as Hattie Shelby turned thirteen, it did happen, again. Another stranger and another baby. This baby was Irene's own mama, Esther.

Edna Perry (◑ *Childhood Neighbor*): Their farm, Middleton folks call it the "Shelby Place" even after Chet Casey took over. For all those years it was Bel raising Hattie raising Esther. Local history is, the exact day little Esther turned thirteen, she got pregnant with Irene.

Ruby Elliot: A family history like that, and you can't blame Glenda Hendersen and me for fearing the worst once Irene got to ninth grade. We walked everywhere with her, not once letting our best friend out of eyesight. When we weren't watching Irene, her ma and grandma was. You could argue they drove Irene a little crazy, mother-henning that way. Could be that amount of safeguarding is what drove Irene to sneak out. Just to be by herself and walk along the river, through the trees along the river, alone.

Sheriff Bacon Carlyle (☼ *Childhood Enemy*): The wild-dog packs running around in those woods, it's nothing but self-destructive, walking in those woods by yourself. For a young girl like Irene was, we're talking about just plain insane suicide behavior.

Ruby Elliot: Except maybe Irene didn't want to spend her life hiding behind locked doors and best friends and her mama's skirt.

Basin Carlyle: Irene Shelby took to sneaking off. Then she got herself knocked up. Then she gone and married Chester. No mystery. It's crazy talk to say a rapist has run down four generations of the same family. Don't make me laugh.

Reverend Curtis Dean Fields: Still, for the life of me, I never did see any child grow up to look so much like his father. Why, anybody meeting Buster and Chester Casey would swear those two were twin brothers.
   That is—if they weren't born a generation apart.

Glenda Hendersen: Granted, Chet was some years older than Irene. You could blame that for why the two of them never acted close, not in front of folks. Never so much as held hands. But they seemed to genuine care for each other, right up until Chet climbed into that airplane and never looked back.

Irene Casey (☼ *Rant's Mother*): You're asking, was I raped? Was I attacked by a stranger who might've been my father, and my grandfather, and great-grandfather? Why bring up such awfulness?

I don't know. I forget. I can't remember.

33—Werewolves IV

Shot Dunyun (◖ *Party Crasher*): Talk about bullshit. Looking back on this. It's beyond bullshit, but sometimes I don't think when I brush my teeth, and I'd spit the toothpaste into the toilet instead of the sink. Force of habit. I never think how spit is really saliva, and I never consider how my dog used to drink out of the toilet.

Jayne Merris (◖ *Musician*): You remember what people were like. One rumor said Nighttimers picked up apples for sale in grocery stores, licked the apples, and put them back, hoping to infect Daytimers. Other rumors said Nighttimers would spit from high-rise windows during the day.

Neddy Nelson (◖ *Party Crasher*): The Berlin Wall . . . the Great Wall of China . . . that zone dividing Israel from the Palestinians . . . North from South Korea—isn't that what the eight o'clock curfew became?

Galton Nye (◑ *City Councilman*): The main problem I have with Nighttimers is they get on their high horse and call me a bigot. Nobody can call me prejudiced. For their information, my own daughter is a so-called Nighttimer, my own little girl. Since almost three years ago.

Neddy Nelson: How soon was it before Daytimers assumed every Nighttimer carried rabies? In food service? In health care? What about child care? Can you name one Daytimer who still hired nighttime labor?

Shot Dunyun: My dog I had was a three-year-old pug named Sandy. She used to chase a tennis ball until she'd be so tired I'd have to carry her home from the park. She'd sleep the whole trip back.

I knew I couldn't boost peaks, and I knew what that meant, but talk about being stupid.

Jayne Merris: You remember? You heard rumors about people not knowing they were infected, kissing their husbands and wives, parents kissing their kids good night and giving them rabies. Churches that shared a common wineglass during Communion, that was another story that made the rounds. How all Catholics or Baptists had rabies.

Shot Dunyun: My pug, Sandy, every day she'd sleep on my bed, her little head on the pillow next to my pillow. Like a little bulldozer, she'd plow her way under the covers, turn around by my feet, then push her way out until just her head was showing. Talk about personality. Sandy even snored like a little person. She knew "fetch" and "roll over" and "wait."

Galton Nye: Despite how much her mother and I tried to warn her, she rejected us. We tried to teach our little girl right from wrong. We begged her not to throw her life away on some silly teenager act of rebellion. We made it abundantly clear that day versus night was entirely a conscious lifestyle choice, but she wouldn't hear a word of it.

Neddy Nelson: Are you aware that, before his gruesome experiments on Auschwitz concentration-camp prisoners, Dr. Josef Mengele had been a well-respected anthropologist? Did you know Mengele had traveled through Africa, collecting human blood and viral samples? That his lifelong dream had been to identify factors that proved a difference between the blood of different races? Then to create a race-specific plague?

Did you know that much of Mengele's findings came to the United States as part of Project Paperclip, where the CIA granted pardons and gave new identities to Nazi scientists if they agreed to share Mengele's research?

Jayne Merris: To insult somebody, the worst thing you could say was "Don't be such a Drooler." Or "Don't go all rabid on me." Instead of holding outlaw, elite status, Nighttimer culture became an object of disdain. The way to dismiss anything was to say: "That is soooooo *nighttime . . .*"

Galton Nye: Our little girl graduated the salutatorian of the Christian Pathways Academy. That means her grade-point average was second highest out of a class of almost forty students. She was a junior youth minister at our church, three years running, and she played varsity soccer her senior year, first string. Her mother and I hired a so-called private detective—this was the week after her running off. All the detective ever gave us for our money was a picture of her in some junky car with the boy, "Just Married" written in white under her window, and her wearing a veil and laughing. The boy had on a white shirt and bow tie. After all the dreams we had for giving our little girl a big church wedding, that picture broke her mother's heart.

The Bible says, "Weep you not for putrid refuse all the better lost."

Five thousand dollars for that one blurry picture, and all it bought us was heartbreak. At the least, we know that Night-timer son-of-a-bitch finally married her.

Shot Dunyun: I don't give a shit what the song says, sometimes a kiss is not just a kiss. That's for sure. My theory is that, every time a bat or skunk bit Rant, he'd by accident let the rabies go a little farther before he'd get treated. If he was trying or not, Rant hatched some bug that medical science couldn't touch.

Phoebe Truffeau, Ph.D. (○ *Epidemiologist*): The only two untreatable rabies-type viruses were the African strains Mokola and Duvenhage, prior to the identification of the Rant serotype.

Galton Nye: The Bible says, ". . . thus if poisoned be the child not of service beneath the parent." You just keep that in mind.

Neddy Nelson: Have you read that Kissinger report he's supposed to have submitted to the National Security Council in 1974? The one where Henry Kissinger warns that the greatest threat to the future of Americans is overpopulation in Third World countries? How's it go? We need the minerals and natural resources of Africa? Pretty quick now, those banana republics will fall apart as their populations rise too high? The only way America can protect its prosperity and political stability will be to depopulate the Third World?

Should we be surprised that the AIDS virus showed up about 1975?

Do you understand what the term "depopulate" means?

Jayne Merris: Under the I-SEE-U Act, the antiexclusion laws guaranteed equal access to all public places for people of day or night status; but if you ask me, people got so paranoid about sweat on gym equipment, things like that, spit on apples, that the nicer places—bars, restaurants, salons—they just closed up at night.

The two cultures shared the same city, but they kept drifting farther and farther apart.

Neddy Nelson: How do you explain this—the first explosion of AIDS infections in Africa started in missionary hospitals where Christian volunteers reused the same needles to vaccinate local kids against smallpox and diphtheria? Does that sound familiar? Could be millions of kids. Doesn't this explain how, between 1976 and 1980, the infection curve rose from 0.7 percent to 40 percent in some parts of West Africa?

Does that scenario make you want to rush out to any public clinic and stand in line for a free vaccination of anything?

Phoebe Truffeau, Ph.D.: Any vaccination carries a small risk of post-treatment encephalitis, so it was inevitable that a few individuals immunized with a pre-exposure prophylactic did develop mild rabies symptoms and required additional treatment. The sheer numbers of people vaccinated made patient tracking impossible, and, yes, at least two persons died as a likely result of their immunization.

Shot Dunyun: Another morning, I'd wake up and the pillow next to mine was soaked in spit, my dog's drooled that much in her sleep. Pugs slobber a shitload, so I didn't give it another thought. Talk about denial.

Phoebe Truffeau, Ph.D.: Rumors within the target community exaggerated and misinterpreted the vaccination-related deaths, and this dampened their enthusiasm to fully participate in further treatment programs, virtually guaranteeing a constant, significant reservoir of the virus within the nighttime population.

Shot Dunyun: Rant Casey used to say, "No matter what happens, it's always now . . ." Talk about cryptic.

I think what Rant meant was, we live in the present moment of reality, and no matter what's come before, no matter how much we loved a person or a dog, when it attacks us we'll react to that moment of danger.

Neddy Nelson: Doesn't it seem weird that a government report recommends depopulating Africa, and by the end of the twentieth century entire generations were dying? Isn't it suspicious how former European colonies with rich natural resources, stuff like gold and diamonds, countries like Botswana, Zimbabwe, and South Africa, were most hard hit by the AIDS epidemic?

Shot Dunyun: A great dog like I had, and I let her drink my spit. Sometimes I'm light-years beyond stupid. That's for sure.

One evening, I woke up to the ten-minute curfew siren, and Sandy was standing on my chest with her pug face dripping spit on my neck. Her black lips curl back to show every tooth down to the yellow root. Her breathing feels hot on my face, and the same way she jumps to fetch a tennis ball, I watch Sandy crouch, ready to lunge at my throat. The minute she springs, I throw the sheets and blankets over her, and I bundle her up so she can't get out. Sandy's never weighed more than a sixteen-pound bowling ball, so I pick her up in that sack of blankets, only she's gone all werewolf, snarling and clawing inside, and my blankets are so old they're nothing but lint. One of her little pug paws, it claws through so I can see her black toenails. The blankets are wet with her drool, so it's like holding a little wolverine inside a bag of wet tissue paper. One more claw and she'll be out and biting me. Just to stun her, maybe knock her out, I swing the bundle so it hits the wall. Sandy's still snarling and thrashing inside, so I swing the bundle against the wall a second time. She keeps fighting, so I keeping hitting her against the wall, until my neighbor on the other side is pounding back. The one-minute curfew siren goes off, then the curfew bell. The wall, where I'm hitting the bundle of blankets, that spot is smeared with red. The bundle, where it's been hitting, the blankets are soaked through with red. Dripping red. My neighbor's still pounding and yelling for me to shut up, but Sandy's not moving or making any noise. It's nothing like in *Old Yeller*.

Talk about panicking. Now you can see what a thoughtless, bullshit idiot I am.

Neddy Nelson: Can you shrug off the fact that, before the rabies outbreak, the relatively younger Nighttimer community was about to outnumber the population of the Daytimers? Wouldn't a good epidemic do to Nighttimers what AIDS did in Africa? Wouldn't it devastate the political power of a rising community and preserve the existing power structures?

Galton Nye: We don't know if she's infected or not, but we're not taking our chances. We have our own health to worry about. I'm not saying her mother and I don't still love her, but the night she walked out with that so-called boyfriend of hers, our daughter was dead to us.

God bless her, but if our little girl shows up here some night, our door's staying locked.

34–What If

Neddy Nelson (ℂ *Party Crasher*): I want to ask, you ever wonder why the dominant culture says certain stuff? I mean, really hammers on you that some stuff is absolutely, deadly impossible? For instance, what science calls the "Grandfather Paradox"? How it works out that you should never, ever even consider time travel, because you might go back in time and kill your own grandfather by accident, let's say, and then—kah-*poof*—you'd not exist? I mean, if you trusted in the government experts, wouldn't you be careful and *never* go back in time?

Echo Lawrence (ℂ *Party Crasher*): I was so little, but I remember the I-SEE-U Act shutting down the rubberneck studies—those government engineers, like my mother, crashing into each other to study the effect on traffic. I remember my mother saying who was missing from her office, and I thought she meant fired or laid off. A few more engineers each week. I asked if she'd be leaving, and she told me no. Never, she said, not without her little Echo, meaning me, and my father. She said she'd never leave us behind.

Neddy Nelson: What if this? If somebody went back and reworked the past, how would the rest of us know? Don't we only know the present reality that we know? What if reality gets reshuffled—in little, tiny ways—all the time? Or what if the people in power have already shuffled the past to get on top, and now they're telling the rest of us not to monkey around with history or we'll go back and kill our ancient ancestors and every generation after that, and then we'll never get born?

I mean, could the people who control all the money and politics ever invent a scarier warning? Didn't these same science experts used to say the earth was flat? Wasn't it really important we should stay at home and be peasants and slaves or we'd fall off the edge?

Echo Lawrence: As a little kid, I remember going to a fucking lot of funerals, mostly for people who worked with my mother. Sitting in church, my father would elbow her, saying, "This is where they really go . . ."

And my mother, behind her black veil, would tell him, "*Not all of them . . .*"

Behind their bedroom door, they'd argue about moving, leaving, taking off. My mother called it Reverse Pioneering, to some place where the air was clean and we'd have empty land all around us. It was a nice dream, but even to a little kid she sounded crazy. At this point in history, there was no place in the polluted, crowded world left like that.

Neddy Nelson: I want to ask you, instead of a "Granddad Paradox," I mean, what if there's a "Grandma Paradox"? I'm not saying anybody's done this, but what if somebody's gone back and screwed with their own past? Not major changes, but just stacked the deck so their present is—better? I mean,

what if you found yourself a long time ago—by accident—
and you met your own great-great-grandmother before it was
wrong to date her? And what if she was a babe? And let's say
you two hooked up? And how about she has a baby who'd be
both your daughter and your great-grandmother? In the
wrong, sick-minded guy, could you see where this plan might
be headed? A hybrid you with superpowers? Couldn't you
keep living, maybe hooking up with your next ancestor
babes—your grandmother and your mom—stoking your own
genetics so the future you—even the present you—was more
strong, smart, crazy . . . some extra *something*?

Shot Dunyun (ℂ *Party Crasher*): No shit. I remember the
big media push for everybody to get ported so we could all
boost peaks. First off, stores stopped selling and renting
videos and books. You couldn't get audiotapes or disks.
Overnight, the entertainment industry switched to producing
nothing except ports and out-corded transcripts. The real
push was targeted at young adults, ranging from fourteen to
forty-five. Among that demographic, not being ported was
equivalent to not being able to read. Or not getting inoculated against some common disease. Or not wearing glasses if
you needed them. Like you were a total cretin.

It's no coincidence that age group is the people most likely
to Party Crash, to drive or ride along as part of a team. But I
have to shut up. Hush. We're not supposed to talk about that.

Neddy Nelson: Jumping backward in time, wouldn't you be
living alongside history, knowing what the news would be
since you've already lived this part? Couldn't you be getting
older, hooking up, trying to inseminate another, better generation of yourself? Buying lottery tickets and betting on horse
races that always pay off?

If you lived long enough, couldn't you watch yourself be born? Couldn't you raise yourself? Be your own old man?

Echo Lawrence: Get this. Most passenger cars are crash-tested no faster than thirty-five miles per hour. The automotive industry reasons a driver will take evasive action and hit the brakes before the moment of impact. The pulse. Not my mother.

The officer at the scene reported that our car never slowed as it crossed the centerline. No skid marks proved my mom had tried to brake. While I snoozed in the backseat, she'd steered us head-on into another car. For all I know, my dad was right. But it's funny, I try to find, to meet and talk to, the engineers who worked with my parents. They'd only be in their thirties or forties by now, but they're all dead. Dead or missing. Killed in car wrecks, or just vanished.

Neddy Nelson: All I'm saying is: What if time is not the fragile butterfly wing that science experts keep saying?

What if time is more like a chain-link fence you can't hardly fuck up?

I mean, even if you fucked it up, even ten hundred times—how would you ever know? Any present moment, any "right now," we get what we get. You know?

Lynn Coffey (ⓒ *Journalist*): Take the time to review the press releases, and the government's official statements seem to conflict with actual events. The rubberneck study wasn't suspended due to passage of the I-SEE-U Act. The study died because its chief engineers were failing to report for work. If you tally the expense reports and cross-reference them with payroll records and police statements, you'll find a pattern of wrecked government vehicles, and a significant number of the engineers driving those vehicles appeared to have fled the scene of each accident. They didn't die, but they've never been seen again.

Neddy Nelson: And by the time you were old, like creaky, fucked-up old, and you'd spermed your last version of yourself—wouldn't you get with that latest-model, young you and have a little heart-to-heart? Let's say this finely tuned new *hybrid* you is eighteen or nineteen years old?

Tina Something (℃ *Party Crasher*): Forget it. Nobody's going to tell you what's the *real* goal of Party Crashing. Go ahead, keep telling yourself we're all just goofing around. A bunch of lamebrains who get our jollies by ramming each other with cars.

Besides, most of these idiots are operating based on rumors. Stories. Nobody's sure how it really works. Nobody's going to tell you what's really going on.

But a few of us are going to become gods.

Neddy Nelson: All I'm saying is: What if it's not Rant's fault he's the result of somebody's longtime, sick-assed plan?

Didn't Rant use to say, "The future you have tomorrow won't be the same future you had yesterday"?

You got all that?

35—A Flashback

Chester Casey (○ *Farmer*): Here comes a load of bull-pucky.

The night before my boy, Buster, goes and kills himself, some old coot tells him this long, impossible yarn. This rich old coot named Simms says how, when he was Buster's age and first moved to the city, he was in a car wreck. This Green Taylor Simms is a young man just driving along, and a car coming in the opposite direction, it crossed the center-line without slowing down a hair, and slammed into the man's car.

Shot Dunyun (☾ *Party Crasher*): The way Rant told me the story, Simms wakes up in a hospital bed, asking, "How long have I been here?" And the nurse tells him, "Four days . . ."

Echo Lawrence (☾ *Party Crasher*): At the hospital, this young guy asked, "What happened to my car?"

And the doctors said, "What car?" The police found him unconscious in the street. He was bruised, with a broken col-larbone and breastbone.

The guy asked, "Where's my clothes?"

And the doctors said, "What clothes?" The police had found him naked.

Chester Casey: Everybody knows this is crazy talk, but Buster didn't know that. Buddy must've believed the old man.

Echo Lawrence: All those years ago, the police asked the guy his name and how to contact his family, and this guy told them. The next day, they came back to his hospital bed and told the guy that those people, his family, they didn't exist.

Shot Dunyun: The cops asked for his name and Citizen ID and Social Security numbers. And a day later, they told the man that *he* didn't exist.

Echo Lawrence: In the hospital, the doctors took one look at the scars on the guy's arms, the punctures and puckers in his skin, and they asked, "What drugs were you doing?"

They asked, "Were you aware that you're infected with rabies?"

Jarrell Moore (ℂ *Private Investigator*): The injuries that Simms described to Rant Casey—the bruises across the iliac crest of the man's hips, the cracked sternum, and the broken clavicle—these are all consistent with injuries inflicted by lap and shoulder belts during a high-speed head-on collision.

Shot Dunyun: So, when Green Taylor Simms was twenty-three years old, he sneaks out of that hospital. As soon as they mention a move to the psych ward, he bails before they can put him behind a locked door. Simms steals some clothes and shoes, and bails. And outside, in just the four days he's lost, the city isn't divided into day and night. Not anymore. Nobody is ported on the back of their neck. People are reading: Books. Magazines. Newspapers. Through windows, he can see people watching television. From radios and stereos—music.

Simms hitches a ride to the only place that seems safe. He goes back home to his family's house, in Middleton. Yeah, the same hometown as Rant.

Chester Casey: Breaks your heart, the load of loony insane lunacy that old Simms coot unloaded on my boy.

Shot Dunyun: In the few years since Simms had moved to the city, somebody had cut down the four locust trees that each stood at a corner of his family's yard. Planted there were four spindly locust saplings, not hand-high. On the house, Simms told Rant, somebody had replaced the buckled, blistered siding with straight new boards painted so clean white they looked blue. The paint, so fresh you could still smell it. His key didn't work in the lock, and when he knocked, a girl answered the door.

Chester Casey: Her name was Hattie, and she was pretty the way folks you love are pretty in old snapshots. When they're still young and excited about life. Before time and work and *you* have destroyed their youth. Seventy years back, Hattie was thirteen years old and just home from school in that empty house, waiting for her folks to come back from work in a few hours.

She must've seen something pretty in this Simms, because she took him inside and almost straight to bed. Straight enough.

Echo Lawrence: Of course, this is the man's version. He didn't rape anybody. He didn't guess who she really was until, laying there, waiting for dusk and her folks, Hattie said, "The only way they'll let you stay is if I get knocked up . . ." And they had sex again.

Midway through that second time, Hattie said she hoped it would be a girl baby. So she could call it Esther. And this strange young man came to orgasm, seeing the clock and calendar on her dresser. He asked her, "Is that thing right?"

Hattie rolled her head on the pillow, looking over, and said, "Give or take a minute."

And he said, "No." He said, "I mean the calendar . . ."

Chester Casey: This old man talking nonsense to my boy, he said he knowed the moment that baby was conceived—felt a surge of energy, smarts, balls, and craziness break over him. Sure as rain or sunshine. "Better," he said, "than any critter bite, poison, or just-plain teeth pain."

He said, since he didn't stick around and meet her folks, stay like a stray dog she wanted to keep, that Hattie gal must've told her folks he jumped her.

Echo Lawrence: The way Simms told it to Rant, when he kissed this Hattie person, Simms tasted the meatloaf with onions and sausage that she'd eaten for lunch in the school cafeteria. Her dinner the night before, of fried calves' liver. Her dinner three nights before, of chicken-fried hanger steak with creamed pearl onions and orange gelatin salad. The moment their future child was conceived, the man's eyesight and hearing, his senses of smell and touch and taste just—exploded.

Shot Dunyun: Driving, just trawling around, Rant told me that Green Taylor Simms had somehow fallen into the past some sixty years. After riding in the backseat of his own Great-grandmother Hattie Shelby, Simms says he felt great. Nights, he only needed two hours of sleep. Like some kind of Superman.

Tina Something (ℂ *Party Crasher*): It's only one of the secret goals in Party Crashing. Most people call it a Flashback. Others called it Reverse Pioneering. Breeding yourself, the way Simms had, we call it Stoking.

Echo Lawrence: Pay attention. That supposed twenty-three-year-old refugee stuck in the past, he desperately wishes he'd studied more of recent history. At least memorized some winning lottery numbers. He washes dishes to save a little capital. He works every waking minute, asking strangers, "Has Microsoft gone public yet?"
These people, they would reply, "What's a Micro . . . ?"
"Microsoft," he'd say.
But people would only shake their heads and shrug.

Shot Dunyun: He asked someone, "Has boosted-peak technology been invented yet?" When they shrugged, it didn't matter. He really, really wished he'd paid more attention during math and science class.
Every few years, he returns to spy on his daughter, Esther, his future grandmother. And because he can't invent anything, he says he seduced her, meeting her in secret, giving her money, he tells her his dream for a future dynasty, about his accidental fall backward through time. The car accident.

Echo Lawrence: Whether she believed him or not, if he raped her or not, that girl had a child she named Irene, and the man, now calling himself Green Taylor Simms, disappeared for another thirteen years.

Jarrell Moore: According to the elderly man in question, every generation, each of the thirteen-year-old virgins was willing, even excited, to participate in his project. His experiment.

Echo Lawrence: With every sperm that met an egg, Simms claims he felt stronger. He was hoarding more gold, making a fortune, and stashing it for his future self.

Shot Dunyun: Totally, balls-out crazy.

Jarrell Moore: Geriatric dementia, to say the least.

Shot Dunyun: The moment of every conception got him high. It jacked him up, all his chromosomes or whatall, changed in that instant. Rearranged. New and improved. And, same as any addiction, it was all this guy knew to do, so he did it, over and over and over.

He just kept fucking with the past. Filling the future with a new himself.

Chester Casey: After telling my boy his crazy story, this old nutcase, he asked Buster to roll up his shirtsleeves. The old miser pointed at the shadow bites, the dirt tattooed by teeth into Buster's hands and arms, and he said, "Badger . . . coyote . . . pit viper . . ." Getting every scar exactly right.

Echo Lawrence: Supposedly, Green Taylor Simms asked Rant to go back in time, to crash in a car accident. People were living longer now. Rant could go back a hundred years. Seed more generations of himself. Rant could memorize lottery numbers and invention plans over time, building an even larger fortune.

Jarrell Moore: Along the way, diddling thirteen-year-old girls.

Shot Dunyun: And Simms promised some way Rant could live forever. Become immortal.

Echo Lawrence: Plus, possibly to hide his tracks, or maybe because he's inbred, hybrid crazy, Simms has been sneaking back to murder those Middleton girls in their old age, using poison spiders, bubonic fleas, and killer bees . . .

Shot Dunyun: Rant tells this crazy old Simms, "Memorize? You don't figure what rabies does to a brain . . ."

Echo Lawrence: And Green Taylor Simms says, "I know exactly what you're capable of doing." He tells Rant, "I am you . . ."

Neddy Nelson (ℂ *Party Crasher*): Nobody wants to go there, but . . . wasn't the Virgin Mary, wasn't she God's child? And back in Biblical times, wasn't she, like, thirteen years old?

Shot Dunyun: Sixty years ago, this other Rant Casey got bumped back in time and had to wait his way back to the present, along the way making a few changes. Stoking.

Neddy Nelson: Besides, what about the creepy Old Testament stuff about Lot's two daughters getting their dad drunk and then . . . "preserving his seed"?

Chester Casey: Close as I can figure, that wild story is how come Buddy drove his car off that bridge. All that crazy coot's dreams, my boy was supposed to fulfill them. But I'd wager that's not exactly what my Buddy done.

36–Hit Men II

Tina Something (ℂ *Party Crasher*): On my last date with Wax, and I mean our final gaddamn date, the two of us were cruising a Honeymoon Night in a hot, and I mean stolen, gaddamn Maserati GranSport, and Wax sees this mess of emergency-vehicle lights down along the train yards off Wentworth Avenue, so he goes to cruise by for a peek.

All's left is smoking metal. Even the middle part of the train looks torched, and the fire guys are wrestling to haul the Jaws of Life over to the biggest balled-up chunk of a Lincoln Town Car. All down this side of the tracks, the smoke blows wedding streamers and junk. A white lace veil soggy with blood. A red rosebud boutonniere.

Allan Blayne (ℂ *Firefighter*): The minute I opened my yap, I knew what I said sounded stupid. What I said to the girl. This job, the worst accidents, I go into automatic pilot.

The situation was a two-car scenario: Vehicle Number One is parked at a railroad crossing, waiting for a freight train to pass. According to witnesses at the scene, Vehicle Number Two rammed the parked vehicle and allegedly forced it against the side of the passing train. Vehicle Two then continued to travel forward in a straight line, colliding with the train. Both automobiles underrode the train's wheels and were crushed and dragged a distance of approximately four hundred feet.

Tina Something: I know all the EMTs, 'cause of working for Graphic Traffic, and when Wax stops to rubberneck, I yell out to this guy I know with an emergency-response service. I ask him what's up, and this EMT says I wouldn't believe it if he told me. Some chick's still alive inside the wreck, all her clothes burned off but not a scratch on her. Shaking his head, this EMT says, "Not even a long fingernail busted."

From the Field Notes of Green Taylor Simms (ℂ *Historian*): The chief argument against the possibility of time travel is what theorists refer to as the "Grandfather Paradox"; this is the idea that if one could travel backward in time one could kill one's own ancestor, eliminating the possibility said time traveler would ever be born—and thus could never have lived to travel back and commit the murder.

In a world where billions believe their deity conceived a mortal child with a virgin human, it's stunning how little imagination most people display.

Neddy Nelson (ℂ *Party Crasher*): You want I should risk telling you about Historians? You know what happens when a fellow spreads those rumors?

What? You can't think up a faster way to get us both killed?

Shot Dunyun (ℂ *Party Crasher*): Besides Reverse Pioneering, becoming a Historian is the other secret guilty dream of every Party Crasher.

From the Field Notes of Green Taylor Simms: One theory of time travel resolves the Grandfather Paradox by speculating that, at the moment one changes history, that change splinters the single flow of reality into parallel branches. For example, after you've killed your ancestor, reality would fork into two parallel paths: one reality in which you continued to be born and your ancestor did not die, and one branch in which your ancestor died and you would never be conceived. Each revision one made in the past, the subsequent new reality it created, theorists refer to as a "bifurcation."

Neddy Nelson: Don't you think the biggest, richest fuckers in the world aren't Historians? And you really think they want the rest of us to know that? These rich fucks? Don't you think they can't fake their dying every six decades or so, then transfer their money and property to their new identity?

From the Field Notes of Green Taylor Simms: Within Eastern or Asian spirituality exists the concept that only an individual's ego ties him to the temporal world, wherein we experience physical reality and time. Within this concept, enlightened beings recognize this self-imposed limitation and attachment to the immediate world, and can choose to free their consciousness and travel to any place or period of history. With apologies to Mr. H. G. Wells, one requires no time machine. Anyone can relocate throughout history or space simply by relaxing his grip on his current reality through meditation and spiritual growth.

Neddy Nelson: You think anybody smart is going to tell about Historians? As much as I've already said, what do you think that says about my smarts?

From the Field Notes of Green Taylor Simms: A third possibility does exist, although it's never been widely discussed. Aside from bifurcation and time travel via a freed consciousness, this third option also resolves the Grandfather Paradox and places the traveler in Liminal Time, suspended outside of the linear movement of time which human beings experience. Simply stated, Liminal Time has no beginning and no end. Nothing is subject to the natural processes of decay and replacement. In Liminal Time, nothing is born and nothing dies.

Quite understandably, only deities ever existed in this immortality.

Until now.

Allan Blayne: Both Vehicles One and Two burst into flame, igniting the cargo of adjacent railroad cars as well as the creosote-treated ties of the track bed. Witnesses place the time of the incident at 11:35 p.m., and four engine crews responded initially. It took one additional crew to bring the event under control, but the wreckage was sufficiently cool for investigators to recover the bodies by 4:15 a.m.

From the Field Notes of Green Taylor Simms: Throughout all mythology, the gods have created themselves as mortals by bearing children by mortal women. The deity simply emerges from the infinity of Liminal Time and manifests himself in the form of an angel or a swan or beast, and completes the seduction or announcement that will result in a mortal offspring. The divine made flesh. The infinite made finite.

It's when you cross this mythology with the Grandfather Paradox that the reverse occurs and mortal flesh might be made divine.

Allan Blayne: Over the course of the search, our unit recovered the charred remains of two adult males and two adult females who witnesses report being in the first, parked vehicle at the moment of impact. In the process of searching the remains of the second automobile, this crewman heard what I took to be sobbing from the collapsed, forward portion of the passenger cell. Using a hydraulic chisel to relieve the buckled, tightly folded structures of the passenger compartment, further investigation revealed a single survivor, an adult female, apparently the driver of the second vehicle. The sound originally believed to be sobbing could now be heard to be laughter, most possibly hysteria-related.

From the Field Notes of Green Taylor Simms: If a deity can make himself flesh by conceiving a life with a mortal, perhaps a mortal can achieve immortality if he's able to travel back in time and destroy one or both of his parents. In this response to the Grandfather Paradox, the time traveler eliminates his physical origins, thus transforming himself into a being without physical beginning and therefore without end.

Stated simply: a god.

Allan Blayne: In my capacity as a crewman, I counseled the survivor, a woman approximately twenty-five years of age, coaxing her to remain calm until she could be examined by paramedics already at the scene. Encasing the survivor was what can only be described as a shell or cocoon of rigid netting. Inspection of the inside surface of this shell proved it to be the burned and melted remnants of synthetic-fiber apparel and headwear, apparently the remains of a long white dress and veil of the type worn by brides at traditional wedding ceremonies.

In my effort to keep the survivor calm, I asked her age, her name, and birthdate.

Perhaps due to shock, she responds, "One hundred and sixty-three years old next month." Twisting her shoulders and torso inside the cocoon of debris, the survivor then said, "That was way fun; now get this burned shit off me . . ."

Tina Something: Waxman watches this miracle girl walk across the tracks, barefoot and wrapped in a blanket, and Wax says, "That's where I want to get . . ."

I guessed Wax meant she was pretty.

This miracle girl is looking right back in his eyes.

But that's not what Wax meant. Not even close.

Neddy Nelson: You want I should introduce you to a Historian? You want to be alive and stupid, or do you want to be a know-it-all dead body?

From the Field Notes of Green Taylor Simms: In a somewhat hideous parody of the Annunciation, the time traveler would make a pilgrimage to a direct ancestor, ideally the traveler's mother or father, at a time before the traveler's conception—for the purpose of killing that ancestor.

Shot Dunyun: Again, do not confuse Stoking with Resolving Origin. Stoking means you flashback to breed a better you. Resolving Origin means you slaughter some ancestor to make sure you'll never be born. I'll grant you, they're both pretty nasty.

Neddy Nelson: Historians, don't they call it Destroying Source or Severing Origin? Haven't you heard it called Resolving Origin? Doesn't it make sense, that, serial killers like the Zodiac and Jack the Ripper, those were people dropped back into time and having trouble finding and *"resolving"* their mothers?

Tina Something: I never hear from Wax, not until a long, *long* time after Rant Casey takes his suicide dive off the bridge. In the meanwhile, certain police have been asking me if Wax has been in touch. It seems some kids died rolling a Jaguar X-Type inside a concrete highway tunnel. The car turned out to be stolen, and Wax's wallet was in the back pocket of some jeans left behind in the wreck. As if Wax totaled a Jag, killing two kids and leaving his gaddamn pants behind . . .

Neddy Nelson: You wonder why we always have war and famine? Can you accept the fact that the people, the Historians who run everything, they get off on watching our mortality?

Tina Something: A couple weeks later, the cops are calling about Wax again. Seems another kid's died in a stolen car, this time a BMW 3 Series 325i. Seems a witness is ready to swear that, the second after the car sailed off the top of an eight-story parking garage, landing nose-straight into a concrete sidewalk, killing the kid in the shotgun seat, after that disaster Karl Waxman climbed out from behind the shattered windshield and walked away.

And again, I told the cops I hadn't heard a word.

Neddy Nelson: How can you expect Historians to feel anything for the suffering of the rest of us? Do you cry when a flower wilts? When a carton of milk goes sour? Don't you think they've seen so many people die that their sympathy or empathy or whatever is pretty much wore out?

Tina Something: Another time the cops called, they claimed they'd matched fingerprints on the steering wheel of the BMW to fingerprints in Wax's apartment. The cops asked, was I harboring him?

From the Field Notes of Green Taylor Simms: One of the common tenets shared by widely divergent spiritual beliefs is the rule that an individual can only attain true power by "killing his father." One possibility is that said rule was not meant metaphorically. The primary difficulty would lie in transporting oneself backward to a time before one's birth.

Then, of course, comes the physically easier but emotionally tricky task of murdering one's own parent.

Tina Something: To try and find Wax, I looked up his mom in the phone book, Gloria Waxman, but she's not listed. Her maiden name was Elrick, so I call the few Elricks I find. One says, wrong number. When I ask for Gloria Elrick or Waxman at the other number, some old lady hangs up the phone on me. About ten times this old lady hangs up, so I drive over for a visit to the address listed in the phone book. Behind the apartment door, the same old-lady voice tells me to go away, but I don't.

I keep knocking and pounding, saying I know Gloria and Wax are around and saying I only want to talk.

Finally, I threaten to tell the police, and somebody inside unlocks the apartment door. Some old man opens the door enough I can see the gaddamn chain's still on, and he tells me to go away or he'll call the police himself. This old man says his daughter, Gloria Elrick, she died almost twenty-some years back. Seems she was parking with her steady boyfriend, and a maniac shot them both dead in the car. A total stranger, a young man with no apparent motive, somebody nobody knew from Adam, had killed Gloria and her boyfriend. And the old man slams the door in my face.

Through the door, I ask what was the boyfriend's name.

And the old man says, "Go away!"

I yell, "Just tell me his name!"

And the old man says, "Anthony." Through the door he yells, "Tony Waxman." He yells, "Now, you go!"

From the Field Notes of Green Taylor Simms: However, once one had made the journey and completed the task, to become immortal, to live eternally in a world where everything and everyone would wither and die while you accumulated knowledge and wealth, becoming the most powerful leader of all time—*for all time*—that seems well worth the effort.

Neddy Nelson: You don't think a real Historian wouldn't kill you just for laughs?

Tina Something: The last time I seen Wax, I was Tag Teaming, wearing a bridesmaid dress, making a last-ditch effort to get picked for a team, and a Rolls-Royce Silver Cloud pulls up to the curb. Scrawled down the polished side of the body, white and pink spray paint says "Just Married." The shotgun window rolls down, and inside, leaning over from the driver's seat, is Wax, smiling and saying, "Hey, baby, get in . . ."

I ask, "Where you been?"

And Wax says, "I did it . . ."

"Did what?" I ask him.

Neddy Nelson: Next, after Historians "terminate origins," don't they go through a long process called something like "residual fading," where every trace of the old them starts to disappear?

Tina Something: Karl Waxman tells me he's got no more future or past. He never has to eat another bite of food or sleep another wink. No more haircuts. No more bowel movements. No aging or injuries or illness. No death. He's outside of time.

And Wax says, "I am without beginning or end." He says, "And I can make you a goddess."

Yeah, I say. Like he made that burned-up kid in the BMW a god? And the kids in the Land Rover?

And Wax laughs and says he was just goofing with them. Wax says, once you're immortal, you forget that other people aren't; you start screwing around, and somebody gets their head cut off. The way they screamed, he says they sounded funny as hell.

With me, he says, it will be different.

Yeah, I say. Like he made his mom and dad immortal?

The Rolls-Royce, the shotgun door pops open, and Wax says, "Just get in, baby." With his hand, Wax pats the seat next to him, saying, "You won't be young, forever . . ." He says, "Unless you trust me."

And I didn't get in his car. I slammed the door shut and said he was a dirtbag for not calling me. I said it was his turn to wait.

"Oh, I can wait," Wax said.

Some Party Crashing kids have walked up, thrift-store brides and grooms, flocking to the Rolls with its tin-can tail and white streamers, ready to climb inside, asking if Wax needs a team, asking if they can all ride along.

And I tell these kids, "Don't." I block the door with my hip and yell at them to get the fuck away from this guy. "You get in this car," I tell them, "and this gaddamn psycho will murder you."

And the kids look at me like I'm the gaddamn psycho.

That last night I see Wax, the last thing he says to me is, "Try and not forget me, baby." And he blows me a kiss, pulling away, steering out into the flow of traffic.

I haven't Tag Teamed a night since then. All I hope is that's the last time I ever see Karl Waxman.

Neddy Nelson: Couldn't you guess that old-time gods and saviors like Apollo and Isis and Shiva and Jesus are just losers with beater Torinos and Mustangs who went Party Crashing and found a way to "sever their origins"? Maybe they all started as real nobodies, but as their reality faded, a new story piled up around them?

Tina Something: Soon as I got home, I phoned the gaddamn police detective that's been bugging me. The detective says he's never heard of any Karl Waxman.

Allan Blayne: The stupid thing I said to the girl, it was just a reflex. In my capacity as a crewman, after we had her freed and wrapped in a blanket, I told her, "You are one lucky young lady."

Tina Something: In every gaddamn photo I have of me and Wax, he's gone, just disappeared. They're only photos of me, smiling, with my arm looped around nothing. My lips puckered, kissing air. When I try, I can't even tell you if his eyes were brown or green. Ask me again in a few months and a hundred bucks says I've never, ever heard of Karl Waxman.

Shot Dunyun: The way Rant told it to me, Simms didn't want him to go back in time to fuck anybody. Now that Simms was his own super-hybrid, he wanted to be immortal. Simms wanted Rant to go back in time and kill his mom. Well, I guess—*their* mom.

37—Resolving Origin

From the Field Notes of Green Taylor Simms (℃ *Historian*): In Middleton, sleeping dogs have the permanent right-of-way . . . both metaphorically and literally.

Echo Lawrence (℃ *Party Crasher*): So we went back to Middleton. To see the Middleton Christian Fellowship. The Sex Tornado. If we were lucky, the Tooth Museum and the wild dogs.

Neddy Nelson (℃ *Party Crasher*): Didn't we go to Middleton to see if Irene Casey was dead? Wasn't our real reason to see if Rant had fulfilled the mission Simms sent him to do?

Shot Dunyun (℃ *Party Crasher*): We parked Neddy's Cadillac at the end of a gravel driveway that ran to a white farmhouse on the horizon, Rant's house. All around that house, the yard where Rant had buried those stinking Easter eggs for his dad to find with the lawn mower.

Echo Lawrence: We parked in the middle of the night and watched the house with a dark outline of Irene in the yellow square of the kitchen window. One of her hands holding a shape in her lap, while her other hand touched the shape and pulled away. Touched and pulled away. Her head bowed down, the light behind her, embroidering. We watched until Shot and Neddy fell asleep.

Shot Dunyun: Until Echo fell asleep.

Irene Casey (◎ *Rant's Mother*): For Christmas one year, my mother and Granny Hattie gave me a sweater they'd made. I figure it was Hattie who'd knitted it, and my mother who'd embroidered the fancy detailing. Satin-stitched down the front were pink roses, padded with felt, with green cord-padded stems. All complicated. Mixed in the roses were violet periwinkle blossoms, made with long and short stitching. Scattered in the background were so many navy-blue bullion knots and smaller French knots, they made the white yarn of the sweater look light blue. Not a single pucker or stray bit of floss.

It was a sweater for indoors, maybe for church on Sunday. Looking back, I should've pressed that sweater behind glass, inside a picture frame, and hung it on the wall. It was that kind of masterpiece.

I couldn't wait to show it off, but my mother said not to leave the house. After family started to arrive for Christmas dinner, all the aunts, uncles, and cousins, the house got so crowded I had no problem sneaking out.

From the Field Notes of Green Taylor Simms: I hesitate to even comment further on this pathetic person, this Rant Casey. It's regrettable that I ever discussed with him my theories about Liminal Time. Beyond that, he suffered hallucinations brought about by a terrible chronic disease, and died a horrible death in the deluded belief that it would be his salvation. Even as we depict him as a victim and a fool, our attention and energy create Casey as a martyr.

Irene Casey: Down along the river, in the trees along the Middleton River, I used to walk and pretend the water was the sound of traffic. I'd pretend I lived in a city, full of noise, where anything wonderful could happen. Anytime. Not like Middleton, where my mother and aunts locked the doors at sundown. Even with our closest neighbors, the Elliots, a half-mile away, my mother pulled all the curtains in the house before she'd turn on a single light.

My mother and my aunts grilled me about never talking to strangers.

But there were never no strangers. Not in Middleton.

From the Field Notes of Green Taylor Simms: To date, fourteen troubled people have driven their automobiles into obstacles and over precipices, dying in apparent imitation of Rant Casey. On a personal note, I deeply resent Mr. Casey casting me as a serial rapist and murderer.

Irene Casey: Usually, the river was noisy and windy, but not that day. That Christmas, it was silent, froze. The ground was so hard you didn't leave footprints. No wind swept the dead leaves or clattered the bare tree branches. You were like you were walking through a black-and-white photograph of winter, without sound or smells. Like I was the only alive thing moving, walking along the river path. My breath blowing out ghosts. The air so dry everything sparked my fingers with a shock of static.

Near as I recollect, such a black-and-white day, my eyes must've been starved for color, since they saw the littlest flash of gold. Way out on the center of the froze river, the thin ice over deep water, my eyes seen just that littlest bright speck of gold.

Tina Something (ℂ *Party Crasher*): Green Simms would tell you that Rant was insane. He's very much part of the elite, and he doesn't want to see that threatened by any new order.

Irene Casey: With one tennis shoe, I toe-kicked the shiny gold spot, round and bright. A coin. I pulled my long sweater sleeve, I slid the cuff back to keep it from getting dirty, and I stopped to touch the coin. To see if it was maybe chocolate. A chocolate-candy pirate coin wrapped in gold foil from the Trackside Grocery. With my other hand, I reached behind and held my hair together at the back of my neck. To keep the hair from falling in my face.

The river ice, gritty with dirt, but slippery under my shoes. Under the ice, water so deep it looked black.

With two fingers, I pinched the coin out of the dirty frost.

From somewhere in the woods and cattails along the riverbank came barking, dogs snarling and snapping.

Between my teeth, the coin was hard, not breaking, sticking to my lips with the cold. A real coin. Treasure. My tongue tasting gold, dated—

And: "Hello."

Someone said, "Hello."

Dogs you couldn't see, off a ways, howling.

In back of me, a man came walking upstream on the deepest stretch of water, flat as a glass road. Ice all around us. He said, "Well, don't you look nice . . ." The Christmas sky floated over him, blue as embroidery floss.

Echo Lawrence: They don't know I saw, but I woke up in the backseat of the car and saw Shot kiss Neddy Nelson on the lips. Shot said, "There, now you're infected."

And Neddy said, "I'd better be, because I'm not doing *that* again."

Irene Casey: The man reached to finger the sleeve of my sweater, and he said, "Isn't this pretty."

I started to step back, making my fist tight around the gold coin, to hide it in case it was his. Nodding at the cattails, I told him, "There's wild dogs, mister."

His eyes and mouth made just a look. Not a smile or frown, more how you'd look if you was alone. The man's fingers worked into the knotted yarn, and he said, "Relax."

I told him, "Don't, mister." I said, "Quit pulling, please."

He stretched the sleeve toward him, so hard you could hear the seam at the shoulder creak, a thread popped, and he said, "I'm not hurting you."

Holding the coin to hide it, saving it, left me with only one hand. My shoes sliding on the ice. To save my sweater, I stepped closer, saying, "You're going to ruin it . . ."

Neddy Nelson: Don't you know rabies is key?

Irene Casey: The sweater, the white yarn worked like a net. An acrylic spiderweb. With both hands, his fingers were tangled, worked deep into the knots and stitches, and when he dropped to his knees, his weight dragged me down. Buttoned to my neck, I twisted away from his clouds of ghost breath, and when he slid flat onto the dirty ice, he pulled me with him. The two of us tied and knotted together.

In the brush around us, dogs barked. The man put his lips together in a kiss and said, "Shhhh. Hush." The heart inside his coat, beating one thud for every four times mine jumped.

His eyes rolled to look toward the barking, the dogs, and I told myself he was saving me. I was fine. He'd only grabbed me and pulled me down to protect me. He heard the dog pack coming, and he wanted us to hide.

As the barking faded, moving down the river, his fingers still knotted in my sweater, he looked at me, from too close to see anything but my eyes. His eyelashes brushing mine, he said, "You ever wonder about your real daddy?"

Neddy Nelson: Isn't rabies what wrecks your port so you can't boost peaks? After that, aren't you free to flashback?

Irene Casey: I remember trying to hold my breath, because, every time I breathed out, he settled on top of me, heavier, making my next breath smaller. Crushing my insides, smaller, until stars of light spun around in my eyes. In the blue silk sky.

He said, "I've been watching your trash."

I remember the long sleeves of the sweater, wrapped and twisted around me, tight as those coats that crazy people wear in movies so they can't move their arms. My, each of my fingers, tied a different way.

From watching the trash, he said, "I know the hours and minutes since your last period." And he said how the baby I'd have, right now, would almost for sure be a boy. He would be a king, that boy. An emperor. A genius who would make me rich and exalted above all other women.

And with my every breath out, he settled heavier on top of

me, making my next breath more shallow, until I was only half awake.

Neddy Nelson: Isn't that why the government pushed to port everybody? Because weren't too many people Party Crashing to mess with history?

Irene Casey: The air smelled like clean water in a clear glass on a hot day. The ice smelled like nothing. The dirt, froze stiff. The river, froze solid. No wind. Like we was outside of time. Nothing happening except us.

He said how boy sperms swim faster, but don't live as long as the girl sperms, and his breath smelled like a burp after you've ate pork sausage for breakfast.

I said I had to pee.

And he said, "When we're done."

Neddy Nelson: Don't you know about the covert government effect? People aren't even aware it's boosting, but doesn't the effect keep you stuck here so you can't mess with history?

Irene Casey: I remember I told him how sorry I was for peeing on him. Peeing on both of us. But it hurt so bad, and the cold air made the hurt worse. Those days, walking out, I'd layer maybe nine, maybe ten pair of panties. To give me hips till I'd fill out.

I didn't want to, but when he worked my zipper down and slipped his cold thumb inside all those panties, inside me, I peed. All hot, creeping through my jeans and underwear. The hot wicking up the yarn of my sweater. The rest of me, ice cold.

In the dirt, in my Christmas sweater, with this man crushing the air out of me, calling me "the mother of the future," I couldn't picture how this'd get any worse.

I remember him turning his hand in front of my face, his fingers wet and steaming in the cold, and me saying, "I'm sorry."

I said, "We're safe."

His wet fingers inside me, I kept calling him "mister." Kept saying, "Those dogs are long gone."

Neddy Nelson: Don't Historians call it "Oblivion," the place without place, where time's stopped. The place outside of time.

Irene Casey: This man brung one knee up to my chest, like to kneel on me, and he brung it down, hooking the toe of his black shoe in the crotch of my jeans. As he stomped the jeans and panties down around my socks and ankles, in that instant, I remembered how many folks were sat down to Christmas dinner at my house. Too many for my mother to ever miss me.

Echo Lawrence: The Easter egg that Rant left for me, he'd written on it with white wax, so that when I soaked it in dye I could read his hidden message.

Irene Casey: Worse than Basin Carlyle fouling you, nailing you too hard, down there with a dodgeball in phys ed. Worse than the cramps. That punching, pushing, shoving inside, it hurts. Gritty and grinding with dirty water, the ice, melted under me. That thin part of ice, turned to mud puddled under me.

I pictured fabric, stuck in one place, stabbed again and again in a big, slow sewing machine.

My arms wrapped tight as a baby or a mummy, just-born or dead-helpless, the man moved on top of me, faster, until he stopped, and every muscle and joint of him turned hard as stone, froze.

Then all of him went loose, relaxed, but he didn't let go. His fingers kept a hold of me.

His heart slowed, and he said, "It didn't happen, not yet. To be safe," the man said, "we'll need to go again."

Echo Lawrence: Instead of dye, I dropped the egg in a cup of coffee. After I drank the coffee, the egg sat there in the bottom of the paper cup, Rant's words telling me: "In three days, I'll return from the dead." Some kind of Easter quote.

Irene Casey: While the man waited, he sniffed his hand and said, "You smell just like your mama and grandma and great-grandma smelled at your age . . ."

Nothing moved. Nothing barked.

"Have this baby," he whispered, his mouth on top of my eyes, his lips on my shut-tight eyelids, "and you'll be the most famous mother in all of history . . ."

Down there, he was moving again, pressing me into the ice, through the ice into the river, and he said, "You don't have this baby and I'll come back to make you have another . . ."

From the Field Notes of Green Taylor Simms: If you must know, the hidden message written on my egg was "Fuck You."

Irene Casey: "Yes," he said, his chin grinding whiskers against the side of my neck. He said, "Yes. Yeah. Oh yeah." He said, "Please."

His hips bucked against me so hard, one crack, two, three lightning-bolted through the ice underneath. Water lapped up from under. White cracks, zigzagging toward shore.

Shot Dunyun: I didn't know why, but my egg said, "Green Taylor Simms."

Irene Casey: When he lifted up on his elbows, the man looked down and said, "You're bleeding."

He looked at my hand, how inside my fist, from holding the coin so tight, I made the gold cut open my palm skin. The edges carved a perfect round scar, deeper at the top and bottom of the circle. The man pried my fingers back, and inside them, the gold coin looked like Christmas in my bright-red blood. Weeks into the new year, I'd have a purple bruise dated 1884.

And the man told me, "Keep it. To pay for cleaning your sweater."

From the Field Notes of Green Taylor Simms: Until now, Party Crashing hadn't a face, and it seems imprudent to give it one. There is no such phenomenon as "flashbacks." No immortal "Historians" exist. Which is more likely—all this time-travel rubbish, or the fact that one young man went insane?

To profess otherwise would be extremely reckless and irresponsible.

Irene Casey: The man pulled up his pants, his thing still steaming with pee and blood. Still dripping sperms. He pulled up the zipper and looked his head around. Looking down at me, he said, "Stay until I'm gone."

And he walked upriver on the water, all the way to over the most far-off horizon.

Tina Something: No, the real lie, the real liars, are Echo Lawrence and Shot Dunyun, because they know the truth but won't tell. You can flashback in time and tinker with events. And every night, they still try.

Irene Casey: My legs, open to the blue Christmas sky. My sweater was froze, stitched into the ice a bunch of places. Half sleepy from not breathing, my eyes watched the water bubble up through the cracks around me. My ears heard the whine and moan of the river pulling apart the broke pieces.

The living, alive blood and piss of me, freezing. The man's sperms.

The river ice shifting, breaking up. Coming to life.

Tina Something: That's how most of the people in power have anticipated and profited from current events. It could be, this is how people have always taken control. Or this dropping back might be limited to modern history. I don't know. You can't know. All I know is: People do this. And they don't want you to.

Irene Casey: Me, just letting the ice sink me lower into the deep cold, my ears hear a voice come out of the bushes. In the cattails along the edge of the froze river, a voice said, "Mrs. Casey?" Said, "Irene?"

The voice said, "Mom?"

And a mostly naked boy stepped out, shaking and wrapped in his own arms.

A blue sheet of paper hid the front bit of him. A hospital getup. He stood in paper slippers, saying, "I couldn't catch a ride."

His teeth rattling together, the boy said, "I'm too late." He said, "Am I too late?"

Echo Lawrence: The hospital ID bracelet that Chester wore that day, it's dated from the day they pulled him out of the river. Nineteen years to the day before Rant plowed his car into the same stretch of water. I still have that bracelet. Chet gave it to me.

The day Rant disappeared into the river, and the day Chet washed up, both days December 21.

Irene Casey: The boy stood pigeon-toed on the froze mud, both his hands knotted in the steam coming out of his mouth. His whole body clenched and shaking, like a skinny fist, he said, "It's going to be okay . . . You're going to be okay . . ."

Scars running up and down his arms. His chattering teeth black.

Maybe only old as a high-schooler.

Except for some blue paper, standing in those cattail reeds naked as a baby.

Neddy Nelson: Icky as it sounds, didn't Rant marry his mom? Didn't he change his name to Chester Casey and stick around to raise the kid? To help raise himself?

Irene Casey: I couldn't sit up, so much of me froze into the ice. I couldn't reach down enough to find my jeans or some panties.

The sheets of ice shifting and tilting, the naked boy come

stumbling out toward me. He kept saying, "Don't move."
Kept saying, "You're hurt."

The river gushing up, flooding the ice, he said, "Don't ever try and hitchhike dressed thisaways."

His blue paper slippers slipping and shuffling to come stand next to me, he gets low to help with my panties, my jeans. As his shaking fingers leaned in, close, to reach me, a spark jumps between us. Between his touch and mine, a static spark, it snaps. Loud. Electric-bright in the daylight. Between his fingertip and mine.

Neddy Nelson: Isn't it like—the Trinity? Rant and Chester and old Green Taylor Simms, like in Catholic Church, three people being the same but divided?

Irene Casey: Froze together, crawling off the busted ice, my ears hear the river lap behind us. My Christmas sweater stretched and dirty. Stained red and yellow. Blood and pee. Baggy and ruined.

The naked boy said, "I'm sorry about . . . this."

And I undid the buttons and peeled my arms out of the muddy sleeves. I held the sweater out, saying, "Take it. You'll catch your death."

Neddy Nelson: Doesn't that explain why Chet Casey wasn't more broken up about his kid being dead? Why Chet just moved in and set up house? Aren't we talking about big backward loops in time?

Irene Casey: Walking back to Christmas dinner, I asked him, "Who exactly are you?"

And this boy says, "You don't want to know . . ."

Echo Lawrence: Loops, like embroidery stitches.

Shot Dunyun: How impossible is that? Rant Casey isn't dead, he's become Chester. The dad. When Rant's car caught fire and Christmas-treed off the side of the Barlow Avenue Viaduct, he flashbacked in time, but not to kill Irene, as Simms had planned. Rant only went back to stop the attack on Irene. It's beyond impossible.

Irene Casey: And that's how Chet come into my life. I didn't know it for sure, not until my next period never come, but that's how Buddy come to life, too.

Echo Lawrence: The dogs barking woke me up. Still parked, watching Rant's old house. Still night. The front porch light blinked on, and the screen door creaked. The outline of someone leaned out, and a woman's voice shouted, "Fetch!"

The howling, barking, and snarling shrank, smaller, the sound blurred.

Shot Dunyun: The woman on the porch, in the glare of the yellow lightbulb, yelled, "Fetch! Come on, boy!"

From next to the trunk of a locust tree, a shape broke away. A figure stepped out, and a man's voice said, "Mrs. Casey?"

Echo Lawrence: And Irene said, "Bodie? Bodie Carlyle?"

By then, the figure had one foot on the bottom porch step. The screen door squeaked, and Irene said, "Get in here. You're going to catch your death . . ."

Bodie Carlyle (☼ *Childhood Friend*): You see, life only turns out good or bad for only a little bit. And then it turns out some other way.

Shot Dunyun: The man stepped inside. The porch light went out.

Neddy Nelson: And isn't this the point when that bogus Sheriff Carlyle arrested us?

38–Communitas

Dr. Christopher Bing, Ph.D. (✷ *Anthropologist*): The phenomenon commonly known as Party Crashing is simply the latest manifestation of a liminal space which provides a cathartic sublimation, generating a normative communitas, thereby deflecting any pent-up hostility toward the status quo and preserving the existent social structure.

From the essay "Liminality and Communitas" by Victor Turner (✷ *Anthropologist*): Prophets and artists tend to be liminal and marginal people, "edgemen" who strive with a passionate sincerity to rid themselves of the clichés associated with status incumbency and role-playing and to enter into vital relations with other men in fact and imagination.

Dr. Christopher Bing, Ph.D.: As defined by the anthropologist Victor Turner in his book *The Ritual of Process: Structure and Anti-Structure* (1969), liminal spaces occur at the interstices between two distinct phases of life. According to Turner, absurdity and paradox define regularity. The regularly occurring chaos of liminoid space is what allows for an otherwise organized civilization.

Ina Gebert, M.A. (ℂ *Theologist*): Arguably, the best example of a liminal space is the secular ritual of Halloween as currently practiced in the United States. On that particular evening, the power hierarchy is inverted, permitting children to demand tribute of adults. Said children don masks to mimic symbols of power. These include ghosts and skeletons, agents of the dead; witches, who ruin fertility; savage animals such as wolves and lions; or cultural outsiders such as cowboys, hobos, and pirates. Masquerading thusly, the children threaten to inflict property damage as punishment for adults who fail to reward them.

Dr. Erin Shea, Ph.D. (ℂ *Theologist*): Established examples of large liminoid spaces include the annual Burning Man festival in the Black Rock Desert of Nevada, the ConFest held in Australia, the international Rainbow Family gatherings, and the so-called "Celtic Renaissance" held in Glastonbury, England.

Dr. Christopher Bing, Ph.D.: Generally speaking, liminal versus liminoid is defined as follows. The term "liminal" refers to a ritual that marks passage from one phase of life to the next: a baptism, a graduation, a honeymoon. In contrast, a typical "liminoid" event such as a rock concert, a rave, or a polyamorous consensual group sex party occurs outside of the mainstream, but a liminoid event marks no such life transition. The defining characteristic of the liminoid space is that all participants act as equals. Social or caste rankings are discarded, and all present enjoy an egalitarian mutual affection for one another. Turner's name for this spontaneous solidarity and love was the Latin word *communitas*.

Dr. Erin Shea, Ph.D.: Smaller examples of liminoid spaces include religious pilgrimages, "road trip" vacations, fight clubs, and Party Crashing events.

Ina Gebert, M.A.: Among liminal spaces the most common are rituals in which members of a society temporarily exchange their respective status. The king becomes a servant. The servant, a king. The Roman Catholic Pope kneels to wash the feet of the poor. The well-dressed, respectable Pentecostal celebrant collapses to the floor, twitching and muttering gibberish. Aboard nuclear submarines submerged for three-month tours of duty, the officers and crewmen exchange roles in periodic rituals such as "Hefe Café," a formal midmission dinner during which the commanders must serve and obey their inferiors. In each instance, this short-lived degradation enhances the long-term power of the ruling entity.

Dr. Christopher Bing, Ph.D.: At its worst, the liminal or liminoid event functions as a release for accumulated anxiety, thereby protecting the overall civilization. At its best, liminal and liminoid spaces become social laboratories wherein participants can experiment and develop new forms of self-expression and social structure.

Ina Gebert, M.A.: The living always feel superior to the dead. Consider that death is the ultimate degradation—as well as the opportunity for a community to safely voice its true feelings about an individual. Witness the funeral scene from *Tom Sawyer*, in which the community believes the title character to be drowned, and they hold a funeral to publicly mourn. Despite their customary disdain for the "deceased," the community expresses its repressed love. Once Tom Sawyer appears, seemingly returning from the dead, the community rejoices.

Dr. Erin Shea, Ph.D.: It's arguable that local authorities are aware of Party Crashing and permit it to continue. The ritual would provide a cathartic release for antisocial and antiauthoritarian impulses, either exhausting those persons, crippling them, or removing them entirely via death. Regardless of the outcome, Party Crashing would serve as a cost-effective, efficient social program for preserving the current social order.

Dr. Christopher Bing, Ph.D.: A typical liminal ritual occurs in three stages. The pre-liminal. The liminal. And the post-liminal. Applied to the Party Crashing phenomenon, these stages manifest as: decorating and parading the vehicles; the actual hunting and accidents; and the post-accident public performance of arguing and acting out, commonly known as "milking the accident."

Dr. Erin Shea, Ph.D.: Inherent in Party Crashing culture is the tendency to subvert traditional liminal symbols. The woman dressed in a wedding gown is not an actual bride. Said "woman" may actually be male. The furniture tied to the automobile roof does not indicate a household being relocated. The Student Driver sign is not intended to protect a fledgling driver.

Ina Gebert, M.A.: The same way Tom Sawyer's ritual resurrection suggested that of the Christ—a luminous youth dying and being reborn to immortality—contemporary culture continues to generate deities following this same model. In recent decades, celebrities such as Elvis Presley, Jim Morrison, and John Belushi have been corrupted by their success, died prematurely, and are subsequently rumored to be alive. This resurrection might simply signal a public denial of their demise, but it does follow a general outpouring of grief and recognition that serves to construct a mythology around the now-immortal individual.

Dr. Erin Shea, Ph.D.: Examples of liminality in language include the French phrase for dusk or twilight: "Between dog and wolf." This same phrase is used to describe the final months of life, as a human being's mental and physical abilities dwindle. In English, the phrase for twilight, "when all cats are gray," demonstrates the flattening of social hierarchy and obvious status indicators.

From the essay "Liminality and Communitas" by Victor Turner: It is as though they are being reduced or ground down to a uniform condition to be fashioned anew and endowed with additional powers to enable them to cope with their new station in life.

Ina Gebert, M.A.: Rant Casey and Karl Waxman represent the latest incarnation of this ancient model. Both men, degraded by a violent public death, are rumored to be alive, and not simply alive, but immortal. Waxman is said to have traveled backward in time and murdered his parents before the moment of his conception, preserving himself in a permanent liminal state. Casey, well, Rant Casey is another story— his is a redemption through public recognition and emotional attachment, a mass refusal to accept that he died in a well-documented automobile accident.

Shot Dunyun (℃ *Party Crasher*): All that Anthropology 401 garbage is beyond boring. Party Crashing is just a fun time. It's a fun playtime. Please, don't kill it with big words.

39—Werewolves V

Hudson Baker (○ *Student*): This is hard to explain, but in every toilet stall in every bathroom at the high school we go to, somebody wrote in every stall: "Amber Nye Is Dripping with Rabies!"

Only, really, Amber wrote that herself.

It's really hard to explain.

Toni Wiedlin (℃ *Party Crasher*): High-school kids would do a dance they called "The Drooler," meaning they'd mimic the partial leg paralysis of an end-stage rabies victim. Kids would stagger around the dance floor, foaming from Alka-Seltzer on their tongue, crashing into each other, and snarling. The word is, doing that dance is a good way to get shot by the police.

Shot Dunyun (℃ *Party Crasher*): People who want to catch the bug, we call them "spittoons." People willing to pass along the rabies virus are "hawkers."

From the Field Notes of Green Taylor Simms (℃ *Historian*): As Charles Dickens once described the French Reign of

Terror: During times of plague there will always be those who can't rest until they've become infected.

Hudson Baker: Amber and me would cover our whole, entire bodies in sunblock, SPF 200 or something. We so wanted people to whisper we were Nighttimers, and for the curfew police to try and bust us. Looking back, we wanted people to be scared of us. Like we could run totally wild at any moment and bite everybody's throat at the Christian Pathways Academy.

Toni Wiedlin: I remember hearing some silly Nighttimers teens bragging about what they called their "lineage," meaning the original source of their rabies strain. Without exception, every kid swears she or he was infected by Rant Casey or Echo Lawrence. Everyone wants to feel special—attain a special status among their peers—but not *too* special. Most kids only want to be special the same way their friends are special.

Hudson Baker: Amber's mom and dad had no idea how we were sneaking out every night. We'd wear these dark-black wigs and white makeup. Looking back, we had to look, like, ruthlessly lame and dumb to real Nighttimers. We wore black tights under black dresses we found at thrift stores, and that Mr. and Mrs. Nye didn't even know we had. We'd stand on a corner and wait for a car full of Party Crashers to stop.

It's really hard to talk about this now.

Toni Wiedlin: I remember everybody saying Rant Casey was the father of Party Crashing and he wasn't dead. These same kids will tell you Elvis and Jim Morrison and James Dean just got sick of the spotlight and faked their deaths so they could write poetry in the south of France. When everyone lies about seeing Rant and kissing him, all their lies prop up a win-win reality. The government says Rant's alive because they need a villain. The kids say he's alive because they need a hero.

Hudson Baker: Amber was so in love with Rant, she'd go into the post office and steal his "Most Wanted" posting off the clipboard they keep for the FBI's top-ten fugitives. Every time the FBI replaced it, Amber would steal another. It had his photo from when he immigrated to the nighttime. Amber wanted to wallpaper her room with those FBI posters, but Mr. Nye would've totally, no-kidding freaked.

Toni Wiedlin: To young kids, Rant and Echo became the Adam and Eve of their era—the F. Scott and Zelda, the John and Yoko, Sid and Nancy, Kurt and Courtney. I remember that everyone who traced their rabies lineage back to Rant or Echo's mouth, they called themselves a "Child of Rant" or "Spawn of Echo."

Every high school has its Romeo and Juliet, one tragic couple. So does every generation.

Hudson Baker: Our high school, a separate student body used our same desks and classrooms at night. Nighttimer kids. They had their own different nighttime teachers and janitors and everything. Their own nurse, even. Nighttimer kids sat in our desks while we slept at home, and we sat there while they slept. Some days, you'd find a note chewing-gummed to the bottom side of a desk—a night kid trying to make contact so you'd leave a note in the same place. That's how Amber and me met that guy Gregg Denney.

Gregg Denney (ℂ *Student*): These day bitches come around, not wanting to be virgins no more. I provided myself a bottomless supply of clean pussy. Day bitches only had to hear I was infected and they'd hunt me out. The rest of us, we called them "spittoons," they was after spit so bad.

Shot Dunyun: Every bullshit little Daytimer who says Rant Casey kissed them, they called themselves "purebloods." Talk about pathetic. Like they were racehorses or vampires—it was beyond pathetic.

Hudson Baker: Gregg Denney is a totally, no-kidding predator.

From the Field Notes of Green Taylor Simms: As with the Tooth Fairy, every culture has its own version of the "bogey-man," a mysterious figure who exists, not to reward children, but to punish them. For example, the Dutch figure of Zwarte Piet, who assists St. Nick by whipping children who misbehave. In Spain, El Coco is a shapeless, hairy monster who eats children who refuse to go to bed. In Italy, L'Uomo Nero is a man wearing a black coat who kidnaps those who refuse to finish a meal. Similar to Santa Claus is the Homem do Saco of the Portuguese, the Torbalan of Bulgaria, and the Persian Lulu-Khorkhore, who carries a huge sack, not to bring gifts to good children, but to spirit away unruly ones.

Hudson Baker: Amber and me had a promise: We'd never get in a car without the other. If a Party Crash team only had room for one of us, we'd wave them off and wait for another car. Both or neither, that had always and forever been our true promise.

Phoebe Truffeau, Ph.D. (☉ *Epidemiologist*): Modern society has struggled with the issue of superspreaders since Mary

Mallon refused to modify her behavior. Because "Typhoid Mary" insisted on working as a cook, she spent the last twenty-three years of her life quarantined on New York's North Brother Island. More recently, in 1999, *The New England Journal of Medicine* reported a nine-year-old boy in North Dakota whose lungs held unusually deep pockets of tubercule bacilli, infecting his family and fifty-six schoolmates while the boy himself appeared to be in perfect health. In a similar case from 1996, the *Annals of Internal Medicine* documented the post-surgical intensive-care unit of a hospital where an outbreak of antibiotic-resistant staph infections was traced to colonies of *Staphylococcus aureus* deep in the sinuses of a seemingly healthy medical student.

Neddy Nelson (ℂ *Party Crasher*): You ever heard of the Emergency Health Powers Act? It was put in place by that president, right after the September 11 fiasco, remember? Did you know that act allows the government to brand anyone as a public-health menace, then lock them up for the rest of their life? You ever hear of due process? You think you're going to get a trial by a jury? Are you kidding?

Phoebe Truffeau, Ph.D.: In rural China, the social stigma associated with leprosy prompted many of the infected to hide their condition. In response, the government offered a cash bounty to anyone who could report a leper, thus forcing the infected into treatment and eliminating the disease from the country.

In India, where a more democratic form of administration prevents such a program, cases of leprosy remain common.

The Emergency Health Powers Act simply enables the federal government to suspend all state and local powers, seize property, and quarantine populations in order to effectively deal with any infectious agent.

Hudson Baker: Amber saw getting infected as the ultimate commitment. Like her and the guy would be doomed to be with each other. Looking back, she figured a brush with death would make her really enjoy her life. Like she would feel more alive. Regular people would feel sorry for her, or some might be afraid or grossed out, but Amber just saw that all as added attention.

Amber said it would stop her from boosting peaks. She really wanted to live a real, alive life. I mean, it's *really* hard to explain.

From the Field Notes of Green Taylor Simms: The term "bogeyman" is derived from "Boney," the British derogatory nickname for Napoleon Bonaparte. Over time, the name evolved into "boneyman" and later "bogeyman," but it was always used as a threat by the British in order to keep their children obedient.

Hudson Baker: Amber and me, she wanted us to double-team Gregg Denney. That's the night I didn't get in his car. I let her go alone.

Phoebe Truffeau, Ph.D.: As was most likely the case with Buster Casey, an asymptomatic, infectious carrier tends to be immuno-compromised by a previous illness. For example, one massive superspreader of *Coronavirus*, commonly known as SARS, suffered from a pre-existing kidney condition which allowed the patient to incubate and transmit huge amounts of the virus.

Gregg Denney: Some bitch gets herself knocked up and says she wants to have my rabid baby. She wants to see, can she go all the way to a baby without curing her infection. I don't know what you're talking about.

Hudson Baker: Amber was always telling me, "Rant Casey is the father of my rabies . . ." Like Amber met him and knew him and everything. Their love was, like, sealed with a kiss.

Gregg Denney: Maybe I put babies inside some daytime bitch, but, no, I never had the rabies for real. I only let on I was infected, to keep me in clean tail.

Hudson Baker: Amber was living with Gregg Denney by then. She expected her baby to be, like, part man, part animal. Like, one time she told me, "I'm taking human evolution one giant step backward . . ."

Phoebe Truffeau, Ph.D.: As with the Rant serotype of the *Lyssavirus,* most modern epidemics have "jumped" from animals to human beings: SARS being a form of bovine *Coronavirus,* or cattle "shipping fever"; Creutzfeld-Jakob disease being the human form of bovine spongiform encephalopathy, or "mad cow disease"; and acquired immunodeficiency syndrome most likely being derived from the simian immunodeficiency virus.

From the Field Notes of Green Taylor Simms: Once he'd died, or at least disappeared, Rant Casey became a very effective bogeyman for our government. Anytime the federal government needed to distract public attention from its own incompetence, the surgeon general simply announced a new development in the rabies epidemic, or the hunt for Rant, or both.

Neddy Nelson: Don't you see how there is no actual rabies epidemic? Can't you see how Rant Casey is just a political scapegoat? Do you really accept that Lee Harvey Oswald acted alone? Or that James Earl Ray really was a "lone gunman" when he assassinated Dr. Martin Luther King, Jr.? How about Sirhan Sirhan? Or John Wilkes Booth?

Do you really believe one man caused an entire nationwide rabies outbreak?

Gregg Denney: A bitch with her hormones exploding and some serious brain damage happening from the rabies, that sounds like nothing I'd want to hang around. Forget it. People I heard of can carry the spit around for years; could be she was one of those.

Phoebe Truffeau, Ph.D.: Other terms for superspreaders include "superinfectors" or "supershedders." Due to the deadly, invisible fog of saliva and mucous droplets that surround these infectious individuals, epidemiologists sometimes refer to them as "cloud cases."

Neddy Nelson: Doesn't it scare you that the Emergency Health Powers Act now preempts all legal rights of the individual?

Shot Dunyun: The way you lock up all your enemies without charging them with any crime, or providing lawyers, it's called a quarantine. Doctors are the new judge and jury. Disease is the new weapon of mass destruction.

Neddy Nelson: Why do you think every political radical gets "diagnosed" as rabid, then locked up until his inevitable death is announced? Don't you see how this is legalized assassination?

Hudson Baker: When I couldn't help it any longer, I called Mr. and Mrs. Nye and told them everything about Amber and the chewing-gum notes and Party Crashing, and they went and hired a detective.

Only, when they went to where Gregg Denney lived, Amber was gone.

Neddy Nelson: How can you say Rant Casey overreacted? How's an intelligent person supposed to react when he discovers that he's merely the product of a corrupt and evil system? How do you continue to live after you learn that your every breath, every dollar you pay in taxes, every baby you conceive and love will only perpetuate some evil system?

How do you live knowing your every cell and drop of blood are part of the big evil?

40—Final Connections

Wallace Boyer (☼ *Car Salesman*): Right now, if you scratched your ear, I'd scratch my ear. If you cocked your head to one side, I'd cock my head—pacing you—selling you with eye contact and proof that I care.

I'd say, "Look here"—another embedded command.

If you said, "Time travel is impossible," I'd bridge your objection, saying, "Yes, many people claim it's impossible, but didn't people use to say the Wright brothers would never get off the ground?"

Echo Lawrence (☾ *Party Crasher*): The last time I saw Green Taylor Simms, we were driving a Mattress Night. Green was roping a mattress to the roof of his red Daimler. We were pit-stopping before the window opened, to fill the tank, standing, leaning against the side of the car, parked next to the gas pumps. Green stood in his pinstriped suit, poking the nozzle and holding the trigger. You could smell gasoline and deep-fried chicken.

I hadn't called Shot about tonight, just so I could ride alone with Green. And, standing there, I told Green Taylor Simms that Rant's dad, Chester, had come to town.

Watching the numbers spin on the gas pump, money and gallons piling up, Green said, "Tell me, how delusional is the elder Mr. Casey?"

Driving by are Torinos and Vegas and Toronados, all with mattresses roped to their roofs. Faces in those cars all turned to look at us with our mattress. People stand on every street corner you can see, a thumb out for a ride. Some people wave a few bills for gas money.

And I told Green Taylor Simms what Chester Casey had told me.

Green said nothing. Just listened. Watching the other teams watch us.

From DRVR Radio Graphic Traffic: This bulletin just in, and it looks like another repeat redundant case of déjà-vu. Three police vehicles are in high-speed pursuit of a burning car, westbound on the Madison Beltway.

This is Tina Something with your Rubberneck Report . . .

Wallace Boyer: It helps, Chet Casey told me, to start simple. Picture time less like a river than a book. Or a record. Something finished. Like a movie, with a beginning, middle, and end, but already done and complete.

Then picture time travel as nothing more than knocking your half-read book to the floor and losing your place. You pick up the book and open the pages to a scene too early or late, but never exactly where you'd been reading.

Echo Lawrence: And, still listening, Green Taylor Simms left the gas nozzle pumping, walked around the car, and leaned inside the driver's window. He said, "I'm listening," and he pushed in the dashboard cigarette lighter.

That's how old his car was. None of us smoked.

Shot Dunyun (℃ *Party Crasher*): Rant said once that you *perceive* time the way the people in power want you to. Like it's a speed limit on some freeway. Santa Claus or the Easter Bunny. Like time is the Tooth Fairy we're brought up to believe. As a path or a river that only moves in one direction.

But speed limits change. Santa Claus is fake.

Rant told me that time's not the way we think. Time wraps. It loops. It stops and starts. And that's just the little bit he's found out. Most folks, Rant says, move through time like a flightless bird on land. Rant says that view of time was set up so folks won't live forever. It's the planned obsolescence we've all agreed to.

Everybody except the folks who don't die. Historians.

"Nothing says you have to swallow this," Rant told me. "You can always just die."

From DRVR Radio Graphic Traffic: Here's another update on that high-speed police chase. The fire seems to be limited to a burning mattress tied to the car's roof. The driver is still westbound on the Madison Beltway, approaching the Center-Point Business Park. With more news as it happens, this is Tina Something with your Rubberneck Report . . .

Echo Lawrence: At the gas station, inside Green's Daimler, the cigarette lighter popped out with a "think" sound.

From the Field Notes of Green Taylor Simms (℃ *Historian*): Let me, somehow, compress this. The human brain operates at four basic levels of brain frequency. Normally, awake and aroused, you operate in the "beta" level of brain waves, which occur at thirteen to thirty cycles per second. At a resting state, your mind slips to an "alpha" brain-wave level of nine to fourteen cycles per second. As you daydream and feel drowsy, your mind slows to "theta" level, five to eight cycles per second. And as you pass into deep, dreamless sleep, your brain waves slow to a "delta" level of one to four cycles per second.

Wallace Boyer: Nothing says you have to believe this. Nothing says you have to even listen, but consider that plenty of smart, rich, powerful folks in history went to their graves swearing that the sun went around us. Also consider that someday, when you're dead and rotted, kids with their baby teeth will sit in their time-geography class and laugh about how stupid *you* were.

Echo Lawrence: The gas pump chunked and the numbers stopped turning. The hose jumped and went silent. Green Taylor Simms slipped one hand inside his pinstriped jacket and lifted out his wallet.

"According to Chet Casey," I told Green, "we met Rant because you recognized him on that street corner . . ."

Green pinched a twenty-dollar bill, another twenty, a ten, a fifty. He pinched all the paper money out of his wallet.

I said, "Pull up your sleeve." I said, "Let me see your arms."

And Green said, "Who do you think invented this little game you enjoy so much?" He said, "Who do you think decides the field and flag and window, then sends the word out?" He said, "What do you suppose would happen to Party Crashing without me?"

Around us, the stink of gasoline.

Green Taylor Simms handed me the cash and said, "Would you be so kind as to buy me some Red Vines licorice?"

From the Field Notes of Green Taylor Simms: Of greatest interest is the idea that an average person easily reaches this mystical meditation state, "theta" brain waves, the state most sought by monks and pilgrims, simply by driving an automobile. Any long drive, anytime you've passed time and covered distance with no memory of the process, you've been submerged in deep theta-level meditation. Open to visions. Open to your subconscious. Creativity, intuition, and spiritual enlightenment.

Echo Lawrence: I left him with the nozzle still stuck in the side of his car. I went inside and bought Red Vines, paid for the gasoline, and came out. And—no duh—when I came out, the red Daimler was gone.

From the Field Notes of Green Taylor Simms: Of special interest is the theta level of brain activity. It's at this frequency that mystics report that visions and inspiration are most likely to occur. In those relaxed moments, while bathing or driving or falling asleep, as you lapse into theta brain waves, you typically retrieve deep, distant memories. You make connections and achieve revelations.

In order to stimulate theta brain activity, Tibetan Buddhist chants follow a droning rhythm which matches the slower brain-wave frequency. Among drumming cultures, shamanic drummers trigger theta activity by a steady, constant four beats per second.

Pattie Reynolds (© *Bartender*): I was at Pump Seven. The man you're talking about was at Pump Five. I heard splashing and turned to look, and this old man was hosing gasoline all over the mattress tied to the roof of his red car. He wore a dark-blue business suit. Gray hair. Good wingtip shoes. The gasoline soaked into the mattress, except a few drips of it rolled down the sides of the car, the windows. The smell was suffocating.

I remember he climbed into the driver's seat and started to drive off. He had to turn on the windshield wipers, so much gasoline was running down the windshield.

Wallace Boyer: Like I told you, I didn't really meet Rant Casey until after he was dead. The remainder of that flight, the time I sat next to Chester Casey, he tried to teach me the impossible. He drank my scotch and told me that time is not a straight line.

Time is not a river. Or a clock or hourglass. It doesn't only run one way.

You could hire a gaggle of brilliant experts to dissect how it might happen, but some people will still look at the proof and argue that the world is flat. Humans didn't evolve from something else. And Elvis Presley is still alive.

From DRVR Radio Graphic Traffic: I'm Tina Something with a Graphic Traffic emergency bulletin. All westbound lanes of the Madison Beltway are closed, due to the crash of a burning car at the CenterPoint exit. Emergency crews are on the scene trying to control the fire. Already traffic is backed up to the Market interchange and the 287 Freeway. Traffic on the eastbound Madison is also slowed to stopping . . .

Shot Dunyun: Shit. I don't know how flashbacks work. I couldn't tell you exactly how a lightbulb works, much less make you one from scratch. But I can use one.

You burn out your brain with rabies. Go all theta-trance-y with driving. You hit something and wake up naked in history.

Wallace Boyer: If it helps, consider how people used to think the world was flat. Two-dimensional. They only believed in the part they could see, until somebody invented the ships and somebody brave sailed off to find the rest of the earth. Consider that Rant Casey is the Christopher Columbus of time travel.

From DRVR Radio Graphic Traffic: Traffic on the West Side is at a standstill. A parking lot. Emergency crews report the fire at the CenterPoint interchange is extinguished, and the accident has been moved off the roadway, but the boys in the meat wagon are still waiting for their cargo.

According to the early rumors, the burned Daimler-Benz appears to be empty. Bringing you the gory details, this is DRVR Graphic Traffic . . .

41–Rant Revisited

From DRVR Radio Graphic Traffic: You don't have to look up at the sky to tell it's a full moon tonight. We already have reports of a fender bender at Milepost 14 of the 217 Freeway, where two bridal parties appear to be throwing handfuls of wedding cake at each other. With the Rubberneck Report every ten minutes, this is Tina Something for Graphic Traffic . . .

Neddy Nelson (ℂ *Party Crasher*): Doesn't everybody know, people still Party Crash? To attain that road-trip trance where you come up with ideas? Or maybe people get off on the chase? You know, to meet people and spend time together?

Echo Lawrence (ℂ *Party Crasher*): Relax. If Shot Dunyun manages to transplant himself into the past, the rest of us will wake to the new reality that he's become the father of boosted-peak technology. Shot will finally use his education, to become the Thomas Edison of neural transcripts. That's if he remembers enough about the actual science. It's one thing to be an auteur, but it's another to birth the entire fucking art form.

No, the instant he goes back and tweaks history, the rest of us might wake up, tomorrow, to a world without neural-transcript boosts. We'll still be watching movies and reading books. But his little pug dog, Sandy, will still be alive.

Shot Dunyun (℃ *Party Crasher*): Maybe Rant wasn't so . . . ballsy or big as we remember him. Maybe this is how any religious figure gets created—his friends brag him up, huger and huger, so they can get laid. You can picture St. Peter in a bar telling some pretty girl, "Yeah, I hung with Jesus Christ. We were best buds . . ."

Maybe people don't travel back in time. Maybe it's lies like that, anything that smells better than the idea of death— black, inky, forever death—it's those kind of sexy lies that set up world religions. Maybe Rant is just dead.

Echo Lawrence: Consider the source. Maybe Shot Dunyun just wants to slip back in time without any competition.

Shot Dunyun: Bullshit. You know, if Echo jumps back in time, she'd be around today, but with both regular arms and legs. Normal. And with living, alive parents. Not whittling and staining sex toys. Echo would be the same age as Rant or Chester, or whatever he calls himself now. They'd be just two regular, boring middle-aged people.

Echo Lawrence: If Neddy manages to go back, there'll be no Infrastructure Effective and Efficient Use Act. People will live the way the cavemen did, everyone indoors or out, anytime they choose. No curfews. One colossal traffic jam, the way the world used to be.

Shot Dunyun: You could argue that we constantly change the past, whether or not we actually go back. I close my eyes, and the Rant Casey I picture isn't the real person. The Rant I tell you about is filtered and colored and distorted through me. Like any boosted peak.

And all these ways I change the past—I don't even know I'm doing most of them. You could say I constantly fuck up the past, the present, and the future.

Echo Lawrence: If Rant ever gets it right—if he ever gets back in time to save his mother from . . . becoming his mother—chances are you'll never have heard the name Rant Casey. He and Green might both be Historians, without beginning or end.

Shot Dunyun: How weird is that? Instead of a biography, this story will become fiction. A factual historical artifact documenting a past that never happened.

Like Santa Claus and the Easter Bunny, another obsolete truth.

Bodie Carlyle (☼ *Childhood Friend*): My head's working overtime to swallow the mess of this. Folks say Rant's skipped back in time, crazy folks, and maybe he'll do something so none of this won't never be. Or maybe just so only he won't be.

Gossip says a secret dog pack of folks run the world. Folks who can't never die, so they keep the rest of us stirred up for laughs. Depends on how they monkey with history, but tomorrow could be I won't be no more real than Superman or King Arthur.

It don't take a brain surgeon to tell, that talk's got to be made-up lies.

Neddy Nelson: Ask yourself: What did I eat for breakfast today? What did I eat for dinner last night?

You see how fast reality fades away?

Tina Something (C *Party Crasher*): What would I change? The next Party Crash night, anytime any gaddamn Maserati or Rolls-Royce pulls up to the curb, I'm climbing inside.

The rest of you gaddamn losers—enjoy your death.

42–Contributors

Hudson Baker (⊙ *Student*) is currently working toward her undergraduate degree in criminal justice.

Brannan Benworth, D.M.D. (☾ Dentist) remains isolated in government infectious-disease quarantine for an indefinite period.

Dr. Christopher Bing, Ph.D. (⊙ *Anthropologist*) is currently overseas studying the culture of Noh drama in Japan.

Allan Blayne (☾ *Firefighter*) remains isolated in government infectious-disease quarantine for an indefinite period.

Wallace Boyer (⊙ *Car Salesman*) is available to lecture extensively about his short-lived in-flight relationship with Rant Casey.

Vivica Brawley (☾ *Dancer*) remains isolated in government infectious-disease quarantine for an indefinite period.

Sheriff Bacon Carlyle (⊙ *Childhood Enemy*) faces charges of wrongful arrest stemming from allegedly harassing visitors to the Middleton Tooth Museum.

Basin Carlyle (⊙ *Childhood Neighbor*) remains active in family, church, and community life.

Bodie Carlyle (☼ *Childhood Friend*) operates and curates the newly opened Middleton Tooth Museum.

Chester Casey (☼ *Farmer*) disappeared in connection with a single-vehicle accident soon after the disappearance of Green Taylor Simms.

Irene Casey (☼ *Rant's Mother*) is now a wealthy philanthropist, and chief financial backer and docent of the Middleton Tooth Museum.

Lynn Coffey (℃ *Journalist*) authored the nonfiction account *Nail and Bail: A History of Party Crashing*.

Gregg Denney (℃ *Student*) is deceased. He was shot by police under suspicion of being rabid.

Shot Dunyun (℃ *Party Crasher*), formerly known as Christopher Dunyun, has been missing since the vehicle he was driving left the roadway and fell from the edge of a three-hundred-foot cliff.

Cammy Elliot (☼ *Childhood Friend*) remains active in family, church, and community life.

Logan Elliot (☼ *Childhood Friend*) remains active in family, church, and community life.

Ruby Elliot (☼ *Childhood Neighbor*) remains active in family, church, and community life.

Reverend Curtis Dean Fields (☼ *Minister, Middleton Christian Fellowship*) altered Communion practices after an outbreak of rabies was traced to a chalice of grape juice shared by his six-hundred-member congregation.

Denise Gardner (☼ *Real Estate Agent*) was named a Millionaire-Bonus-Plus Seller in the regional midlevel single-family-home market.

Sean Gardner (☼ *Contractor*), with his wife, operates the GothStop telephone hotline, an intervention-and-treatment program for parents of adolescent children trapped in the goth lifestyle.

Ina Gebert, M.A. (☾ *Theologist*) is an asset at any party.

Mary Cane Harvey (☼ *Teacher*) dreams of her upcoming retirement to "any place but Middleton."

Glenda Hendersen (☼ *Childhood Neighbor*) remains active in family, church, and community life.

Silas Hendersen (☼ *Childhood Friend*) remains active in family, church, and community life.

Brenda Jordan (☼ *Childhood Friend*) remains active in family, church, and community life.

Leif Jordan (☼ *Childhood Friend*) remains active in family, church, and community life.

Allfred Lynch (☾ *Exterminator*) remains isolated in government infectious-disease quarantine for an indefinite period.

Canada Mercer (☼ *Software Engineer*) recently celebrated the first birthday of his Irish setter, Lulu.

Sarah Mercer (☼ *Marketing Director*) expects to give birth to her first child in September of this year.

Jayne Merris (☾ *Musician*) continues to perform live punk rock as her accounting career allows.

Officer Romie Mills (☾ *Homicide Detective*) was recently promoted to chief administrator of the federal Rabies Containment Program, overseeing the apprehension and quarantine of any and all infected individuals.

Jarrell Moore (☾ *Private Investigator*) remains isolated in government infectious-disease quarantine for an indefinite period.

Neddy Nelson (☾ *Party Crasher*) was last seen riding as a passenger in the car in which Chester Casey disappeared.

Galton Nye (☼ *City Councilman*) successful lobbied for a program to keep quarantined rabies suspects confined until the current public-health threat is resolved.

Danny Perry (◌ *Childhood Friend*) remains active in family, church, and community life.

Edna Perry (◌ *Childhood Neighbor*) remains active in family, church, and community life.

LouAnn Perry (◌ *Childhood Friend*) remains active in family, church, and community life.

Polk Perry (◌ *Childhood Neighbor*) remains active in family, church, and community life.

Jeff Pleat (⟲ *Human Resources Director*) now works as a successful swimwear model.

Symon Praeger (⟲ *Painter*) continues to paint portraits as his law practice allows.

Hartley Reed (◌ *Proprietor of the Trackside Grocery*) pleaded innocent to charges of reckless endangerment after witnesses testified to seeing him lick apples later offered for sale to the public.

Pattie Reynolds (⟲ *Bartender*) continues to tend bar as her drug habit allows.

Lowell Richards (◌ *Teacher*) recently celebrated six months of continuous sobriety.

Livia Rochelle (◌ *Teacher*) recently celebrated six weeks of continuous sobriety.

Todd Rutz (◌ *Coin Dealer*) retired to a private island in the Mediterranean.

Dr. David Schmidt (◌ *Middleton Physician*) closed his medical practice in order to accept the position of regional quarantine warden, under the Emergency Health Powers Act.

Dr. Erin Shea, Ph.D. (⟲ *Theologist*) remains isolated in government infectious-disease quarantine for an indefinite period.

Green Taylor Simms (⟲ *Historian*) continues to be a Person of Interest sought by the police in connection with the disappearance of Buster L. Casey.

Tina Something (◖ *Party Crasher*) was last seen entering a
Dodge Viper which later crashed, exploding, against the
side of a freight train. Emergency responders found no one,
alive or dead, at the scene.

Edith Steele (◖ *Human Resources Director*) remains isolated in government infectious-disease quarantine for an
indefinite period.

Lew Terry (◖ *Property Manager*) is currently serving a
twenty-five-year prison sentence for felony child sexual
abuse.

Carlo Tiengo (◖ *Nightclub Manager*) remains isolated in
government infectious-disease quarantine for an indefinite
period.

Luella Tommy (◉ *Childhood Neighbor*) remains active in
family, church, and community life.

Phoebe Truffeau, Ph.D. (◉ *Epidemiologist*) was appointed
the federal Rabies Tsar, to coordinate the expanding duties
of law-enforcement officers under the Emergency Health
Powers Act.

Victor Turner (◉ *Anthropologist*), an international authority on ritual and metalanguages, dreamed of operating a
samba school in Brazil. He died in 1983.

Toni Wiedlin (◖ *Party Crasher*) continues to participate in
Party Crash events but denies all rumors that she's
assumed the role of game organizer.

CHOKE

Victor Mancini, a medical-school dropout, is an antihero for our deranged times. Needing to pay elder care for his mother, Victor has devised an ingenious scam: he pretends to choke on pieces of food while dining in upscale restaurants. He then allows himself to be "saved" by fellow patrons who, feeling responsible for Victor's life, go on to send checks to support him. When he's not pulling this stunt, Victor cruises sexual addiction recovery workshops for action, visits his addled mom, and spends his days working at a colonial theme park. His creator, Chuck Palahniuk, is the visionary we need and the satirist we deserve.

Fiction/978-0-385-72092-2

DIARY

Misty Wilmot has had it. Once a promising young artist, she's drinking too much and working as a waitress in a hotel. Her husband, a contractor, is in a coma after a suicide attempt, and his clients are threatening Misty with lawsuits over a series of vile messages they've discovered on the walls of houses he remodeled. Suddenly, Misty's artistic talent returns. Inspired but confused by a burst of creativity, she soon finds herself a pawn in a larger conspiracy that threatens to cost hundreds of lives. What unfolds is a dark, hilarious story from America's most inventive nihilist, and Palahniuk's most impressive work to date.

Fiction/978-1-4000-3281-5

HAUNTED

Haunted is a novel made up of twenty-three horrifying, hilarious, and stomach-churning stories. They're told by people who have answered an ad for a writers' retreat and unwittingly joined a "Survivor"-like scenario where the host withholds heat, power, and food. As the storytellers grow more desperate, their tales become more extreme and they ruthlessly plot to make themselves the hero of the reality show that will surely be made from their plight. This is one of the most disturbing and outrageous books you'll ever read, one that could only come from the mind of Chuck Palahniuk.

Fiction/978-1-4000-3282-2

LULLABY

A culling song is a lullaby sung in Africa to give a painless death to the old or infirm. The lyrics of a culling song can kill, whether spoken or even just thought. You can find one on page 27 of *Poems and Rhymes from Around the World*. When reporter Carl Streator discovers that unsuspecting readers are reading the poem and accidentally killing their children, he begins a desperate cross-country quest to put the culling song to rest and save the nation from certain disaster.

Fiction/Literature/978-0-385-72219-3

STRANGER THAN FICTION

Palahniuk's world has always been, well, different from yours and mine. In his first collection of nonfiction, he brings us into this world, and gives us a glimpse of what inspires his fiction. At the Rock Creek Lodge Testicle Festival in Missoula, Montana, average people perform public sex acts on an outdoor stage. In a mansion once occupied by The Rolling Stones, Marilyn Manson reads his own Tarot cards and talks sweetly to his beautiful actress girlfriend. Across the country, men build their own full-size castles and rocketships that will send them into space. Palahniuk himself experiments with steroids, works on an assembly line by day and as a hospice volunteer by night, and experiences the brutal murder of his father by a white supremacist.

Essays/978-0-385-72222-3

SURVIVOR

Tender Branson—last surviving member of the so-called Creedish Death Cult—is dictating his life story into the flight recorder of Flight 2039, cruising on autopilot at 39,000 feet somewhere over the Pacific Ocean. He is all alone in the airplane, which will crash shortly into the vast Australian outback. But before it does, he will unfold the tale of his journey from an obedient Creedish child and humble domestic servant to an ultra-buffed, steroid- and collagen- packed media messiah.

Fiction/978-0-385-49872-2

ANCHOR BOOKS
Available at your local bookstore, or visit
www.randomhouse.com